THE INSTRUCTION OF OLIVIA

by

GEOFFREY ALLEN

I0621354

Published by **CHIMERA**
ISBN 9781780807171

CHAPTER ONE

'Olivia Holland!' The court usher poked his head around the door and beckoned with his forefinger. 'Yes, you. Come along girl.'

Olivia, a tall slender girl of eighteen rose wearily from the bench and followed him into the magistrates' court. Suddenly dressed in her tattered rags and with mud spattered legs she felt very conspicuous and alone in the world. She had been chased the whole length of the High Street for stealing a loaf of bread, which, the constable assured her, was a hanging offence; already the noose seemed to tighten around her neck.

Her hand went involuntarily to the lump forming in her throat then, conscious of the rip in her dress, she tugged the material tighter over her bosom and stared blankly at the magistrate.

'Take your hand away from there and stand up straight!' he barked, squinting his eyes in the gloom.

Olivia came to attention and the lapels fell open, revealing a bust of larger than average size, made more prominent by the slim waist beneath. Indeed, it seemed remarkable that her narrow shoulders could carry so much weight. With all eyes riveted on her bust, Olivia blushed red and knew, to her acute embarrassment, there was nothing she could do to prevent her nipples from hardening upwards, pushing at the thin cotton like young strawberries eager for the sunshine.

For a few moments the magistrate stared back. In his mind he had already undressed her and was availing himself of those ripe fruits, working his tongue all around them, sucking them raw; a stark contrast to the thin, undernourished waifs he usually sentenced.

'Stealing is a serious crime,' he said, mopping his brow with a red spotted handkerchief. 'A hanging offence, in fact and normally I would have no hesitation in dispatching you thither. Do you comprehend my meaning?'

Olivia nodded. A cold sweat had broken out under her armpits and was trickling down her sides; she was sure this was to be her last day on earth. It mattered not that her nipples stiffened further or at any second her bladder would suddenly gush its contents all over the floor; here, in this dismal room, her short life was about to end.

'Stop snivelling girl, and look at me when I speak to you.'

Olivia lifted her tear streaked face, and avoiding his penetrating eyes, gazed absently at the clock, watching the hands beat away her remaining minutes. They seemed to go very fast; much faster than they had when she was sat outside on the bench.

The magistrate stroked his chin thoughtfully. He had no intentions of sending such a splendid body to the gallows, or shipping it off to Australasia. She was the last case to be heard that morning, and with a whole afternoon free other ideas came to the fore.

'I am sentencing you to six months hard labour in the House of Correction. And,' he added joyfully, 'twenty-four strokes of the birch; half now and half on your admission. Stand down.'

'I'm not being hanged, sir?' Olivia sobbed, clutching the rail for support.

'Not at all. But you will be flogged, and flogged hard, you may rest assured of that.'

He watched her cross the courtroom, his eyes no less riveted on her bottom than they had been on her bust. It seemed remarkable how similar in proportion and appearance was the lower regions of her anatomy to those at the top. Her dress, two sizes too small, hugged her cheeks as she walked. The faded pattern of stripes danced with each frightened step, going into the cleft and out again, stretching over the colliding globes, and threatening to burst at any moment He watched her out of sight and went quickly down the back stairs to the cells beneath, tripping over his gown on the way and almost braining himself in the process.

Olivia was ahead of him, and at a doorway she halted while another girl came out, clutching her bottom and sobbing bitterly.

'Twelve strokes they give me!' she exclaimed, as if in some way it were Olivia's fault. 'Twelve strokes on my bare bum. The bastards!' She opened her mouth to utter another oath but was cut short by a hard shove in the small of her back.

'In here,' said the constable who had sent the girl flying along the corridor.

Olivia stepped into a cell furnished only with a long low bench and a leather bucket in which the previous occupant had generously relieved herself.

'That sometimes happens,' the constable remarked dryly, seeing the look of curious fascination on Olivia's face as she peered at the yellow swirling liquid. 'And I daresay that you will be no exception.'

'I daresay you're right.' The magistrate entered the cell and closed the door behind him. Seen close up and under the soft glow of a lamp, the magistrate had to admit, if only to himself, that Olivia was one of the most stunning looking young ladies he'd ever encountered. There was, he decided, a vague Oriental air about those huge almond eyes, her high cheekbones and voluptuous lips. But the most noticeable aspect was her hair; a vast, tumbling mass of raven locks, which under the lamp assumed a blueish sheen tinged with auburn. For a fleeting moment he was reminded of a picture he saw of an odalisque sprawling across a divan smoking a hookah, the expression on her face suggesting that nothing was beyond her capabilities when it came to pleasuring men.

But the expression on Olivia's face was now one of abject terror. Her wide, lustrous eyes widened still further at the sight of the birch now swinging to and fro in the constable's hand.

'I will deliver the punishment myself,' said the magistrate, snapping from his reverie. He glanced at Olivia and then at the bench. 'Lift you skirt,' he commanded, hardly able to contain the trepidation in his voice.

Olivia bent over and, gathering her skirt in bunches at the knees, slowly drew it upwards. At mid-thigh she stopped and looked up at the magistrate.

'Well, go on, girl,' he said tartly.

Olivia swallowed and hoisted the bunched cotton to her waist. Then, as if knowing what was expected of her, she tied it in a knot and took her hands away. The next command had her lower lip trembling, her eyelids flickering, and the two men moving much closer.

'Please sir,' she whispered, 'I've never taken my drawers off in front of a man before.'

'Do as you're told,' the constable advised, not unkindly.

Head bowed, she slipped her fingers under the top of the material and pulled it outwards, wriggling it over the swell of her hips. As she bent lower and slid her drawers reluctantly to her knees both men nearly choked. The heavy weight of her breasts had fallen forward and swung ponderously to and fro, and it was not impossible from where they were standing to see right down her front as far as her naval.

'Shall I take them right off?' she asked in a foolish whisper, the tone of which left the magistrate in no doubt that the girl was unused to stripping on demand.

At a subdued murmur she bent low and dragged them to her feet, stood up again and lifted out her left foot, and with the right, kicked them away. To the utter amazement of her tormentors, her next gesture was to untie the knot of her skirt and let it float around mid-calf.

'I don't recall giving you permission to cover yourself,' said the magistrate, genuinely shocked. 'Kindly return your skirt to its former position and bend over that bench.'

The shock on Olivia's face was none the less equally startled. 'Am I to be beaten on my bare bottom?' she asked askance.

'Did I not tell you that earlier?' he replied.

He had indeed informed her of that sobering fact but Olivia had forgotten it in the trauma of having to remove her drawers. Now she stood like a stunned cow in a slaughter house, looking all around her, hoping for a last minute reprieve. The door was closed and bolted and she knew full well that even if she got past it she would never reach the end of the passage.

'This isn't right,' she said suddenly, surprised at her own temerity. 'Beating me on my bare bottom.'

'Very well,' said the magistrate, 'I shall not beat you on your bare bottom, but on your bare back as well. Now strip off those filthy rags.'

Olivia's jaw gaped. 'You are going to beat me naked?!'

'The girl's an imbecile,' said the constable. 'I thought she was.'

'I am not an imbecile,' replied Olivia, not really understanding the meaning of the word.

'Then you do comprehend what is required of you. Either you undress yourself or the constable will assist you.'

Olivia leapt backwards into the corner of the cell and heaved her dress over

4

her head. A low whistle escaped the lips of the constable as he stared agog at the naked young woman cowering in the corner. Her arms were crossed, covering her breasts and accidentally forcing them upwards, making them appear much larger than they really were. When she looked down to see what the magistrate was looking at her hands flew to her fleecy triangle, abruptly releasing her breasts and causing them to burst free and then swing embarrassingly slowly back into place.

For what seemed an eternity she stood there, frozen like a Greek statue, the only sign of life, a tear which trickled down her cheek.

'Save your tears and bend over that bench!' the magistrate said harshly.

Olivia came forward an inch at a time, her feet shuffling over the flags until she drew level with the seat. Her hands were still between her legs, and keeping them there, she lowered her knees to the floor and leaned over. When she was sure her pubic hair was hidden from their view she took her hands away and placed them on the floor in front of her. The seat was narrow enough to only support her middle, allowing her breasts to hang over the edge, yet sufficiently high so that her knees swung clear of the floor, thus suspending her weight solely at the pelvis.

'A handsome piece of work, your worship,' complimented the constable whilst eyeing Olivia's raised bottom.

Under the golden glow of the lamp her bottom assumed the colour and shape of a ripe peach, its flawless skin glistened with a fine layer of sweat that gathered at the under-crease and trickled in tiny streams down the backs of her thighs. There was no doubting the comfort those soft cushions could provide between a man and his mattress, or the depths into which he could happily impale himself.

'Handsome indeed,' the magistrate agreed. 'All the more pity in having to rip them asunder.'

If he said that to frighten her he most certainly achieved the desired result. Her bottom quivered and twitched uncontrollably. The muscles in her flanks tensed, giving greater emphasis to their splendid structure. The sides of her buttocks caved in to hollows, and at the base of her spine two deep dimples appeared. To Olivia it seemed the whole world was concentrating on her naked rump; bare and defenceless. She gritted her teeth, determined not to cry out. No matter what happened she would deny her cruel tormentors the satisfaction of hearing her shriek. In stoic silence she would take her punishment.

'Half now and half later,' she heard the magistrate repeat, as he stepped up behind her.

There came the sound of a mighty rushing wind and the abrupt, sharp crack of twigs breaking on bare skin. Olivia's mouth opened and gulped in a whole lungful of air which was as quickly expelled with a whoosh.

'That,' the magistrate explained, 'was for committing the crime in the first place.'

Olivia heard only a muffled garble through the tumbling tresses of her hair.

She thought for a moment she had been struck with a railway sleeper full of red-hot nails. An intense fiery pain burned into her cheeks worse than she could ever imagine.

'Hold her still!' she heard the magistrate command, and a hand, presumably that of the constable, pressed hard and flat between her shoulder blades, pinning her to the seat.

'And this,' the magistrate exclaimed, 'is for having the audacity to think that you could get away with it!'

The second blow fell with the full strength of his arm, catching her unawares across the crown of her bottom, striking the base of her spine. Her legs shot outwards and buckled at the knees.

'And this,' the magistrate continued with great satisfaction, 'is purely for the pleasure of beating you!'

The birch hissed into the fat of her cheeks like a firebrand, and with such ferocity that Olivia jolted forwards, escaping the hand of the constable, toppling over, and landing upside down, her legs in the air and wide open.

'Look what we have here,' said the magistrate, eyeing with satisfaction the multiple welts forming across Olivia's cheeks.

The constable followed his gaze into her fork, wondering whether the magistrate was actually intending to hit her there. But no, he ordered Olivia back over the bench, legs spread and haunches raised, ready for the remainder of the blows.

The next half dozen came thick and fast, landing square on the centre of her cheeks. Try as she might, Olivia could no longer grind her teeth or deny them the satisfaction of hearing her cry. A long, loud piercing howl rushed from her lips, followed by a longer one when the birch assailed her upper thighs, leaving in its wake a livid array of welts. Two more landed on her back with a vehemence that sent dozens of splinters flying through the air.

'Well, what have you got to say for yourself now?' the magistrate asked, pausing for breath.

There was very little Olivia could say. Her head hung almost lifeless over the edge of the bench, and her whole body felt as if it had been set ablaze. She knew that she was crying uncontrollably.

The last two strokes came at mid-thigh, but Olivia felt little for her hindquarters had lost all sense of feeling. She was aware only of sound; the breaking of twigs and the dull thump as they landed on their target.

'You can get up now, Holland.'

Olivia struggled painfully to her feet, clutching her burning bottom and weeping copiously. She had long ago given up caring that she was naked in front of strangers. Now there was no attempt to hide her nakedness under bashful palms.

'I hope that you feel justly chastised,' said the magistrate, wiping the sweat from his brow. 'I have expended a good deal of effort on your behalf, not to mention the constable who expended an equal amount holding you down. In the

House of Correction you will not be afforded such luxuries. There you will find your superiors are much more versed in the correction of their charges. Do you understand?'

Olivia shook her head. Never in her whole life had she been subjected to such fearful punishment. Quite suddenly she fell to her knees and buried her head in her hands, sobbing and snorting away the pain. The magistrate stepped up beside her, so close that the organ throbbing inside his trousers brushed against her trembling shoulder, and for a while he stayed there letting it pulse while he waited for a reaction, but seeing none he withdrew and turned to the constable.

'This young harlot,' he said, 'must be dressed and made ready. Bring over her drawers.'

The constable tossed them into her lap, whilst keeping his eyes keenly on her breasts. He was sure her nipples had swollen to an even larger dimension than they had hitherto. Indeed, the pimpled discs seemed to have spread to twice their width, but thinking that that was an impossibility, he put it down to a trick of the light and excused himself while he went off to the toilet.

Olivia wrestled on her drawers, wincing at the enormous pain manifesting itself in her back and bottom. To her, it did seem as if her breasts had swollen and her throbbing backside was indeed twice its normal size.

The magistrate watched her in studied silence as she pulled her drawers around her reddened cheeks. Her hair had become wild and tangled, falling in twisted coils around her flushed face, lending her an air of gay abandon which he'd seen on the faces of wandering gypsies, whom, he knew from experience, would do anything rather then be shut up in a prison. It was not too wild a leap of the imagination to picture her with bronzed limbs, making free with her charms on some remote and blasted heath. Neither would it be too bold to make the same offer he'd made to all the other good-looking young women he'd flogged raw in these cells.

'I am in a position to help alleviate your sufferings, Miss Holland,' he said, helping her to her feet.

Olivia suddenly brightened up. 'You mean I won't be flogged any more, sir?'

He put his arm around her shoulder and led her to the bench, thoughtfully removing his gown and placing it under her bottom.

'What I mean is that I am in a position to reduce your sentence, perhaps no more than a month, if you are good.'

'Oh, I will be good, sir!' she replied, crossing her legs and putting her hands in her lap.

She stared straight ahead at the slop bucket and her stomach churned. The magistrate could clearly hear the rumbling and gurgling emanating from her belly.

'Perhaps you would care to use the pail before you show me how good are your intentions.'

He left her and went out into the yard to enjoy a cheroot; women as a general rule didn't much care for company when they needed to relieve themselves.

How old was she? Eighteen, and thieving to keep herself alive. Girls much younger than she were known to take off their drawers for a hot pie or a night's shelter. Why, he thought, should she be an exception? The town was full of them. Yet, when he'd called her a harlot there had been no reaction, neither had there been when he'd pressed himself close. Perhaps the girl was just plain stupid. He finished his cheroot and went back into the cell, and saw Olivia sitting on the bench just as he'd left her.

'Have you considered my proposal?' he asked seriously.

'Indeed I have, sir. And I would rather face being buried alive than submitting myself to any further indignities. From now on I shall live a good and honest life. I shall never steal or give you just cause to chastise me. I am sure that after I have proved my worth in the House of Correction you will feel justified in reducing my sentence, and—'

'And I am quite sure,' said the exasperated magistrate, 'that the constable was correct in his assumption! You are indeed an imbecile and will serve out your full term!'

With that he left her rubbing her bottom and staring after him with mystified tears staining her cheeks, completely unaware of the fresh horrors which awaited her at the hands of men far more ruthless and determined than he.

CHAPTER TWO

Herded like cattle, Olivia and three other young women were driven across the police station yard and into the back of a van. The journey to the House of Correction was not a long one, but far enough to allow a quick witted or dexterous criminal to effect an escape. The driver who was solely responsible for their delivery had been duped on more than one occasion by a woman pretending to be sick, only to find that as soon as he opened the door she was off like a hare, and his meagre wages correspondingly reduced. To completely eliminate that risk Olivia and her companions were shackled together hand and foot with chains and, as a double precaution, were further hindered by being made to sit upright against the van wall while he passed iron collars around their necks and fastened them to hooks.

The passengers journeyed on in silence, lulled by the monotonous creaking of the axels and clip clop of hooves, until at length they halted outside a lonely inn.

'Here we go,' said the girl sitting next to Olivia as the door swung open.

'Are we to drink?' Olivia asked innocently, straining her parched throat against the iron ring.

The girl snorted with derision and turned her weary head to a crowd of onlookers gathering at the door. Slowly they edged forward and one by one clambered into the van. The last closed the door and blocked out the window with his jacket. The driver, who had collected a penny from each of them, set

8

the horse in motion, heading at a leisurely pace across the desolate moor.

How odd, Olivia thought, that a prison van should stop to pick up passengers as if it were a public omnibus. Perhaps here, in the remote countryside, there was no other way to get about, and with the prisoners shackled it would make little difference either way.

In the semi darkness one of the passengers knelt at her feet and began kindly stroking her numbed calves. Then he eased apart her ankles as far as the chain would permit, running his hand further up her leg, caressing her knees, manipulating them between fingers and thumb.

'Better?' he whispered.

'Much, thank you,' she replied, grateful for his concern.

'And your bottom, how does that feel? Sore I expect.'

'Very sore,' she said, shuffling uncomfortably and nudging the girl next to her, who had already lifted her legs and was having her thighs soothed.

'Mayhap I can help that too,' the voice whispered, drawing closer.

'It's not that sore,' she said, edging backwards into the van wall.

But the kindly man would have none of it and, placing his hands under her thighs, he lifted her clear of the seat and slid his hands under her bottom. Olivia sat down again and nearly choked. His hands were touching her bare buttocks, the fingers curling into her crease, seemingly going ever deeper.

'I'm quite all right there, thank you,' she said firmly.

He ignored her. 'No, I don't think you are, so you just keep still, there's a good girl.'

Olivia couldn't keep still. The tips of his fingers had wormed far into her crevice and were getting alarmingly close to her bottom hole. Blushing with embarrassment she turned to her companion who, offering no protest to the head buried in her cleavage, rolled her head from side to side, breathing in great gulps.

It wasn't quite the same situation on the other side of her. There, the girl was writhing and panting, and although trying to escape the hands which lovingly stripped away her upper garments, exposing her breasts and fondling them, she seemed to be surrendering as if there were little she could do. The girl nearest the door had gone strangely quiet except for murmuring groans, punctuated with short, sharp gasps.

I mustn't appear ungrateful, Olivia told herself, these simple country folk had willingly offered their comfort to those they knew were far worse off than themselves. The fingers continued to explore her crease, kneading and pinching her flesh, gradually restoring life into her dead cheeks.

'I feel much better now, thank you,' she said, as the man slid his hands away.

'I ain't finished yet,' he replied brusquely, bringing them over her flanks and into the join of her legs. 'Now, lift your arse.'

'I'll do no such thing.'

'You'll do as you're told.'

Sighing with resignation, Olivia raised her bottom from the seat. His hand went quickly into her groin, stroking her fleece, passing under her legs, and making free with her private parts. He went on rubbing to and fro until she felt dizzy and uncomfortably wet.

'I'll have to sit down,' she apologised, 'or this ring around my neck will surely throttle me.'

'Bugger the ring,' he muttered, reluctantly taking away his hand.

Olivia lowered herself gingerly back onto the seat. For some inexplicable reason the temperature inside the wagon had soared and sweat trickled down the sides of her face.

'What's the matter with you?' he asked, genuinely concerned.

'Air, for God's sake, I need a little air.'

He obliged her at once by loosening the buttons of her dress, and kept on loosening them so that when he'd finished it fell open from collar to waist.

'You're so thoughtful,' she sobbed, and then looked down. 'Was it really necessary to release me that far?'

'You said you needed air,' he reminded her, taking both breasts in his hands and gently squeezing them.

'Why don't you fan me instead of doing this?' she protested, pulling at the chains.

'If you don't shut your trap I'll fan you with the flat of my hand.'

Olivia gritted her teeth and let him go on mauling her. She had come to the conclusion that he wasn't very intelligent, treating her breasts in this fashion had very little effect in the way of reviving her; if anything he was making matters worse. It didn't help her state of mind when she looked at her companions who seemed to be in an advanced stage of collapse. The girl nearest the door had swooned with her mouth wide open and was uttering fearful groans.

'Christ, help me,' she muttered, turning her head to Olivia. 'Have courage, I'm sure we'll be there soon.'

'I'm there already,' she whimpered, gazing with glazed eyes. Olivia gave her a sad, baffled look and turned back to the man who was still worrying her breasts with painful squeezes and pinches on her nipples.

'You've made me more sore than ever I was before you came into this dreadful wagon,' she complained. 'I don't believe you're trying to assist me at all.'

The man took away his hands abruptly, just as the van rumbled to a halt. The door opened emitting a glare of bright sunshine that made everyone blink and swear, except Olivia who vainly tried to conceal her nakedness by bowing her head and letting her hair cascade over her sweating chest.

'You'd be a lot more sore if it weren't for them chains,' he said rudely, clambering out of the van.

The door quickly closed again and they set off at such a rate the van nearly toppled into the ditches that lined the road to the House of Correction. Through the now unconcealed window a grim building appeared on the horizon. It disappeared behind some trees and came into view again but larger and more foreboding than before. There was nothing around it for miles and Olivia found herself wondering why the van had dropped its passengers in such a remote and distant place. It never occurred to her that they would be picked up on the way back and would repeat the same exercise over and over again. Neither did she realise that the chain that prevented her legs from opening had been her saviour. The girl, for whose life she had so feared, had made a remarkable recovery and seemed none the worse for her ordeal.

'We're here,' she announced gloomily, as the van slowed to a crawl.

The driver reached for a bell rope and gave it a sharp tug. Somewhere inside a bell boomed and a minute later came the rattling of bolts and locks. The van proceeded slowly under an arch and into a cobbled quadrangle surrounded with high walls topped with spikes. They set off again through another arch and came to rest outside a huge black studded door.

The driver unhooked the iron rings from their necks and stared malevolently as they rubbed their fingers over the mark left in its wake.

'That mess in your drawers, how did you get that?' he said, addressing the girls at random

'It was the journey,' one of them replied. 'It made me wet myself.'

'And that goes for all of you. Understood?'

They nodded in unison, except Olivia who returned his staring eyes.

'That's not true. It was that man who made me mess myself, putting his hand where he had no business, undressing me and making free with my person—'

'I don't think you heard me!' said the driver, slapping her face.

'I wet myself,' she said sullenly.

Satisfied with that, he pushed them out onto the cobbles and rapped the knocker of the nearest door. It was answered by a girl of their own age, dressed in the drab, grey rags of the prison.

She told them that the board wished to speak with them forthwith as was customary with new entrants. Following her up a steep spiral staircase, Olivia was thrown into confusion. She didn't know a board could speak, so far the ones over which she had prostrated herself had not uttered a word. Up and up they went and at each step the girl exhibited an awkward lurch of her hips as if one leg were shorter than the other, then when they reached the top she could see the reason. What fearful instrument could possibly leave those welts? she wondered, for the girl's bottom showed clearly beneath her tattered skirt the evidence of a recent and brutal flogging which had left her half crippled. She walked on along a corridor until she came to a pair of double doors.

'Remember not to speak unless spoken to,' she said nervously, and then knocked, waited for the word of command, and went in with the others trailing behind.

'The new inmates,' she announced, dropping a painful curtsey. Then, turning a wincing face to Olivia, said solemnly 'Bow to the board.'

The board consisted of three men and a woman looking very grand in their dark blue uniforms with shining brass buttons and an air of moral superiority. The girl who had led them there bowed so low her skirt audibly ripped, revealing the tops of her thighs and, to Olivia's profound astonishment, a pouting pudenda freshly shorn.

'Get out, Smithers!'

At the sound of the woman's voice Smithers fled from the room rubbing her bottom more readily than before.

'I wish I could say that I am pleased to make your acquaintance,' said a bewhiskered gentleman in a high chair. 'But unfortunately that is not the case. The world is full of miscreants like you, who, despite strenuous efforts of the courts, return again and again to their lives of crime. There can be no doubt that this way of life is of your own choosing, and that its rewards have hitherto outweighed the punishment. That sorry state of affairs will now be rectified.' He rustled a piece of paper on his desk and looked up, eyeing the girls in turn.

'Olivia Holland, who is she?' Olivia raised her hand. 'Two dozen,' he said.

Olivia did a quick mental calculation. 'But sir, I'm only due a dozen.'

'Are you assuming that the magistrate is in error? Because if you are, you are insolent, and for that you will receive another half dozen, making thirty four in all.' Olivia wondered where the extra four came from but thought it wise not to ask. He read out the other names on his list and laid down his paper.

'The tiresome task of flogging your backsides we shall deal with immediately, and after that you will be shown to your place of work. Kindly remove those filthy rags.'

'We have to take off all our clothes?' one of the girls exclaimed agog.

'Idiot!' returned the matron, getting up and rushing towards her.

She placed her long skinny fingers under the girl's collar, and with one jerk of her elbow, ripped it clean from her back. Hardly had the girl recovered from the shock when she was spun round and the exercise repeated at the front.

'The old story,' said the gentleman in the high chair, 'no drawers, I see. But it will make our task all the more easier. The last one to disrobe will receive an extra six strokes for her trouble.'

A frantic hurrying of unbuttoned skirts now ensued with such rapidity that in a matter of seconds the girls were rendered completely naked.

'The Judgement of Paris,' chuckled the third gentleman on the board. 'But in their case I think I would forego that choice, just look at them.'

The gentleman in the high chair was looking, as was the matron and both with eyes that settled emphatically on Olivia's slender body. It was not a pleasant feeling seeing where the direction of their eyes lay.

'Mrs Priestley, take them to the punishment room, and please ensure that these wretches receive their just deserts. Don't spare them.'

'Indeed I will not, sir,' the matron replied with obvious relish, her eyes still roaming over Olivia's bottom.

Halfway along the passage, the girl leading the way stopped abruptly at an open window overlooking the quadrangle where small groups of women and girls were busy heaving coal from a cart.

'Do we have to walk across there naked?' she asked incredulously.

'Those are the rules,' the matron replied smugly, 'to teach you humility and obedience, but one look at your stupid faces tells me that you possess neither. But you will soon learn, of that you may rest assured.' She was about to give Olivia a swift kick in the rump, but stopped short. 'What did you do to deserve that?' she inquired, noticing the birch marks.

'I stole a loaf of bread, miss.'

'A thief, no less, and doubtless an artful liar into the bargain. In my opinion, the magistrate let you off lightly, which is more than I would have done.'

Then she did kick her, and so hard that Olivia flew down the corridor like a bullet. If it was designed to put fear into the rest it certainly had the desired effect. They rushed past Olivia and darted down the staircase, leaving their stricken companion to follow as best she could.

Almost bent double with shame, Olivia hobbled across the cobbles oblivious to the fact that none of the coal heavers paid her the slightest heed. The matron came close behind, pausing now and then to slap the face of anyone within reach. The girls headed for a low, squat building on the other side of the quadrangle wherein the flogging of the inmates was duly performed.

'You're first,' said the matron, indicating a small, redheaded girl.

Trembling from head to toe, she made her way to a peculiar wooden construction that closely resembled a painter's trestle, except where a plank might have rested were chains with iron rings on the end of them.

'Step up and put your wrists through those,' the matron ordered.

Sally mounted the bottom rung and stretched her thin arms upwards to the rings. Her wrists slipped easily through and the matron, ensuring that there would be no possibility of them slipping out again, secured them by turning a key. The new inmate was clearly terrified at the prospect of another flogging. Olivia, watching to see how matters would progress, saw at a glance that her boyish buttocks and narrow back were unused to sustained punishment. Far from having learnt to relax and so soften the blows, her cheeks tensed making them all the harder and more susceptible to the searing pain soon to follow.

The instrument whose cruel marks Olivia had seen on Smithers, was a cat o' nine tails, whose leather straps were worn to a high gloss from so much use.

'Brace yourself, wretch,' said the matron, as much for the benefit of Olivia and her companion as the girl on the trestle.

To Olivia's astonishment, the matron faced not the girl, but the opposite wall, then suddenly, with the speed and agility of a ballet dancer, swivelled round on her heels sending the whip ricocheting into Sally's quaking bottom. The whole trestle shook from the blow and when Olivia opened her eyes it was to see Sally's cheeks covered in a mass of stripes. If one stroke could deliver that, she thought, what would be left after a dozen, or two or three? This would be no light flogging, but a severe example designed to strike terror in the hearts of those who witnessed it.

'See and remark how we punish our transgressors,' the matron announced, raising her arm for the next blow.

Olivia could see very well. What had been pale, translucent skin was now a blazing scarlet. Between each stroke was not a finger's width of flesh unmarked; and between each stroke Sally's body leapt away from the frame until she hung there, feet dangling lifeless over the bar.

The matron clicked her tongue. 'Fainted. The girl's fainted. You, fetch that bucket.'

The girl next to Olivia scurried across the room and brought over a pail, which the matron emptied across Sally's back and bottom. She stirred slowly into life, emitting a low, deep groan, which the matron judged was enough to continue the punishment.

The thongs lashed around her flanks, curling round her upper thighs and licking into the pit of her stomach. For a moment the trestle rocked on its legs, threatening to collapse.

'Enough!' Olivia shrieked. 'The girl's had enough!'

'Nonsense,' replied the matron. 'Two dozen is her lot and two dozen she shall have.'

She gathered the whip in her hand ready for a renewed attack, but it was pointless continuing for Sally had passed out and no matter how many buckets of salt water were thrown over her, she would not recover.

The matron cast aside her whip and released the keys. Sally fell backwards hitting the floor with a dull thump of her head, shoulders and back.

'How very inconsiderate,' said the matron, 'fainting like that. All the more effort in carrying her to the infirmary.' Stepping aside, she picked up the whip. 'Next!'

Jane, a diminutive brunette, walked bravely to the trestle and, standing on the rung, reached upwards, but even on tiptoe could not touch the rings.

'Get down and bend over that rung,' the matron hissed. Jane hopped off the rung and, kneeling before it, bent herself over, pushing her bottom high into the air.

'Perfect,' said the matron, lashing the upraised globes.

As Jane's legs spasmed and kicked she hit her again, catching a fearful blow across the upper thighs, and speedily repeated it, this time landing it on the calves. Jane's body arched in pain, and for a full minute she thrashed about like a stranded fish on a bank, screaming and yelling at the top of her voice.

'Scream all you like,' said the matron, 'no one will hear you.'

That wasn't true. The inmates assembled in the yard could hear everything that was going on. So could the workmen on the roof three buildings away.

The matron paused to regain her breath and waited until the thrashing limbs exhausted themselves. When Jane no longer moved she let her have it in a quick succession of blows down the whole length of her back. From shoulder blades to waist the flesh was ripped raw. Unable to endure the sight of Jane's tear-streaked face, Olivia turned away, burying her face in her hands, but her ears could still hear the barrage of unending shrieks which gradually rose to a piercing crescendo and then finally subsided into a blubber of choking sobs.

'Get up now,' the matron said, pleased with the result and complimenting her for not fainting.

Jane struggled to her feet and tottered about the floor like a drunk. She got as far as the door and fell flat on her breasts, half in and half out of the entrance.

'I spoke too soon, t'would seem.' She took a bottle from her apron and gulped a deep draught, belched, and put it back again.

Her eyes had a demoniac glow as she advanced upon Olivia. 'And now we come to you.'

Right from the start the matron had taken an instant dislike to Olivia, as she always did with any good-looking girl. She had reached that point in her life when no longer young, she began to despise it in others. Her tired breasts and broad thighs made a sad contrast to the finely sculptured contours of Olivia.

'You are a thief,' she went on, 'and thieves are not tolerated here. Moreover, they are punished more severely than anyone else, and you will be no exception.'

'Please, ma'am, I only stole for the food. I hadn't eaten for three days, and as I am orphaned—'

The matron cut her short with a resounding slap in the face, and another that, because Olivia was knocked sideways, missed its target and caught her unwittingly across her right breast.

'Stand still, girl!' she rasped, as Olivia swayed under the blow.

When her breast had settled back into its proper place the matron regarded her with an especially evil glint, which Olivia had often seen on the faces of licentious drunks who accosted her in alleyways and whispered lewd suggestions.

A forefinger and thumb, crooked like the claw of a hawk, closed around Olivia's nipple and pinched so hard tears of pain formed in her eyes. At the same time as it twisted her teat, the matron slapped her again on the other breast, and kept on slapping, turning it a gorgeous shade of pink. The nipple that had all the while been subjected to excruciating pain was released, and then to Olivia's sheer disbelief it began all over again on the other. Then she set about her with the bare flat of her hand, hitting everywhere at once. She slapped her breasts so many times that Olivia was certain they had gone egg shaped, and when she had finished with those she moved to her flanks, working all the way around, lingering long over the firm globes of her bottom, covering them with bright red fingerprints. The finale was a slap of gargantuan strength on the small of her back which sent Olivia tumbling pell-mell head over heels.

'Don't bother to get up,' the matron advised. 'I can beat you just as satisfactorily where you are.'

She marched across the room and retrieved the whip from where it had previously fallen, beside the still recumbent body of Sally.

'No doubt you've spent much time in that position,' she croaked, seeing Olivia lying on her back with outspread thighs. 'And as it is so familiar to you, you can stay there.'

'It isn't familiar to me,' Olivia replied, nonplussed. 'I usually sleep on my side with my hands under the pillow.'

The matron's face contorted incredulously. 'For one moment I almost believed you, which just goes to show what a skilful liar you are.'

'I'm not lying,' said Olivia, hearing her voice rise. 'Why ever would I choose to sleep with my legs wide open.'

'Why d'ya think, stupid girl?'

'Really, I have no idea. As I said, I always sleep on my side, although sometimes I have woken to find my hands have gone between my legs.'

'Probably because you were dreaming,' the matron replied absently, staring wide eyed into Olivia's crotch. 'Now, spread your legs wider and draw up your knees.'

Olivia's legs bent and fell open, presenting an uninterrupted and magnificent view of her more than generous mound.

'Please, ma'am,' she pleaded, 'spare hitting me there. I'll be good from now on. I promise I'll never steal anything again as long as I live, not never.'

The matron expressed extreme doubt in that quarter and then whirled round sending the leather tails whistling into Olivia's groin.

'The one great advantage of the cat,' the matron said, 'is that it can cover a large area with the minimum of effort.'

Indeed, the first blow had embraced the whole of Olivia's labia, the crease of her thighs, and entered the slit itself. She groaned like a wounded animal, letting her knees drop and bridging her back into a high arch. Patiently the matron waited for her to recover, and then tickling the fallen knees with the thongs, indicated that Olivia should lift them up again. This she did with greater agony than before. A second blow whipped higher, slashing her belly from mound to naval. Olivia thought it would burst, and when the third stroke lashed her pubic ridge it seemed she had been branded with hot irons.

'Please, ma'am, I beg you, no more! Beat my bottom if you will, but don't hit me there again!'

'Very well,' said the matron in a rare fit of generosity. 'Turn over, and I shall fulfil your wish.'

Olivia didn't wish at all. She would rather have been boiled in oil than receive one stroke more, but groaning and sobbing she rolled over onto her stomach and put her hands under her head. The whip struck into her crease leaving a remarkable duplication of itself, a host of thin red bands which rapidly swelled wider, turning from pink to red to purple until it was impossible to tell which was which.

'Your hardened bottom does, I admit, take quite a whipping,' said the matron, not without a hint of admiration. 'But nevertheless I still have my duty to fulfil, and you were due two dozen and six, were you not?'

Olivia had received half that amount, and braced herself for the rest which the matron delivered with deliberate slowness of hand, allowing long intervals for the agony to spread down the whole length of her legs.

'Are you chastised enough?' she asked, when the final stroke fired its way across Olivia's burning cheeks.

Olivia moaned and lifted her head. The matron turned to fetch the bucket and saw to her astonishment the governor standing in the doorway.

'Has she succumbed?' he inquired nonchalantly, nodding at Olivia.

'The girl is still conscious,' the matron replied dryly.

The governor leaned over her, pressing his fingers into her bottom. 'Normally you would be set to work at once, but on this occasion I will make an exception. Report to my office.'

Olivia struggled to her feet and made her way out into the quadrangle where the coal heavers were gathering around a cauldron of bubbling gruel. Such was the commotion that again her appearance went largely unnoticed. She went through the doorway and up the spiral staircase, but instead of going right to the top she entered the second storey and became quickly lost in a labyrinth of passages and staircases. Each was no different than the one before or after, but it was the eerie silence that unnerved her. Not a sound stirred, and for a moment she experienced the sensation of being completely alone in the world; alone and naked, with only her throbbing bottom to remind her that other people did exist somewhere beyond these grim, dank passages.

She walked on, occasionally glancing out of windows to get her bearings. Twice she saw the quadrangle with the coal heavers scurrying about like frightened ants, and once overlooked the roof of a building that, if she had the courage to scale, might have deposited her outside the walls. But the prospect of having to run stark naked across miles of inhospitable moorland was too awful to contemplate.

Using the quadrangle as a compass point with which to navigate, she kept to that side of the building and eventually found herself on the correct floor. But where, she wondered, was the governor's office? The only recourse was to knock on the nearest door and ask someone.

'You!' she exclaimed, thankful for a familiar face.

Smithers regarded her for a moment, her head cocked on one side as if she had never seen another human being and it was a rarity to do so.

'Why don't you come in for a second?' she said, admitting Olivia into a room magnificently furnished with a huge brass bedstead and sumptuous drapery.

'What is this place?' asked Olivia, taking it in with a wide sweep.

'The governor's private quarters,' she said softly, seating herself on the bed and swinging her legs to and fro. 'And I daresay, if you are so favoured, you might one day be invited here for tea, and a little else besides.'

Then she broke into a fit of wild, shrieking laughter that stopped abruptly.

'What on earth is going on in here?'

Olivia stood rigid, arms by her sides. 'Please, sir, I got lost and was asking Smithers the way to the office.'

'You will find it at the end of the passage. Smithers, you will remain here until I return. You know how I expect to find you.'

Smithers, who had got off the bed, dropped a curtsey and hurriedly opened the door. Olivia went out first and rushed down to the office. Although she couldn't say why, there was something deeply disturbing about that room.

The office overlooked fields and meadows beyond, where in the distance she saw a trail of white smoke threading its way to the town station. A faint sound of a whistle heralded its approach and then died in a cloud of black smoke.

'The new railway,' the Governor informed her, coming in and closing the door.

Olivia felt very vulnerable in her nakedness now that he stood beside her.

'Please sir, may I have my clothes?' she asked timidly.

'Your clothes?' he replied, as if it were an odd request and everyone was expected to go around completely naked. 'All in good time you will be issued with a uniform, but for the present you will remain as you are. Kindly bend over my desk.'

'I have had my punishment,' she reminded him, as politely as she could.

'Not quite. There are still four owing, which I shall deliver myself.'

'But,' she protested, 'if I am aright, two dozen and six makes thirty, and when you think there are nine straps to the stroke, I have in fact been belted almost three hundred times. Even though the straps be not as long as a birch, they were nonetheless painful.'

The governor listened with growing astonishment to this startling piece of intelligence, and came to the conclusion that she was far too clever for her own good.

'Shut your mouth girl and do as you are told. A common prostitute contradicting my authority, indeed!'

'I am not a common prostitute,' Olivia protested.

'Indeed you are not, in fact, you are a decidedly uncommon prostitute.'

The fact that he was confusing her with that of one of her companions recently flogged was lost on them both. Sighing with dumb resignation, Olivia did as she was told. She leaned over the desk and spread both arms and legs, saving him the trouble of asking her to do so.

'The matron has served you well,' he remarked, his eyes riveted on her gaping slit, 'but she was not supposed to hit you there. That I strictly forbid. After all a female is, I suppose, entitled to some respect regarding those places. Are you in pain?'

'Very much, sir,' replied Olivia, thinking what a thoughtful gentleman he really was.

'Then I shall only beat you with the lightest of hand, and afterwards tend the place where you have been untowardly mishandled.'

He was true to his word and landed his own Malacca cane with the lightest of strokes, presenting it tactfully well away from her most tender place. It seemed to Olivia that even in the most ruthless of men there existed a spark of compassion. Behind his ferocious whiskers lay perhaps a kindly face and a kinder heart, which at that moment had gone to a cabinet and was fetching the means of her comfort.

'This is a task I usually leave to the nurse,' he told her. 'But as she is busy seeing to your other companions in crime I shall do it myself.'

'You do me great honour, sir,' Olivia replied, settling herself comfortably over the desk.

'Now open your legs a little wider and lift your bottom, up on your toes, if you have to.'

Olivia did as she was ordered, shuffling her feet over the carpet and thrusting out her behind. A cloth soaked in oil went between her legs and gently rubbed back and forth, not unlike the stranger in the prison van who uninvitingly came to her aid. But this was different; instead of a rough, leathery hand that left her dizzy and feeling sick, there came a curious cold, tingling sensation that seemed to penetrate right to the depths of her belly. Round and round it went, all over her mound and buttocks, soothing her burning skin, seemingly charming away the pain.

'Oh, sir, that is wonderful,' she gasped, clutching at the edges of the desk.

For some odd reason, which she was unable to fathom, the oil had worked its charms on her breasts and nipples, and down the length of her thighs, particularly on the insides where they were most sensitive. And it was there he now concentrated, going in broad sweeps from knee to groin and again into her parted labia.

'Look upon me as doctor,' he said amiably.

'I've never been to a doctor, sir.'

The cloth suddenly stopped. 'Then I may assume that you are in excellent health, inside and out.'

She nodded.

'But if you did have reason to undress in front of a medical man, you would not have any qualms in letting him examine you - intimately, I mean.'

She had to give that consideration before replying. 'If it were for the betterment of my wellbeing I should allow him to do whatever he sought fit.'

'As I am so doing at this moment.'

'Indeed, sir, I feel better already.

'This is only the first part of the treatment. Your thighs have been particularly abused and will require further attention. Please remain where you are.'

Olivia could not remember when she had ever felt so relaxed and calm. Her limbs had taken on a curious weightless feeling so that she seemed almost to be floating, except for a mild and persistent throbbing between her legs.

'How does this feel?' he asked, running the tip of his finger up and down her inner thigh.

Olivia shivered. 'It does feel rather odd, sir,' she chuckled. 'A bit like being tickled with a straw.'

'You know all about that, I suppose? A handsome piece like yourself would never lack for suitors.'

'I suppose not,' she answered vaguely. 'But in truth, I have not been thus favoured, and nor do I care to.'

'Hmmm, well, tell me what this feels like.'

Olivia could not readily think of a comparison. It didn't tickle her in the way that his finger had done, but neither was it lacking in the same effect.

'Well reach behind you and see if you recognise what it might be.'

Olivia stretched her arm to her thigh and groped blindly for whatever it was that travelled up and down her skin. She was helped when it was put into her hand.

'It feels warm and hard,' she muttered, 'and yet soft enough to squeeze.'

She closed her hand around it and wondered what could possibly grow even harder, or larger. For a while he let her caress and pinch it gently between her fingers, then, he lifted her hand away and put it back on the desk, and as he did so the stalk she had just been feeling nudged into her hip, and again she shivered.

'It does feel rather like the arm of a baby,' she said quizzically, 'but I don't suppose it could possibly be that - could it?'

'Indeed not,' he exclaimed, unable to resist a furtive laugh. 'It's a root,' he informed her, 'containing a liquid with particular medicinal properties which I shall now bestow on your wounded thigh. And when I have done so, you may rub it into your skin to increase its properties. Do you understand all that?'

She nodded and immediately he stroked his weapon against her flesh, running the plum rapidly back and forth over her fleece and then returning to her thigh, which he found particularly to his liking. She was certainly untouched, he was sure of that, which made a pleasant change in a place like this where almost every inmate had at least taken a hundred or more of the very thing that was now quivering against her leg.

'Now hold yourself in readiness,' he warned her, and with that he suddenly erupted, uttering a grunt that made Olivia shudder.

Hot spurts of sap darted against her thigh, a few stray drops spattered over her buttocks and trickled into her crease. Olivia, obeying her master, reached behind and palmed it into her skin, rubbing it most emphatically on her inner thigh.

'And your bottom,' he advised her.

He stood back watching her long slender fingers running deep in her crease, lending it a silky shine which for one moment he was very much tempted to penetrate. But that could wait, it would require time and effort to bugger a virgin, and at that precise moment it would be a lot less tiring to take Smithers.

'You can get up now, Holland,' he said, buttoning his trousers. 'Go down to the storeroom and collect your uniform. Tomorrow you will begin your term of hard labour, but occasionally, when it pleases me, I shall require your presence here, and if necessary administer the same.'

Olivia bowed low and then, standing up, looked at her hand. 'What shall I do about this?'

Her palm was still greased and glistening.

'Lick it clean,' he said. 'You may find it quite to your liking.'

Olivia walked along the corridor taking great care not to get lost, trying to discern what, if anything, that strange taste resembled.

Chapter Three

The uniform that Olivia collected had been originally intended for a female much shorter and less well-endowed than herself. The hem that should have reached past mid-calf barely covered her knees, and her generous breasts, straining at the front, prevented the buttons from entering their corresponding holes. But, she was soon to realise, in that she was not alone, for every Sunday all the uniforms were taken away and washed and had shrunk so much none of them fitted anyone.

Olivia had been set to work in the laundry itself and in the steaming heat she laboured stripped to the waist, or more often than not, attired only in her drawers. It was not unusual for some of the women working over the boiling vats to take off their underwear and set about their tasks entirely naked. Through dense clouds of steam they moved like spectres, their bodies glistening with sweat, their hair tied up behind or falling lank around their gleaming shoulders. In such an environment modesty was in short supply, as was privacy. When Olivia asked where she could relieve herself the overseer merely pointed to a tub in the middle of the room, where, out of sheer desperation, she squatted alongside whoever happened to be there at the time. Those who were forbidden to leave their place of work, such as the mangle or washboards, simply wetted their drawers as they worked and were obliged to continue thus for the remainder of their shift.

On her first Sunday in the laundry Olivia was summoned quite unexpectedly into the yard where, all the other inmates now bereft of their uniforms, stood around in semi-naked or naked groups for the purpose of witnessing a public flogging. The girl, who had not been quick enough in removing her uniform, suddenly took fright and bolted towards a low door that led into the main quadrangle.

'She'll get an extra twenty for that,' someone behind Olivia whispered.

What happened next sickened Olivia to the stomach, and gave her the first insight as to just how far the other inmates had been brutalised into tormenting each other.

'Fetch her back, and a day's rest for the one who does!' roared the overseer.

At once the entire congregation rushed for the door, pushing and shoving, punching and kicking, to be the first to lay hands on her. Olivia brought up the rear and watched in horror how a previously docile assembly of cowed women could so quickly transform into a pack of snarling she-wolves. The girl ran back and forth along the perimeter wall like a frightened rabbit as the pack slowly closed in. Making a final hopeless attempt to scale it, she leapt up and began a slow ascension of the brickwork. The pack gave her enough time for her bare bottom to reach head height and then a pair of hands seized her between the legs. The girl screamed as a clenched fist squeezed her mound and another went under her legs and ripped at her pubic fleece. But still she clung by the fingertips to the bricks, desperately trying to escape more clutching hands that now grabbed her ankles. Peals of laughter arose as her legs were spread wide, threatening to split her asunder.

It was a wonder to Olivia just how wide a woman's legs could spread or with what strength she managed to cling on, her arms thrown upwards and outwards.

'That will do! Leave her!'

At the sound of the overseer's voice, the pack drew off leaving the girl suspended, star shaped, flattened against the wall. 'Bring a rope,' he ordered.

For one terrible moment, Olivia assumed she was going to be hanged. But the overseer, instead of forming a noose, fashioned the end into a huge, hard knot, into which he inserted a pebble for good measure. The pack retreated into a semicircle as the overseer stepped closer. It didn't take much imagination to see what he had in mind. The heavily weighted end swung upwards straight into the join of the girl's legs. The knot not help but bury itself in her parted slit. She let out a piercing howl and clung evermore desperately onto the bricks.

Another slash of the rope had the girl writhing in agony, and Olivia now understood why she had been left there. Her breasts pressed flat against the coarse surface suffered torments as the rope lashed her again and again. Her delicate pert nipples rubbed raw, as did her belly and fronts of her thighs. But still she clung, sobbing and wailing.

One of the inmates, clearly a self-styled leader of the rest, encouraged the overseer with harsh shouts of, 'Beat her harder!' and, 'Make the blood flow! Whip her to death!' She probably did not mean it literally but the effect on the others was galvanic. They all began adding advice of their own and the louder it went the more savage and cruel the taunts. Things really came to a head when the overseer, tired of beating the clinging girl, threw the rope haphazardly into the crowd. The woman who caught it was as quickly floored with a fist in the jaw. She was probably unconscious before her bottom struck the earth, which was hardly surprising, being as the woman who hit her was built like a navvy. Tall and powerful, she struck terror into the hearts of the assembly who had now gone deathly quiet. Above that eerie silence came the dull thud of the rope landing on the small of the girl's back. It was well aimed and deliberately so, for the immediate reaction of the girl was to thrust her hips violently forward, and in so doing her pubic ridge scraped the bricks. Olivia winced in sympathy, but not it seemed, did anyone else. Her astonished face stared in amazement at the sights she saw going on right in front of her very eyes. Blatantly, in full view of God and Man, arms began to encircle waists, hands slipped between thighs, fingers searched into clefts, and lips touched lips.

'It's horrible,' exclaimed Olivia without thinking. 'How could women do that to each other? It's so immoral, and in a place set up for our correction.'

She forced her eyes back to the girl at the wall who had nearly fainted and was now held in situ by a couple of willing helpers whose hands pressed against the backs of her upper thighs. The stout woman was lashing the girl on her back, sending the rope whistling over the heads of her participants and bringing forth fresh screams of pain. Where the knot had landed were huge black bruises, and between her legs a once pretty and pouting mound had become a swollen and open wound wherefrom a river of milky juice oozed and dripped.

Olivia, so appalled at the spectacle of what the other inmates were doing amongst themselves, failed to notice the long, sinuous arm creeping around her shoulders. Neither did she pay heed to the lengthy thigh rubbing assiduously against her own. Not a few feet away, two of the inmates had secreted themselves into an alcove and were locked in fond embrace. A knee had positioned itself into an open crotch and was moving rapidly to and fro. The girl, whose head Olivia could see resting on the shoulder of the other, flicked her tongue into her companion's ear and raked her fingernails up and down her back. Beyond that despicable display she saw another pair with hands on each others bottoms, seemingly trying to insert their fingers into their respective clefts. Everywhere she looked it was the same; except for the girl undergoing a whipping. The insides of her thighs were coated with a greasy liquid which now poured from her labia.

Olivia was suddenly spun round and into her open, astonished mouth a wet and wriggling tongue thrust itself. The shock was so paramount that for several seconds she went limp in the arms that held her. A knee pressed into her groin and began its urgent movement, going up and down and rubbing deep between her legs. Olivia's only means of egress was to bite the tongue searching inside her mouth. It flew back accompanied with a muffled cry of pain.

Olivia found her eyes level with the head of a remarkably pretty woman who blinked at her in astonishment.

'Do you always do that when you're being kissed?' she asked.

'I have no desire to be kissed,' Olivia replied, trying to push the woman away.

But the woman held on, pinning Olivia into a doorway. One hand planted itself on her breast, and the knee rubbed harder than ever.

'Let me go this minute,' Olivia protested, wriggling her bottom against the door frame.

'I like my lovers to put up a struggle,' the woman said, introducing herself as Flora the turnkey.

Olivia had already discovered that a turnkey was a trusted inmate who locked the dormitories at night and was allowed certain privileges. But this, she decided, was definitely not one of them.

'Put your hand between my legs,' she said softly, 'or I shall be forced to report you.'

'For what, in heaven's name?'

'Anything you like; stealing, shirking, plotting to escape. Anything that will have you flogged senseless.'

'Are you trying to frighten me?'

'Not necessarily. Just do as you're told.'

Olivia glanced quickly over Flora's shoulder. The girl on the wall had collapsed and was lying in the dirt and being revived with hard slaps across her breasts and face. Slowly the women were trooping away back to their various duties. If only she could stall a few minutes longer. She put her hand into Flora's groin and held it there, keeping still, wondering what would happen next.

'Now open your mouth,' Flora murmured.

'I told you, I don't want to be kissed, and least of all by another woman. Why, it's outrageous.'

'Then in that case I'll report you for soiling your bed instead of using the pot.'

She made to move but Olivia pulled her back.

'If you do I'll be put back on the trestle and whipped.'

'Certainly.'

'This is blackmail.'

'Yes it is.'

'And you think that just because you're a turnkey, you can get away with it.'

'I don't think, I know. Ask anyone, they'll tell you.'

Olivia knew that putting that to the test would be wasted effort. She swallowed hard and opened her mouth slightly, barely parting her lips.

'Wider,' said Flora, placing the tip of her forefinger on Olivia's chin and drawing it downwards.

Olivia's jaw gaped, and in a trice Flora's tongue shot into her mouth, circling around the cheeks, coiling over her own tongue, and then darting quickly from side to side. She pushed Olivia's head into a corner of the door frame, keeping it there until she considered herself satisfied.

'Now, what was so awful about that?' she asked, giving Olivia a final kiss.

'Everything,' Olivia hissed. 'You're vulgar and foul and nasty, and I'd rather be whipped than have your odious tongue back in my mouth.'

This sudden outburst left Flora temporarily speechless. By now the quadrangle was cleared of its occupants, save for the whipped girl who still lay writhing in the dust where no one had bothered to care for her. Flora let Olivia slip from her grasp and watched her with squinted, glowing eyes as she raced back to the laundry.

Smithers laughed quietly to herself from the window high above.

She had witnessed everything that had taken place down below in the quadrangle, and had been so engrossed in the proceedings that she didn't hear the governor coming up behind her.

'Why aren't you ready,' he snapped, slashing her viciously across her behind with his cane.

Smithers jumped away from the window. 'I beg your forgiveness, sir,' she said, tearing off her tattered uniform and rushing to a beautifully inlaid cabinet. She opened the doors and stood dutifully aside. 'What is your preference today, sir?'

'Your bottom,' he replied thoughtfully, rummaging in the cabinet.

A profusion of chains, shackles and padlocks clattered to the floor. Smithers did not need to be told what to do next. She gathered them up and placed them in a tidy pile on a bedside table along with a selection of whips and belts.

'The bed, sir?' she inquired meekly. 'Or would you prefer me the usual way?'

'Neither,' he replied. 'Fetch the stool.'

Smithers knew what he had in mind and did not require any further instruction. In the centre of the room she placed a low, quite innocent looking three legged stool that might be found in any lounge or boudoir. But closer inspection would reveal a more than generously padded seat and legs that splayed outwards at an angle wider than what would be considered usual on such furniture.

After she had taken off her uniform she stood naked before him as she always did; arms by her sides, her left leg bent slightly at the knee, her pretty oval face a picture of humility.

'You know perfectly well,' the governor began, 'that nobody is allowed in this room without my express authority. I turn my back for five minutes and find that you have wilfully disobeyed my orders.'

He walked behind her and patted her bottom. There was no doubt that Smithers had, in his considered opinion, the finest arse in the whole building. It was firm and well rounded, broad, yet well shaped, and the crease deeper and tighter than most. But what he had discovered about Smithers, after much experimenting with many of the other inmates, was that she more than any other, had no illusions as to what comfort her bottom could offer. Some had squealed and shrieked, others had grunted and winced, not a few sought to prevent his advances by compressing their muscles, but that was dealt with by a hard thump on the base of the spine. But Smithers had welcomed him with open and eager cheeks. How she had writhed and purred, wiggling her hips and reaching behind to actually stretch apart her crease instead of tearing her hair and sobbing. He had also discovered that she was even more receptive after a good flogging.

'You know the punishment for disobedience,' he said, steering her towards the stool.

'I deserve it,' she replied. 'I would like to be whipped hard and taught my place.'

'Your place is over that stool.'

Smithers knelt before it like a nun at prayer, hands in front of her, head bowed. A hard shove on the shoulder sent her over the seat. Putting her hands behind her over the crown of her rump, she leaned far forward, letting her breasts swing free, checking her balance by allowing her weight to rest squarely on her stomach. She caught her breath in a sharp, expectant gasp as a pair of iron cuffs locked securely around her wrists. Extending from either side of the seat were two broad leather straps rather like a belt that labourers wore equipped with a sturdy brass buckle through which one end of the strap quickly passed. The governor put his knee into the small of her back and pulled tight on the straps, using all his strength. The belt sank into her midriff, and went on tightening until at last the buckle was fixed.

Smithers in the throes of passion had the most unfortunate habit of thrashing her legs in all directions, which at her first attempt over the stool had unbalanced her, causing serious distraction to the governor who now allayed that eventuality with another set of straps. He passed the first two around her upper thighs binding them to the legs of the stool, which because of their wide angle allowed them to spread sufficiently for his purpose of entering her. The next set went around mid-thigh, and the last just above her knees. Her thighs thus secured thrice on each, he turned his attention to her bowed head.

'You know the reason I have to fit you with this collar,' he said, taking hold of her hair and arching her neck upwards.

'I can't help it, sir,' Smithers choked. 'It always affects me like that when your thing goes in me.'

'All the more reason why you need it. If I remember correctly on the last occasion when your head jerked about like a drunken puppet I thought you were in serious danger of doing yourself an injury, which is why I have also to fit you with a gag.'

Smithers couldn't deny the truth of that; her head did roll about all over the place and she did often give vent to wild shrieks, especially when his member was more than ordinarily excited (and after caressing it against the flanks of Olivia it was almost bursting with renewed desire).

The collar closed around her neck and was fastened at the front with small metal studs. At the sides were rings through which the governor slid lengths of chain. These he drew downwards to the front leg of the stool, stretched them taut and fastened with a padlock.

'I'm sorry that I don't have a silk handkerchief to hand,' he apologised, 'which would have been more suitable for a gag, so I'm afraid one of these belts will have to suffice.'

He returned to the table and selected a long, narrow length of leather, which, for no reason other than her bottom looked so beautiful, he sent sizzling into her cheeks. Smithers, taken completely unawares, let out a scream, but her head, much to his satisfaction, remained rigid.

'Open your mouth, April,' he said, taking her even more by surprise.

'You've never addressed me so familiarly, sir,' said Smithers, flushing with relish that she should be so honoured.

'A slip of the tongue,' he snapped, angry at the mistake, and forced the strap between her teeth.

When he came to fasten the buckle the strap proved to be too long, so he wrapped it twice more around her head and then with considerable difficulty adjusted the buckle into her open mouth.

'What shall I use to soften your bottom?' he mused, rummaging through the collection of whips and thongs. He held up a whip, thought for a moment, and put it back again.

'No, I don't think so. You're far too used to that. I need something to really open you up, and at the same time give you such a thrashing that when I've finished you'll have forgotten what day it is.'

At that Smithers visibly quaked. She wondered why he seemed as intent on punishing her as he did riding her bottom. Normally, unless she had been less forthcoming than usual, the whipping did not last long and he was soon inside her pumping like a savage. It might be something to do with that girl she had foolishly invited into his bedroom. If that were the case, she in turn deserved a flogging for putting him to so much trouble and keeping her waiting. Smithers made a mental note of that.

'Perhaps this will do,' said the governor, breaking in on her thoughts and offering up a rather vicious looking riding crop.

Smithers hated Olivia more than ever when that passed before her eyes. One swipe with that and she would be cut to the bone. For the first time in her life she was glad she possessed what everyone else considered to be a 'fat arse'.

'Will this do?' he repeated, tapping the end under her chin. 'After all the effort in keeping you on that stool, I don't want you to feel cheated.'

Smithers uttered an incomprehensible grunt that the governor rightly took as full consent. Without any more ado he was behind her and lashing her bottom without mercy. Yet, as every stroke whistled into her burning halves and at every grunt she uttered, his mind was not on what still lay ahead, but on that tall, raven haired beauty against whose slender flanks he had spurted. She was as innocent as a spring lamb; for no woman, no matter how stupid, would fail to realise what had taken place behind her back. And the way she'd rubbed it into her skin without so much as a hint of delight made her all the more desirous.

One look at Smithers' striped bottom told him what sport could be had with Olivia. How would she react, he wondered, if he took her in the same way as he had taken Smithers, bound and flogged, but without knowing what he fully intended?

Smithers' mind was not on Olivia but on the whipping she was taking. Her bottom was ablaze with a searing pain that covered her whole backside, the tops of her thighs, and her hips. The crop had cut deep into her soft, abundant flesh, particularly near the crease of her thighs where the pain excited her most. Stroke after stroke sliced into her thigh creases and flanks and each blistering welt left her aching for more. If she were not gagged she would have asked for a thrashing between her legs, where the pain would have been greatest. But as it was she had to content herself with being thrashed on her bottom and legs. The governor, aroused with thoughts of buggering the innocent Olivia, tore into

Smithers with a vengeance.

It seemed incredible that her bottom could withstand such a flogging, but Smithers was more than equal to the task. The harder he whipped, the greater her need for his manhood, which by now had been released from his trousers and was eagerly awaiting its own immersion into the willing orifice between her cheeks. But there still remained one part of her bottom as yet untouched.

'Your cleft,' he announced. 'I think we'll give that some attention.'

Smithers' heart skipped a beat when the iron cuffs around her wrists fell open. As was customary, she reached behind and, sinking her fingers into her cleft, prised it fully apart. The crop landed with superb accuracy, cutting into the darker regions of her valley where the flesh had not yet been welted. He gave her a dozen strokes, dividing the number in half on either buttock. Her teeth bit hard onto the strap as the heat burned from her welted cheeks into her quivering bottom.

It quivered a great deal more when the crop was cast aside and her hands were taken away and repositioned over her back. The iron cuffs locked her wrists together again, and as a further precaution he tightened the straps around her head by releasing the buckle and then wrenching it harder into her mouth. 'Bite on that for a while,' he instructed.

His own hands took the place where Smithers' had been and, sinking his thumbs into her cleft, he drew the cheeks slowly open.

'Splendid,' he complimented, admiring her puckered bottom hole.

Then with a mighty shove he filled her. Smithers' eyes watered at the thrill of being ridden so hard and being subjected to so much pain. But they might have watered a lot more if she had but known that the governor would from now on turn his attentions elsewhere. As his rod jabbed into the walls of Smithers' bottom he wondered what the dark haired beauty was doing at that moment.

CHAPTER FOUR

The dark haired beauty was making her way back to her dormitory, exhausted after sweating over the mangle. Her bottom throbbed from constant lashings delivered by the overseer. That was another lesson Olivia had learned; her bottom was no longer private property, but available to anyone who chose to trespass upon it. It seemed that beatings and punishments were given out on the slightest pretext. No one was safe, and could be tormented at any time of the day from morn to night. She quickly learned the scheme of things; those on the board threatened the overseers, who took it out on the turnkeys, who in their turn bullied and terrified the inmates, whose only relief came at night in each other's arms.

Olivia lay awake listening to the furtive tread of footsteps going from cot to cot, and then, moments later the steady creaking of the palliasse, the pants and moans, the writhing of limbs and sobbing, grateful expulsions of frustrated passion. In the dim light hungry mouths found willing nipples and labia, fingers and tongues searched into hot, juicy recesses; and always the constant changing of partners and silent, frequent trips to the pot.

The dormitory inmates took it in turns to empty it out in the freezing yard; a good excuse to escape the fetid and stale odour laden air that hung like a heavy mist over the cots. They would return refreshed and ready to select another lover, creeping discreetly past the ends of the cots, spying out who was free or otherwise coupled.

Olivia had kept herself awake, lest someone should suddenly worm their wicked way under her blanket. The clock tower struck one, and just as Olivia deemed it safe to close her eyes she felt the blanket slip from her shoulders.

'Leave me alone,' she rasped, clutching the blanket and pulling it back again.

The ghostly figure at the end of the cot floated towards her and seated itself.

'I'll give you one more chance,' it whispered. 'Now make room.'

'Go away,' Olivia returned. 'I want to sleep.'

But the figure wouldn't go away. A hand slithered under the blanket and alighted on her thigh. Before Olivia could grasp it the fingers were between her legs, probing clumsily, leaving her in no doubt as to where they wanted to go. In the next instant a blast of hot air blew across her face.

'Oh, no,' sighed Olivia.

'Oh yes.'

And then she was kissed full on the lips.

'Now make room,' Flora whispered, clambering in beside her.

Olivia shuffled her bottom across the palliasse and turned her head away, staring tearfully at the couple in the opposite bed who were making such a noise that half the dormitory was awake and starting to add to the din.

'Please don't,' Olivia wept, feeling Flora's fingers encircling her labia and her tongue sweeping around her throat.

'Be quiet and open your legs.'

'I'll do no such thing. You can kiss me if you really must, but I won't be touched there.'

Flora paused and then, much to Olivia's profound relief, took away her hand.

'Sniff,' she said, poking her wetted fingertips into Olivia's nostrils.

'I know what I smell like,' she replied, wrinkling her nose, and before she could utter another word Flora slipped them into her mouth.

'Suck them,' she whispered, 'go on, see how you taste.' 'It's like poison,' Olivia gulped.

Someone in a nearby cot heard that remark and burst out laughing. But Flora wasn't laughing.

'Enough of this foolery,' Flora rasped. 'Open your legs and let me lie on top of you.'

'It says in the Bible,' Olivia began, 'that we are not supposed to lie with our own kind...'

Then the whole dormitory erupted. Everyone was listening now, sitting up, looking over each other's shoulders and stopping whatever they had been doing.

'You've done this deliberately!' Flora hissed, aware that everyone was waiting to see what she would do next.

She shouted at the nearest girl to go to the end of the dormitory and fetch the pot. When she came back Olivia was standing at the end of her cot with Flora glaring at her. The laughing had ceased and the inmates were clutching each other fearfully, waiting to see what Flora intended.

'Empty that stinking pot over her bed,' she said to the girl, who gazed back in a disbelieving stupor.

Then she seized it herself and tossed the entire contents all over Olivia's palliasse. The deathly hush became a knife edge of abject terror, for Flora was a dangerous woman to cross.

'You all saw that!' she snapped. 'This wretch has soiled her bed on purpose!'

Thirty heads nodded in unison. Some had retreated back into the shadows, and some were getting back into bed and covering themselves.

'Out of there!' Flora roared, her deep, sonorous voice booming around the walls, 'and follow me to the mill!'

She grabbed Olivia by the hair and dragged her along behind her. Out across the yard they went, the rest trooping behind, mostly naked. Olivia, through streaming eyes, saw herself being hauled through a doorway and into a building piled high with sacks and barrels. At the far end hung lengths of chains suspended on pulley wheels used to raise and lower loaded sacks from the machinery above.

'Stand up straight and part your legs!' Flora commanded, positioning Olivia in the midst of the chains.

One of the girls, obeying Flora's instructions, picked up the end of a chain and passed it through Olivia's open legs. While she stood holding it an iron band was fetched from a pile of dismembered barrels and fitted around Olivia's waist like a belt. The end of the chain the girl was holding was then passed between the band and Olivia's stomach, and locked in place with a hasp.

'Put your hands out in front of you,' Flora grinned maliciously.

'What are you going to do with me?' Olivia asked, feeling the chain between her legs pulling tighter.

'Flog you of course, and in a way that you'll never forget. When I've finished with you in here you'll be begging me to share your bed.'

'You could share it now,' Olivia replied, wishing she hadn't resisted in the first place.

'Too late for that now.'

A short length was wrapped around her wrists and the links intertwined, thus binding them tightly together.

'Very good,' said Flora, pleased with the result. 'Now raise your hands above your head.'

Olivia did so, and from behind a hand drew her wrists back to the suspended chain that had passed between her legs to the band at the front. A rattling of more chain fastened her already bound wrists to the suspended length.

'Almost there,' said Flora cheerfully, and she reached for a length a chain hanging by Olivia's side.

A sharp tug, a grinding of links through a pulley, and Olivia's feet shot from the floor. Her mouth flew open, gasping for breath. The chain between her legs suddenly sank into her slit as her whole weight bore down upon it. Her arms stretched upwards, sending in their wake a scalding pain through her breasts and sides. A torturer from the Inquisition could not have been more thorough in his methods than Flora. Around Olivia's ankles went yet more chain, which was then hooked to a solid lump of iron used as a counterweight to the sacks going up and down to the loft.

For a moment it seemed to Olivia that time stood still. Her eyes closed, taking in the excruciating pain burning through her vagina and belly. She was sure the chain had sawed her in half. All through her legs, arms and back every muscle spasmed and twitched. Her ankles felt as if they would tear asunder from her aching calves. By now the chain between her legs had embedded deep into her bottom crease, and because of the weight on her ankles was sinking deeper and deeper. Only when the links finally struck the base of her spine did the chain halt its agonizing progress.

'Please! For Christ's sake let me down!' she pleaded, lifting her eyes heavenwards as if he might suddenly appear from the rafters.

'Not until you've been flogged,' Flora said, smiling up at her.

Then she put her hand on the inside of Olivia's thigh and stroked, savouring the smooth expanse of creamy flesh hanging defenceless before her. The hand went upwards until the fingers found the parted and swollen labia.

'Splendid lips,' Flora observed, kneading them as she might a lump of dough. 'I do declare, you make me feel quite envious, eh, girls.'

They came forward as one, crowding around and peering up into Olivia's slit. At Flora's encouragement they all began feeling her legs and bottom; pinching the taut muscles in her calves, taking hold of handfuls of flesh on her thighs and squeezing it deliberately hard, increasing the already unbearable pain. Her bottom was poked and slapped and kissed and finally bitten with teeth as sharp as razors. Olivia shrieked and jolted with such force her feet swung to and fro like a pendulum, the links in her groin rubbed back and forth, spreading open her labia and affording Flora a view of the luscious, pink, inner petals on which she now turned.

Never had Olivia been so humiliated or felt so degraded as when Flora angled her head into her groin and licked the dew from her quivering petals. Burning with shame, she lowered her blushing face, hoping the mass of tumbling hair would offer at least a modicum of privacy from the taunting eyes.

Flora made an exaggerated play, smacking her lips and rolling her tongue either side of the chain, much to the delight of the onlookers who expressed their desire to do like wise. Flora permitted half a dozen of the assembly to feast themselves on Olivia's weeping nectar before she announced the commencement of the flogging, which she assured Olivia, would leave her bottom blazing for some considerable time.

The instrument she chose was a whip used by the mill overseer, which had once been a cart whip and had been reduced in length by cutting it in half, leaving the narrow and supple part for slashing the backsides of the mill workers. But it was still long enough to wrap around the body of its victim at least twice.

Flora took her stance behind Olivia and gathered the whip in her hand. The rest of the assembly shuffled ominously away from Olivia's hanging body and turned their eyes upwards, unable to disguise the joyful twinkle that flashed there.

The first lash struck Olivia across the buttocks as she thought it would, but even well prepared for that eventuality, she was not able to prevent the reaction that followed. Her ankles kicked out, lifting the weight and swaying it back and forth, putting greater strain on her arms and crotch. Olivia wasn't sure where the pain was most acute; on her whipped buttocks or between her legs. Now she understood why Flora had suspended her that way. From now on every lash would have her bucking and jolting. She would swing to and fro and the chains would do their work.

The whip whistled again, its sound magnified in the huge expanse of the tall and empty building. Olivia's screams echoed to the rafters and bounced from wall to wall.

'Excellent!' exclaimed Flora. 'That's what I like to hear. And the more you scream, the harder I shall whip!'

Olivia could hardly credit it; the pain was so severe the only release lay in screaming, so by that token it was clear that the whipping would only stop when her screams ceased after she had fainted.

She braced herself for the next lash, which caught her on the left of her flanks and then again on her right in quick succession. Olivia's body twisted in all directions from hips to shoulders like a stoat caught in a trap. Flora whipped again, and with consummate skill, judged where Olivia's flailing body would contort next, so that each blow sent her back again in the same direction.

Olivia, as a child, had been told about the early Christian martyrs who had been torn to pieces on the rack, and now she was beginning to understand what it must have felt like. Her arms and legs had lost all feeling, except at the wrists and ankles where the persistent pulling of the weight and chain threatened to rip them asunder. Between her legs it was no better, there the links had ground well into her sex and had all but disappeared. It was the same in her bottom-cleft; there the chain had seesawed with each violent jerk of her hips and had left her raw.

As the whip went on lashing her, she saw through tear-filled eyes that she was changing direction. All around her the walls and roof were spinning, churning her stomach, making her feel giddy and sick. That was just what her terrible audience would like. Nothing would give greater satisfaction than to see her throw up and soil her own body. Whatever happened she would cling to her self-respect, she would not, no matter how awful her sufferings, discharge her bladder or bowels. But that was much easier thought than done, for the whip now fell across her front and sides as she continued spinning round and round.

To Flora it was the most rewarding punishment she'd carried out in a long while. All she had to do was remain in one spot and send the whip where it would. It cracked into Olivia's soft belly and wrapped around her waist, and when pulled free sent Olivia whirling by the wrists, offering both back and bottom to a renewed attack.

Poor Olivia didn't know where it would fall next. It could land anywhere; her buttocks, back, belly, breasts or hips and flanks.

'Stop it!' she managed to shriek. 'I've taken all I can! You're killing me!'

Her pitiful pleading echoed back, shrieking again and again in her head, but Flora's blood was up. She would leave this insolent bitch who had made a fool of her half dead, and when she came again into the dormitory Olivia would welcome her with open legs.

And it was at these she aimed the whip, catching the straining calves and thighs, whizzing Olivia faster than a whipped top. The weight kept her spinning longer than she would ordinarily have done, and when it had wound to its fullest extremity it spun back the other way. Olivia tried desperately to halt it by twisting her body in the opposite direction, but she was spent. The whip falling across her back and buttocks was now merely going through the motions of welting her. Her piercing screams had given way to choking sobs and snorts. She had not been sick or degraded herself, she just hung there slowly spinning, her head bowed, eyes barely able to focus on the debris that littered the floor.

'Take her down.'

Flora's voice seemed to come from both near and far as the chain creaked through the pulley. The weight fell from her ankles and it seemed as if they were floating. Her toes touched the tiles, putting a stop to her spinning body. The chain creaked again and Olivia felt her legs buckle at the knees. Then they too touched the earth and she sank back on her whipped haunches, spreading her calves and letting her bare, burning bottom find comfort on the cold tiles beneath. A gasp escaped her lips when her wrists fell away from the chain and it was dragged from her crotch.

'Thank God,' she breathed, collapsing onto her side.

One of the girls pulled her upright again and seated her back on her haunches. Olivia looked up and found her eyes level with Flora's pubic triangle, a wealth of tangled golden curls glistening with sweat. Indeed, her whole body was covered in a fine layer of perspiration, for she had whipped herself to exhaustion.

'The rest of you, clear out!' she barked in her deep voice.

The last one to leave closed the door softly behind her and remarked to her lover that it was a miracle that Olivia was still alive.

When they were alone, Flora knelt in front of Olivia and kissed her on the forehead as lovingly as she might a child in a cradle.

'I had to punish you,' she whispered. 'You do understand that, don't you?'

Olivia nodded dumbly. 'I am here as a punishment,' she mumbled sadly. 'But why do you want to lie alongside me and put your fingers in my...' she hesitated, finding it difficult to utter the word considered improper for young ladies to mention.

'Cunt?' Flora offered.

'If you like,' although she had never heard it called that before.

'Because you're so beautiful,' Flora said. 'And if I don't, someone else most certainly will, if they haven't already.'

'No one has ever touched me there.'

'Except a lover, perhaps.'

'No, I've never had a lover.'

Flora considered that for a moment. 'Are you telling me that no one has ever kissed your nipples or done what comes naturally between men and women?'

It was Olivia's turn to think about that. The only idea she had about sex was what she had been told at Sunday school. While she pondered, Flora leaned forward and gently kissed her lips, and at the same time flicked her thumb over her own nipples, teasing them to erection.

'Now, suck these,' Flora coaxed.

The poor dazed girl planted a quick peck on each nipple, still baffled as to why she was expected to do something that no self-respecting woman could possibly enjoy.

'I think you're still in need of further instruction,' said Flora, her voice lowering to a gravelly husk.

'I will not let you touch me,' Olivia retorted, aware now that Flora's sympathy was a mere ploy to lull her into doing things she did not want to do.

'You might not wish it, but when I have finished with you, you will not be in a position to refuse. Now, return to the dormitory and take this with you.'

Olivia made her way back; carrying the chain that Flora had used to bind her wrists.

The other occupants, thinking that the entertainment was over, had retired to their cots, but on seeing Olivia return sooner than they anticipated and with Flora coming up behind, eyes blazing once more, they sat up with renewed interest.

'Lie on your bed,' Flora instructed.

'In that?' Olivia replied, looking at the huge wet patch where the pot had been emptied.

'Are you questioning my authority?'

Any argument would have been futile; Flora was determined to subject Olivia to more humiliation, and would keep on degrading her until she finally broke.

'No ma'am,' Olivia sighed, planting her bottom in the midst of the filthy swamp.

'Isn't this wonderful?' Flora beamed, slapping Olivia's belly and then tweaking her nipples. 'Yet despite all my efforts, she still hasn't grasped it. Have you, dear?'

'Grasped what?' Olivia asked, wondering what it was she was supposed to grasp.

'You stupid girl, am I obliged to treat you like a child?'

'I'm not a child,' said Olivia indignantly.

'But you behave as if you were, and a naughty one into the bargain. So we have to correct you, don't we?'

'Do we?' Olivia muttered, a cold chill going through her stomach.

'We most certainly do.'

Flora spread the lengths of chain over the stinking palliasse and selected one, which she then wound around Olivia's neck. Then, taking up the slack, she told Olivia to put her hands together, palm to palm as if she were in prayer, and place the fingertips just below her chin. The end of the chain was used to tie her wrists, and the remaining links were laid between her breasts, exactly in the middle.

Another length of chain was selected, measured for suitability by stretching it across the railings at the head of the cot, and one end secured to the furthest rail. It was then passed again around her neck and taken to the opposite rail, where it was pulled taut, obliging Olivia to shuffle her body up the palliasse until her head bumped the railings

'Now your legs,' said Flora, taking up another length.

Olivia spread them, already knowing what Flora had in store. She opened wide, placing her ankles at the very edges of the palliasse, which now began to feel very wet and clammy, sticking to her bottom and sucking into her crease like a pair of soaking drawers.

'Thank you,' Flora said, in the manner of an omnibus conductor collecting fares.

The chain pulled on Olivia's ankles, but despite Flora's strenuous attempts they would not reach the railings.

'Please excuse me,' she said, going behind the railings, 'but I shall stretch your legs until your feet are right up against the posts, which is going to cause you considerable pain, I'm very pleased to say.'

And with that she rested one foot on the frame, and leaning back, pulled with all her might. Olivia groaned in agony as her thigh almost tore from her pelvis. Then the exercise was repeated on the other leg, leaving Olivia close to a state of near strangulation.

But there still remained two unused lengths that Flora now put to good use.

'Lift your bottom,' she said, ready to slid the chain beneath it and at the same time fashioning a large knot at its centre.

Olivia emitted a painful grunt and managed to arch her back high enough to allow the chain to pass beneath her. When she dropped down again it was to land herself directly on the knotted links, at the base of the spine where the pain would be most savage. Flora then calmly brought the two ends over Olivia's hips and tied them tightly just above her pubic triangle. The last length she decided to use as a whip.

'Your belly shall be the recipient of this,' Flora explained; flicking the chain over her shoulder, ready to bring it whistling onto Olivia's stomach. 'The purpose of chaining you like this is twofold,' she continued, rather like a schoolmistress. 'Even though the pain I am about to inflict will be very severe, and you may feel it necessary to wriggle, I would not advise it, because if you do, the chain around your neck will pull tighter and strangle you. Secondly, when you are being whipped across your belly, you will suffer twice over; once from the chain itself and once from the knot digging in your spine. If you wish, you may scream as loud as you like. No one will hear you, and even if they did, it would not make the slightest difference. My authority is absolute and you are the lowest of the low.'

Olivia listened to this speech with a curious mixture of terror and dumb acceptance. The turnkey had made everything perfectly clear; as long as she remained in the House of Correction she would be constantly abused and violated by anyone who saw fit. In short, she would be whipped and whipped, sexually tormented and above all, made to feel as if it were a pleasure to undergo these appalling torments. Well, let them do their worst, Olivia would not succumb, she would remain pure until her wedding day; if she lived that long.

The chain struck directly across her naval with a hollow slap, and Flora was right in her delivery. Olivia, recoiling under the blow, writhed her bottom from side to side. The chain around her neck almost choked her, and the knot dug sharply into her spine. She was still panting from the shock when another slapped diagonally from waist to hip. Olivia went rigid; her only defence against slow strangulation or a fractured spine. But in keeping her legs as straight as ramrods and her bottom perfectly still, she added to the pain, for now all her muscles had tensed and gone hard as iron. She felt each blow much more acutely than when she was hanging suspended in the mill, for there at least she had been allowed to swing and twist, which to some extent had helped to allay the pain, but here, all she could do was lie still and suffer it.

She closed her eyes and concentrated on counting the blows. Five, ten, fifteen, twenty-five. It seemed it would never end. Her belly was crisscrossed with stripes, as were her upper thighs and ribs. Only her breasts were spared, under the protection of her clasped hands.

The effect of the whipping on the inmates was no less the same as it was in the quadrangle, only more so. Here, in the sanctuary of their dormitory, they were free to indulge in whatever they chose. Some remained, eyeing with relish Olivia's whipped belly and thighs, but most, finding it too arousing to watch any longer, had drifted to their cots where they blatantly indulged in each other; a practice not lost on Flora who, finding the grunts and moans too much to bear, cast aside the chain and knelt between Olivia's open legs.

'Don't bother to struggle,' she advised, putting her hand into her victim's crotch.

Olivia shook her head. 'Could you at least take away the chain from under my bottom?' she whispered, her throat parched and sore.

'I shall have to leave it there, because as long as your bottom is raised I can feel you more thoroughly.'

Thus, her hand began moving to and fro, the fingers slipping right inside Olivia's slit.

'You are very tight,' Flora observed, wiggling her fingers and sliding them in and out. 'I can only assume you were telling me the truth after all.'

Her hand moved faster and faster, while her other went under Olivia's clasped hands and began pinching her nipples.

'Tell me how you feel now,' Flora panted, her face flushed and hot.

'I feel only the pain in my back and on my belly,' Olivia gasped, which wasn't quite true.

Somewhere deep in her womb was a vague hint of arousal; a peculiar tingling feeling that spread through her whipped belly and flanks. But she did not want Flora to know that, for if she did it would be a tantamount admission of defeat; a licence to further her disgusting intentions. And one look at the other inmates told her that she would never sink to their depths of depravity. In the bed next to her lay a girl on her back with her legs open and drawn up to her chest. Between them a tousled blonde head bobbed up and down as fast as Flora's fingers.

Olivia concentrated on that to take her mind away from what was evidently arising within her own belly. The face on the prostrated girl was fascinating in itself. It had rolled in Olivia's direction, and for a fleeting moment Olivia was reminded of her journey in the wagon when the passengers had come aboard. There she had heard the same noises and seen the same peculiar expressions of parted lips, misty, far away eyes, and the awful groans and sucking of breath.

A girl in the opposite cot was thrashing her legs in the air and rubbing them against the head of her companion. Suddenly her back arched and there came a heartrending cry and a wild leaping of her shoulders. Then presently, after a lot more groaning and gulping, she lay quiet, her breast heaving as if she had fallen into a deep and satiated slumber. Her companion emerged equally as exhausted and collapsed over her, smiling contentedly.

Flora, too, betrayed similar sentiments and, panting and blowing like a racehorse, she withdrew her soaking fingers and thrust them directly into Olivia's gaping mouth. 'I think it's actually happened!' she said agog.

But Olivia didn't hear her. She had ceased to be aware of anything except the chains around her neck and the dull ache in her loins and bottom. Around her the breathless panting started to fade. Her head rolled lazily to one side, and she passed out.

Chapter Five

When Olivia awoke the next morning it was to find that all the chains had been removed and she was strangely alone in the dormitory. She sat up and looked around at the empty cots, wondering why she had been left there and not aroused for her labours. The wet patch beneath her bottom had become icy cold and stank to high heaven.

Pulling a face, she groaned and got off the palliasse just as Flora came into the dormitory.

'So, you're awake at last,' she said, coming towards her and looking very grim and purposeful.

'Did I have to suffer so?' Olivia asked, rubbing the places where the chains had chaffed her skin.

She was sore, and aching particularly on her bottom and belly and between her legs, which she decided not to rub in front of Flora, lest she be attacked there again.

'You will suffer whenever you need correction,' Flora replied tartly, wrinkling her nose at the stench arising from the soiled palliasse.

'That wasn't correction, it was torture. And what is more, I am convinced that your treatment of my body was illegal. Look at me.'

Flora looked dryly at Olivia's welted belly, and when she turned round she saw the livid indentation where the knotted chain had dug. Her bottom was still a bright shade of red and pink.

'Perhaps you would care to voice your complaint to the governor, who at this moment awaits your filthy presence in his office.'

Olivia's hands flew involuntarily to her blazing cheeks. 'Why, what have I done?' she asked, petrified.

Flora glanced at the patch and then at Olivia. 'You'll see.' And without giving her time to cover herself she dragged Olivia by the wrist out of the dormitory and up the spiral staircase.

Smithers was down on her hands and knees scrubbing the floor in the passage when Olivia approached. She stopped abruptly and shot her a malicious grin, but a savage kick in the rump from Flora prevented her from saying whatever she was going to say.

'I am persuaded,' said the governor, rising from his desk and coming round to meet Olivia, 'that you are a troublemaker, and decidedly lacking in both respect and obedience towards those set in authority above you.'

Olivia looked totally nonplussed. Flora stared directly ahead, standing to attention, legs close together, hands behind her back.

'I'm sorry, sir, I don't understand. Since my being here I have striven to do my duty and thus far have not met with complaint,' Olivia said meekly.

'Oh really. Your supervisor tells me that when you were instructed to empty the night soil you refused and went into a tantrum, the end result of which was the soiling of your own cot to the great discomfort of the other inmates who were obliged to inhale its noxious stench, and the result of that is no less than seven of them have been confined to the infirmary.'

'It's a lie!' shrieked Olivia, staring hard at Flora who remained gazing at the clock on the mantelpiece.

'But there are witnesses to your atrocious behaviour.' He paused as if a thought had just come into his mind. 'And furthermore, when you were told to get up and report to the laundry, you refused and remained content in your bed of filth.'

Olivia burst into tears. How so treacherous, she thought, that after all she had endured, Flora could so easily betray her. She had a good idea who were the seven that reported sick; they had been up all night creaking their cots and had used Flora's venom as a way of seeking rest, no doubt aided and abetted by the turnkey herself.

'What is to be done with you?' said the governor, shaking his head, knowing full well the answer to his own question. The more he looked at Olivia's bottom the greater his urge to explore it.

'May I suggest she wear the belt, sir?' Flora suddenly piped up.

'I was going to suggest a sound thrashing, but I can see she's recently had a good dose of that medicine, and by now is probably getting used to it. No, I think you are right, Miss Bellows. Perhaps a week or so of wearing the belt will teach her some manners.'

Flora could hardly contain herself. 'Shall I fit it, sir?'

The governor smiled to himself. 'I shall fit it,' he said firmly, thinking that it would be a good excuse and a less obvious reason to fondle Olivia's bottom, together with the added bonus of her private parts.

'As you wish, sir,' Flora replied, piqued and bowing her way out of the room.

The belt the governor fetched from his cupboard was more reminiscent of a medieval Inquisition than a nineteenth century mode of correction.

'This has been designed to cause you maximum discomfort both day and night,' he said, dropping it on the desk.

Olivia regarded the terrible looking contraption with bated breath.

'I have to wear that?' she exclaimed.

'You do, and I shall have the infinite pleasure of seeing you in it, as will everyone else.'

Olivia didn't know what he meant by that, but parted her legs as instructed while the governor took up the belt. He knelt in front of her, humming to himself as he slipped around her waist a broad iron band, which he fastened over the crown of her buttocks with a small brass padlock. Behind her was another section that was hinged beneath the padlock and able to pass under her legs and would be secured at the front by the same means as of the rear. But fitting it was not quite as simple as one might imagine, for, protruding from the hinged section were two upright metal rods, about six to eight inches in length and an inch and a half in diameter.

'These,' the governor said to the horrified young woman, 'will be fitted snugly inside you, and you will not under any circumstances, be able to either expel or escape them.'

Olivia gritted her teeth when the first rod was pushed up her bottom. Happily, she could not see the evil glint in his eyes as he watched her straining to take it all.

He could hear her sucking her breath and letting it out with a grunt.

'How much more?' she gasped, reaching behind and pulling apart her cheeks.

'Another inch or so,' he lied.

Up and up it went, the pain making her clutch her hair and pull it until her eyes watered. A long sigh whooshed from her lips when she was at last completely filled.

'What if I want to go to the toilet?' she asked, just realizing that sobering fact.

'You will ask permission and someone, probably the turnkey, will assist you, and of course return it afterwards.'

Olivia blushed with fury; no wonder the crafty bitch had suggested that. Now, every time Olivia needed the pot, she would have to be accompanied by Flora, who would take great delight in fumbling about for ages, trying to fit the belt back into place.

'Now the front section,' the governor said in a business like manner.

Although it ought to have slipped in much more readily he seemed to experience considerable difficulty, and so was obliged to put his fingers inside her, guiding it in and pushing from its base. He uttered the same observation that Flora had made; that she was remarkably tight and narrow, coming to the same conclusions with equal surprise.

Olivia looked down and watched its progress with detached curiosity, as inch by inch vanished between her legs. Then the section was padlocked over her naval and the governor stood up. He placed his hands on her hips and spun her round, testing it for any slack that might need taking up. There wasn't any, and he stood behind her fondling and patting her bottom as he might a mare taken to stud.

'That should open you up a bit,' he murmured as much to himself as she.

'You said just now,' Olivia reminded him, 'that everyone else will see me.'

'So I did and they will, for every morn, noon and night at meal times and at prayers you will display yourself before the whole assembly.'

'What?!'

'I think you heard me.'

'I have to stand naked like this, with these things in me?'

'Those are the rules, and rules are there to be obeyed. When the time comes to have the belt removed I am, by law, obliged to carry out an inspection of your parts, which will involve the insertion of another implement, particularly up your bottom, which you will accept without question. Do you understand?'

Olivia nodded glumly, but thought it just as well she be inspected; God knows what would be going on inside her with those cruel things prodding day and night.

For two whole weeks, Olivia wore the belt; subjected to the prying eyes and disgusting remarks from the other inmates, and the constant fingering and bullying from Flora. Not once was she given any respite, and on one occasion when she protested, the belt was removed, but only to be replaced with longer and thicker rods than before, and a ring fitted in front to which her hands were chained at night, as were her ankles and neck. This last was fitted with a collar from which more chains extended and held her fixed to the railings so that it was impossible to move her cramped and aching limbs. When at last the day came for her release, Olivia presented herself before the governor.

'I hope that you have learned your lesson, Holland,' he said, keying the padlocks at her front and rear.

The belt went slack and the rods glided from her vagina and anus with an audible squelch. Olivia sobbed tears of relief; no longer would she have to parade naked in the quadrangle or suffer the hateful Flora.

'I'm so grateful, sir,' she bowed. 'I could not have endured it another day longer. You have no idea how I have suffered so, what with the turnkey making me use the pot every five minutes for no reason except to humiliate me, and then afterwards obliging me to put those filthy things in my mouth and suck them for ages on end.'

'She made you do that?' he said, eyebrows lifting.

'And that's not all. She made me do something so vile that I dare not repeat it.'

'You must tell me everything that's happened to you.'

'Everything?'

'Leave no stone unturned, so to speak.'

Olivia fidgeted with the belt, sliding it between her fingers and absently fondling the rods. 'Well, sir,' she stammered. 'A few days ago, after I had just retired from my duties in the laundry, she came to me saying that I was to lie with her for a while as I deserved a rest.'

'And did you?'

'Only until I learned her true intentions.'

'And what pray, were those?'

'Really, it is so sickening.'

'I insist that you tell.'

Her hand closed around the rod that had been inside her vagina and squeezed it until her knuckles blanched. The governor listened wide-eyed while Olivia related how Flora had detached the vaginal rod and inserted it inside herself; insisting that Olivia ply it back and forth. This she had done until Flora seemed to throw one of her fits, as she often did on such occasions, but this time she had suddenly grabbed Olivia and tried to insert it in her, thus, hopefully joining them together at the groin.

'And why do you think she tried to make you do that?'

41

'Really, I haven't the faintest idea.'

The governor regarded her with considerable interest, and decided to play his hand there and then.

'The instrument I intend to put up your bottom is in my trouser pocket, see if it seems familiar.' And with that he gently placed her hand against his waiting erection.

Olivia gave it a squeeze. 'I can't say that it does,' she said, with a blank look on her face.

He unbuttoned his trousers and slid her hand inside his underwear. Suddenly a flash of recognition crossed her face.

'The very same,' he said joyfully. 'And you remember how soothing it was on your whipped flanks.' She nodded and he continued. 'Well, now it is time to have it up your bottom - for its soothing properties, you understand.'

'All of it?' she asked, growing pale at the prospect.

'Every inch,' he assured her.

'I don't think I can.'

'If you do not I shall be obliged to put the belt back on again, and you will wear it for a month.'

Olivia recoiled in horror. 'Oh, anything but that!' she wailed.

'Then bend over and spread your buttocks.'

'If I must... but would it be an impertinence to view it first? I am curious to see what it looks like.'

Her request sounded reasonable, so without further ado he showed her.

'Oh, dear God,' she cried. 'That's horrible. It isn't what you led me to believe at all, and I won't have it. I won't, I won't, I—'

The governor slapped her face and she broke into a flood of hysterical sobs. It wouldn't do to have her carrying on like that with members of the board gathering in the next room for their monthly meeting. Quickly he rang the bell and both the matron and Smithers came hurrying into the room.

'Take this babbling wretch to the infirmary,' he said, looking down to see what had attracted their attention. 'I was attacked,' he said, slipping his tool back into his trousers and feeling very foolish.

'The girl must be deranged,' said the matron.

'I thought there was a queer look about her,' said Smithers.

And so poor Olivia was whisked off to the infirmary as fast as they could carry her.

If Olivia thought the belt and the dreadful Flora were bad enough, they were mild in comparison as to what awaited her there. The master in charge of the infirmary, on being informed by the matron that Olivia was a raving lunatic with unhealthy desires towards the personal property of men, had her placed in solitary confinement.

'It's for your own good,' he warned her. 'As much for the safety of others as for yourself.'

'But I'm not mad,' she protested. 'It was the governor, he showed me his thing and wanted to put it my bottom, if you please.'

'Yes, I'm sure he did,' the master replied sympathetically, and instructed her to stand with her back to the wall.

Olivia went on protesting her innocence while the nurse produced a long coil of rope and a stout pole.

'Are you going to beat me?' she asked, preparing to touch her toes.

'Not at all,' the master replied kindly. 'Just do as you're told.'

Olivia stretched back her elbows and the pole was slipped behind her back and allowed to rest in the crooks of her arms, while the nurse took up the rope and bound them each in turn. Olivia thought her arched back would break, but worse was to follow. The loose end trailing over her buttocks was passed between her legs, pulled tight in her bottom crease, and drawn through to her upper thighs, where it was wound in slow succession round and round her legs. At every coil, both master and nurse wrenched it tight, finally knotting it at her ankles.

'Now your neck,' he said, fashioning a noose from another length and dropping it over her head.

With considerable dexterity he threw the other end over a beam and, after giving just the right amount of tension to have Olivia up on her toes, he tied it behind her back in the centre of the pole.

'What if I should fall?' Olivia wailed.

'It has been known,' the nurse nodded.

'Which is why your legs have been tied the way they are,' rejoined the master, 'and also why we paid particular attention to your knees. I think you'll find they will not bend, so you are quite safe.'

Then he turned to the nurse and said, 'The hood, if you would be so kind.'

'Oh, please, don't put that on me,' Olivia sobbed.

'We have to I'm afraid. But first we have to gag you.'

A short length of rope went around her head and into her mouth, was pulled taut, and then a hood blocked out the light.

She was informed that she would remain that way during the waking hours, and at night the noose and hood would be removed and she would be allowed to sleep, albeit, still with her arms and legs secured. The gag would only be removed when the nurse would feed her from a bowl of the cold and thinnest of gruel. With that they left her standing on tiptoe, the noose angling her head, arms and back at breaking point.

Olivia's suspicions were confirmed when, not a half hour later, the cell door creaked open and footsteps crept furtively across the floor. Held as she was there was nothing she could do to prevent the mauling hands that groped and played with her breasts. In angry darkness she suffered them lifting and weighing her ample orbs and the mouth that slobbered over her nipples, sucking and biting, leaving livid teeth marks on her tender flesh.

Neither was she surprised at the cane that slashed across her upper thighs. Only the force of the blows shocked her. Whoever was hitting her was using the full strength of his arm, working his way down to her knees, over the rope, and striking the fleshy sides of her calves. The exercise was repeated on her flanks and haunches, striking everywhere at random. The assailant paused for breath and began again on her belly and then her breasts, paying particular attention to her nipples. When they had been sufficiently caned to arousal and had swelled, pointed and throbbing, the teeth returned and bit the teat, crushing and rolling it, seemingly for hours.

Olivia endured it still up on her toes, the noose around her neck threatening to throttle her if she offered resistance, which was very little, except for a half-hearted twist of her hips.

Shortly after she had been whipped the nurse came in and removed both the hood and the rope that gagged her.

'Thank God,' Olivia breathed, inhaling whole lungfuls of air.

'Why, just look at you,' said the nurse, standing back and staring at Olivia's face.

She was indeed a sight to behold. Tears streaked her cheeks in grimy rivulets, and from the constant snorting of her nostrils a thick globule of snot had blasted over her chin and chest.

'Now I suppose I shall have to wash your filthy face,' retorted the nurse angrily.

She marched out of the cell, and in the distance Olivia heard the sound of running water cascading into a bucket. The nurse returned and threw the whole lot straight into her face. Then she fetched another and tipped it slowly over the top of her head, drenching her completely, and leaving her shivering from cold and shock.

'What have I done to deserve this?' Olivia blinked.

'You are quite mad,' the nurse replied. 'It's all over the house, the way you assaulted the governor, tried to feel his thing, and what with throwing pots of soil at all and sundry. Now, open your mouth while I feed you.'

But rather than waste precious time spooning the gruel, she put the rim of the bowl onto Olivia's lips and tipped it so abruptly that the greater part of the contents spilled over her chest. Olivia swallowed but a mouthful of foul tasting gruel that had been dredged from the very bottom of the vat.

'Is this all I get?' she asked, grimacing.

'Until I return this evening, yes.'

She replaced the gag and hood and marched off, leaving Olivia half starved and aching. All day and everyday Olivia was obliged to remain thus bound and up on her toes. The only respite came when, at night, she was taken down from the noose and laid on the floor to sleep.

At the end of a fortnight Olivia learned who it was that caned her regularly and so thoroughly, beating every inch of her legs and body.

'You had to be subdued,' the governor apologised, while the master and nurse stripped away the ropes.

Olivia, racked with pain and starved to the point of distraction, seized her bowl of gruel and swallowed it in a single gulp.

'More,' she said, thrusting it into the nurse's face. 'I want more. My guts are rumbling I'm so hungry.'

Governor, master and nurse stared in stupefied astonishment at this untoward request.

'Did I hear aright?' the governor uttered, horror stricken. 'The wretch has dared ask for more?'

'She did, sir,' confirmed the nurse.

'Then the girl is mad,' added the master, hoping to keep Olivia there until the governor had finished with her, thus allowing his own salacious advances.

'Stark, raving mad,' the nurse said again. 'Mark my words, she will be hanged. I feel it in my bones. That girl will be hanged.'

Olivia thought it a miracle she hadn't been hanged already. 'I only want some more,' Olivia pleaded, falling at the governor's feet and kissing the tips of his boots.

An animated discussion took place. Olivia was mad and far too expensive to be maintained in the House of Correction. The additional cost of having her transported over the moors to the lunatic asylum was allayed by an advertisement pasted up in the town, offering Olivia as a maid of all work to anyone willing to part with a sovereign.

Chapter Six

The response came much quicker than anticipated, and a day later Olivia was bundled into a cart and driven post haste across moors to the town, where her new employer awaited her.

'The girl stinks,' said Mrs Reynolds, the undertaker's wife, pinching her nose and taking an emphatic step backwards.

The magistrate, who had authorised Olivia's release, looked rather embarrassed. 'But she'll clean up ma'am. Just put her under the pump and she'll clean up.'

Mrs Reynolds eyed her suspiciously. Olivia looked very underfed and hardly able to work fourteen hours a day.

'A waste of money,' she grumbled, ripping Olivia's dress from her back.

The magistrate quickly extricated himself before she changed her mind and he would have all the bother of finding her another place.

'Get those rags off!' Mrs Reynolds barked, kicking Olivia in the rump and heading towards a large pump in the middle of the yard.

Olivia peeled away the tattered remnants of her dress and stepped naked into a stone trough. A young man and woman who had been watching the proceedings emerged from a doorway and came over to where Olivia was standing.

'Allow me,' the young man said, picking up a fearsome looking scrubbing brush.

'Scrub her well, Henry,' replied Mrs Reynolds, shaking her head and going back to her kitchen.

'Charlotte, work the handle,' said the young man, taking hold of Olivia's hair and twisting it round his fist.

The girl creaked the pump handle up and down, showering Olivia in a torrent of icy water. Her limbs shivered and broke into thousands of tiny goose bumps. Henry began scrubbing her back, and had already made up his mind to have her as soon as the opportunity presented itself.

'Open your pretty legs, there's a good girl,' he smiled wanly, and drove the bristles hard into her labia.

He scrubbed her all over, and when he had finished helped her out of the trough, taking great care to squeeze her breasts as he did so.

'Now what?' said Charlotte crossly.

Henry was the undertaker's son and heir to the business. The last thing Charlotte needed was a rival. She had hated Olivia on sight.

'I'll take her into the workshop,' Henry said, wringing his hands. 'And you can be about your business.'

Swearing and muttering to herself Charlotte went off into the house, leaving Henry and Olivia making their way across the yard to a line of low, squalid outhouses stacked to the eaves with coffins.

'This is where you'll bed down,' he remarked, 'which I daresay, is plenty good enough for the likes of you.'

'Thank you, sir,' Olivia replied, staring into an empty coffin.

He put his hands on her waist and steered her tactfully away from the window and behind a pile of timber, where he immediately began to fondle her wet bottom.

'What are you doing?' she protested over her shoulder, trying to shove him away.

'Inspecting you. It's part of my duty, to make sure you're fit for work. Can't have another corpse on our hands, at least not yet.' His laugh resembled water gurgling down a drain, and Olivia shuddered.

'Is it necessary to feel me there?' she asked.

'Very,' he chortled. His clammy hands went everywhere, rubbing between her legs, pinching her calves and thighs, all around her buttocks, and spent a long, long time cupping and squeezing her breasts. Olivia stood stock still while he feasted himself on her nipples, thumbing them and gazing in awe as they rose up, erect and succulent.

'I bet you've had quite a few in your time,' he croaked in her ear, patting her bottom and grinning like an imbecile.

'I don't know what you mean.'

'Cock,' he said crudely. 'I'm talking about cock. How much have you had? A couple of hundred, I'll bet a pound.' And before she could utter an astonished

46

reply he pushed her over the timber and kicked her heels apart.

'This is outrageous!' she shrieked, wriggling like an eel.

'Lovely,' he said, grabbing her waist. 'I like a woman who struggles. Makes it all the more worthwhile when it's in you, not like Charlotte, she just lies there like a dead parrot.'

Olivia could hardly believe this. She knew exactly what was prodding into her buttocks, and from the feel it was much bigger and harder than the thing the governor had made her touch.

'Do you always treat your servants this way?' she snorted, deftly bringing her legs together.

'It's part of your duties,' he explained, and thumped her hard between the shoulder blades.

Olivia, temporarily winded, felt her legs being opened again, this time at the thighs, where his strong hands pulled them open and then fumbled with his weapon for a fresh attack.

'Now keep still, or so help me I'll knock your teeth out.'

Olivia wondered how he hoped to achieve that with her head hanging over the timber, but nevertheless the threat was very frightening and very real. She was on the verge of being raped, that much was clear.

'Please don't,' she sobbed. 'It's not true, I haven't had hundreds of cocks.' She said that without thinking and suddenly blushed scarlet. 'I haven't had one,' she added softly.

'You mean, you're a virgin?' he gasped, pulling her off the timber and wheeling her round.

Her blush had turned almost purple. 'Yes I'm a virgin.'

'Now that is rare these days, I must say.' He thought for a moment and glanced around the workshop. 'What about sucking? Have you ever done that?'

'Oh, lots of times.'

His voice rose to an excited crescendo. 'You have?'

'Well of course. Lollipops and bull's-eyes and—'

He slapped her breast. 'Play any more of these silly games and I will knock your teeth out.'

'Well what do you mean?!' she snapped back, surprised at her own daring.

'This, you stupid girl,' and so saying he forced her to her knees.

'Oh, my God, surely you can't want me to—'

His hands rammed her face into his bulging breeches and held it there until she thought she would suffocate. Then he took it away and lowered his voice to a hoarse whisper. 'Stay on your knees,' he told her, creeping across the room and bolting the door. His erection poked ridiculously from his open breeches. Olivia lowered her eyes in despair.

On the way back he snatched up a length of twine, and going behind her, took hold of her wrists and crossed them over her rump. His fingers moved with amazing dexterity and in a trice Olivia's hands were firmly tied. Just in case she had it in mind to up and run and go yelling around the workshop he tied her ankles into the bargain.

'Now,' he said gravely, 'either open your mouth, or I'll beat the living daylights out of you.'

Olivia watched him take up a stout piece of timber as thick as her arm and wave it menacingly over her head. One blow from that and she'd be rendered unconscious, and then God knows what would happen. She was quite sure she'd come round nailed up in a coffin and being transported to the nearest churchyard.

'I'll do it because you're forcing me to,' she sobbed, 'but don't go blaming me if, in a fit of despair, I bite it off.'

Henry considered that possibility. It had almost happened before with a young and inexperienced filly who had got overexcited and gnashed her teeth. The memory was still painful and he'd had great difficulty in explaining to Charlotte why he kept it hidden for several weeks. He couldn't risk that again. There was nothing for it, the girl from the parish would have to be broken in gently - a little at a time.

'Very well,' he grumbled. 'Just for now I'll let you lick it, but mind you do it well or you'll spend the night in a place not to your liking.'

Olivia, thankful her threat had worked, stuck out her tongue.

'I said lick it, like you do your lollipops.' He laughed at that and shoved the swollen end of his member against her lips.

Olivia swept her tongue up and down and found, to her great relief, that it wasn't as bad as she feared. There was a taste of sorts; a salty, musty smell that wasn't entirely disagreeable.

'Now the plum,' he said, nudging gently forward, daring to rest it on her pouting lower lip.

She didn't jolt away as he thought she might but licked a little harder than before, seemingly exploring the deep groove at its base and lashing against the shiny sides. Then without being told, she went back down the shaft, angling her head from one side to the other, covering him with saliva.

'You could try licking those,' he suggested, when her tongue inadvertently flicked against his fruits.

She took a deep breath and, after letting it out again, wiggled the tip of her tongue through his wiry hair, flitting to and fro, this way and that, an action that sent blood racing into his member. Olivia withdrew and looked up at him, wide-eyed and pleading.

'May I stop now, please? I've done what you asked.'

Henry was bursting to release himself and the temptation to put it straight into her mouth was overwhelming. But time was on his side; there was no need to hurry. He untied her wrists and took hold of her trembling hand.

'What do I have to do now?' she asked, feeling him close it around the pulsating shaft.

'Give it a jolly good rub,' he said, as if instructing her to polish the top of a coffin.

Olivia took him at his word and rubbed like a Trojan. Suddenly it went enormously rigid and very hot. Henry swayed on his heels, let out a grunt as if he'd been stabbed, and squirted directly into her face. It went everywhere, spattering her cheeks and lips, and splashing into her eyes and hair. She jolted backwards and caught another dose on her chest. In stunned silence she felt it trickle between her breasts. A drop of the foul stuff had landed on her left nipple and hung there like a huge white tear. Then it plopped sadly onto her stomach.

Olivia, almost as if in a dream, scooped it up with the tip of her forefinger and licked it. A flash of recognition went across her face.

'The governor,' she murmured, 'it tastes like the governor.' And she went on staring at it with the intensity of a child.

Henry fastened his breeches and stared back in return, his face a mask of anger. 'You lied to me,' he exclaimed. 'You said you've never sucked a man before, and if you've lied about that, you must have lied about everything else.'

'I haven't lied,' Olivia retorted. 'It was the governor, he...'

Her voice trailed away. How could she explain that the governor had rubbed his thing against her thigh and, more poignantly, she had permitted him to do it? How would it sound if she admitted being confined in the infirmary for supposedly trying to expose his thing? Who would believe her if she said that all this had been the result of trickery and deceit?

'You were saying?'

'Nothing,' Olivia sulked.

'So you are a liar.'

'Yes... I am a liar. But there is something I must explain—'

'I'm going to punish you,' interrupted Henry.

But whatever he was going to add was cut short by an angry rattle of the door bolts. Henry cut the twine around Olivia's ankle and went to answer it.

'What's been going on in here?' hissed Charlotte, her flashing eyes glaring at Olivia.

'She's to spend the night lashed to the pump,' he said quickly, knowing how much that would please Charlotte.

'And richly deserved, no doubt,' Charlotte rejoined without asking the reason.

Then, much to Olivia's disgust, she fell on her knees in front of him and kissed his bulging breeches, her stupid face a picture of simpering and grovelling worship.

'Did that dirty slut vex you, my darling?' she whimpered, gazing upwards with wide, evil eyes.

Henry kicked her away and ordered Olivia into the yard.

'What you need is a damn good thrashing,' he said, much for the benefit of Mrs Reynolds coming out of her kitchen.

'See that she gets it,' said the old woman, still convinced that buying Olivia for a sovereign in return for nothing less then a slave was tantamount to daylight robbery.

49

Olivia, outnumbered and weak from near starvation in the infirmary, had little choice but to step into the trough and reach up for the handle. Henry used Charlotte's shawl to bind her wrists by tearing it into strips. Charlotte considered it a great honour that her lord and master should treat her garment with such contempt.

'Fetch a switch,' he said, and Charlotte bolted into one of the outhouses and came back with a bunch of twigs.

She lifted her skirt, rolled down one her stockings that had cost her a fortune in the city, and handed it to Henry, who snagged it around the twigs, forming a makeshift handle. It wasn't as satisfactory as he would have liked, so Charlotte rolled down the other stocking and handed it to him, her eyes in tears of gratitude.

Henry stepped to one side of the trough and let fly, but the twigs merely broke in half and splintered across the flags.

'Damn!' he cursed, hurling the rest onto a midden.

'Now look what you've done,' exclaimed Charlotte to Olivia. 'Wasted the master's time in tying up all those twigs,' and she leapt up and boxed her in the ear.

For one whose physique closely resembled that of a serpent she possessed considerable strength, especially when she wanted to impress her lord, and she nearly knocked off Olivia's head. Olivia, still dazed, felt a searing pain slash across her bare bottom. She staggered sideways, tripped over the edge of the trough, and hung with her knees on the ground and her arms still tied to the handle above.

'Pull her upright!' Henry yelled at Charlotte, who rushed to the farthest extreme of the handle and jerked it downwards.

Olivia was whisked off her feet and left swaying to and fro, her toes bumping into the edge of the trough every time they passed over it.

'Forty strokes, that's your due,' Henry announced, trying to sound like a magistrate.

Charlotte beamed at him with pride and seated herself on the handle to keep it there.

Henry's own belt, which he had withdrawn from his breeches, was fitted with brass studs at regular intervals and he was careful to ensure it was those that ripped into Olivia's back. He began at her shoulders, landing it with an almighty crack that scattered a flock of pigeons from the roof. It did indeed sound like a gunshot and Olivia, thinking she had been hit with a host of musket balls, screamed aloud. Her legs thrashed outwards and as quickly returned, smacking the bones of her ankles together, which brought forth a heartrending cry of agony.

But Henry whipped on, encouraged by Charlotte who heaped mountains of praise upon his head; proclaiming his great strength and manliness as he whipped all the way down Olivia's back. Olivia shrieked and screamed, tugging at her bonds, head thrown back and mouth open in shock and pain. When he reached her waist he stopped for rest and ordered Charlotte to fetch him a bottle. She leapt off the handle and Olivia hit the trough with a loud smack of her bottom.

With Charlotte temporarily out of the way he bent low and whispered in Olivia's ear. But despite the offer of putting an end to her sufferings she would not consent to having his thing in her mouth, or up her bottom, or anywhere else for that matter.

'Very well, then I shall pepper your bottom,' he promised, and seeing Charlotte scurrying out of the kitchen, he stood up and took the bottle she brought.

He was about to send it winging into the midden but thought better of it, and carefully placed it on the ground, well out of harms way. Charlotte jumped onto the handle and Olivia whizzed into the air again. Henry gave her no quarter, and Olivia shrieked and yelped her miserable way through two dozen more landing with monotonous regularity on the fat of her buttocks. A quick refreshment from a stream of water dribbling from the pump and he began again, curling the studs and leather around her thrashing thighs.

While all this was going on Olivia suffered the appalling countenance of Charlotte's face, which looked with pure hatred and malice at her sobbing eyes, but every now and then broke into a wolfish grin of satisfaction as the belt left its fearful marks. Occasionally she glanced at Henry with adoration, but mostly she looked at Olivia, her eyes sparkling in the sunlight.

Olivia's ordeal was far from complete, for Henry had returned to her bottom and was trying very assiduously to catch her under her legs at the moment they opened, which pleased Charlotte mightily. He managed to strike her there, but in the main she was too quick for him, and he soon abandoned the idea and went instead to her ribcage. That, he found, was much easier, and in no time at all the belt lashed round her protruding ribs and just caught the outward swell of her breasts. The howl that Olivia let forth persuaded him it was worthwhile continuing in that quarter, and he moved round the trough to better his aim.

Whether by accident or design, his aim was indeed perfect, for the furthest range of studs cut splendidly upwards under the swell of her breasts, lifting them and making them wobble, which had Charlotte rocking on the handle and laughing like a lunatic. Olivia did not share her humour, for the studs were now landing where she most dreaded.

Ten times over he struck each teat, and ten times over Olivia screamed as if her soul were entering purgatory, which at every renewed blow she undoubtedly was. Her legs had stopped thrashing and hung lifeless, apart from a twitching in her thighs which Henry found most arousing, so much so, he decided to end her flogging there and then.

Charlotte climbed reluctantly off the handle and Olivia fell in a crumpled heap into the trough. Her legs had unwittingly fallen open and Henry, anxious for her revival, instructed Charlotte to ply the handle.

'Why not leave the bitch where she is?' Charlotte suggested.

'Because I don't like to see dumb animals suffer,' he replied seriously.

'How kind you are, Henry. That's you all over - so considerate, so thoughtful, and so generous.' And with that she spitefully showered Olivia, freezing her to the marrow.

They left her there, naked and tied to the pump handle, while supper was served in the kitchen, a dish of tripe and onions, whose delicious aroma drifted into Olivia's nostrils. It was hunger that made her struggle, trying to wrench free from her bonds. Her shivering body twisted back and forth, which only served to exacerbate the problem, for the strips of silk had wound tighter. She lay in the trough, panting from the exertion, giving up the struggle and resigning herself to a freezing night under the stars.

Henry, however, had other ideas concerning Olivia's welfare. He was getting heartily tired with Charlotte's simpering compliance. There was nothing to look forward to any more. Whatever he wanted she gave, which lessened the excitement and made him bored with life in general. Whenever the opportunity presented itself, he betook him to the city and squandered the profits of the business in taverns and with the ladies who resided there. But that wasn't very often, and besides, Charlotte always insisted on accompanying him, which greatly added to his frustrations. He might well have abandoned the business altogether were it not for the unexpected and glorious arrival of Olivia.

In the early hours of the morning, when it is darkest and at its most deserted, he stole from his bed and crept across the yard. Olivia had fallen asleep in the trough, gone into a deep slumber, worn out with abuse and fatigue. The moon was not quite full, but light enough to illuminate her body, and it seemed to him, in a flight of fancy, that she resembled a figure not of flesh and blood, but of white marble translucent in all its magnificent shapes and contours. Her legs were long and shapely, and her bottom splendidly round. But it was her breasts that fascinated him the most.

In her sleep they gently heaved, the nipples, still erect from the cold, seemed to beckon. As did her mouth, which, slightly open, was irresistible to the ache he felt bulging in his breeches.

Olivia grunted and shook her head at the intruder poking softly between her voluptuous lips. Then, wonder of wonders, her mouth opened further, uttered a faint gasp and took it in.

Henry was beside himself as he squatted, for it was not every night an astonishingly beautiful young woman sucked him in her sleep. Completely unaware of what was taking place, Olivia sucked harder, believing it to be her long awaited victuals. Into her mouth it went, encouraged with a gentle shove of Henry's loins. But mindful of her earlier threat, he allowed her only his plum and held himself in readiness for a speedy withdrawal.

He need not have worried on that account, for Olivia had in her dreams gone back to childhood and was tasting the long forgotten sweetness of strawberry and custard. Henry watched, devastated, as her cheeks fanned in and out. Her head made a slight bobbing motion as it moved around his plum. He thought it worth his while to nudge just a little deeper, and he slipped further in.

Olivia's throat started a warbling sound and from inside her mouth came the slow ministrations of her tongue. Only with the greatest of difficulty did Henry remain still. How he managed to with a hot, wet tongue furling around his member and soft lips gliding back and forth and sinking gradually down his shaft, amazed even him. To his utter joy she had taken it all, for by now her lower lip was buried in his course pubic hair. She emitted a purr from the depths of her throat and slid back up again. She halted at the plum, grunted and then returned, sucking more generously as she went.

Henry gripped the sides of the trough and shot his bolt just as his shaft was in the deepest, when her lips were on the return stroke and her cheeks hollowed. Olivia gulped, gulped again, and swallowed every drop. She blinked and opened her eyes, staring directly onto the throbbing plum slipping quickly from her parted lips.

'You filthy beast!' she exclaimed. 'How could you? How could you?'

'Quite easily,' he smirked, whipping out a clasp knife and sawing through the shawl.

Olivia's hands dropped lifelessly into her lap, and in the next movement Henry slid his arms under her knees and around her back and carried her off into the storeroom.

'If you've done it once, you can do it again,' he assured her, dumping her bottom on top of the nearest coffin.

One way or another he was determined to make her suck him again, and if she refused she knew well what punishment awaited. He had taken off his breeches and shirt and stood between her open legs, his member level with her breasts.

'I only did that in my sleep,' she whispered sadly, looking at the throbbing stalk and wondering if she really could do it again.

'And there's nothing from preventing you now, is there?'

'You can only take me by force, and if you do I shall cry rape.'

Henry was unused to such threats, and to let her know that he gave her a resounding slap on the side of her face. 'I find it difficult to believe that anyone could possibly rape the likes of you,' he replied, planting his stalk in the cleft of her breasts.

He was right in more ways than one, for Olivia was determined to resist at all costs.

'What do you mean by that?' she asked, feeling her temper rise and equal difficulty in containing it.

'I mean you are a whore, and whores cannot be raped by the very nature of their calling.'

'I don't understand you.'

'You live principally for the pleasure of men, and no doubt have been much trafficked in that quarter. It wouldn't surprise me if half, nay, all of the town has lain between your willing thighs at some point or other. True?'

53

He slapped her face twice in succession and again on her thighs.

'What's the most you've had in one day?' he asked, feeling a rush of blood to his organ. 'Ten? Twenty? More?'

Olivia could plainly see the effect of his questioning, as much to excite him as to frighten her.

'A dozen,' she lied, hoping he would desist.

'Ah, I thought so,' and he pushed her on her back. 'Well, here's the first of the day.'

Olivia deftly rolled over and fell to the floor, whereupon he quickly sat on her, straddling her stomach. He took her hand and closed it around his shaft.

'I suppose you're used to this,' he said, 'so let's see how well you perform. The outcome will decide how many times I flog you during the course of the day.'

'You've flogged me already,' she muttered.

'That was mild compared with what will happen to you if you don't obey me'

Olivia reluctantly began to move her hand slowly up and down. She had little choice with him sitting on her and pinning her to the floor. But unbeknown to the master and skivvy, Charlotte had woken and was making her way across the yard, and hot on her heels came Mrs Reynolds wielding a poker.

They burst in at once and the startled Henry leapt off Olivia, proclaiming in a loud and innocent tone how Olivia had taken advantage of him; how when he brought her out of the cold trough she had seduced him into doing something he would otherwise, not for all the world, have done. Charlotte looked very suspicious, but was so besotted she readily believed anything he told her.

'Now you're for it!' Mrs Reynolds shrieked, barging past Charlotte and seizing Olivia by the hair.

She threw Olivia over the nearest coffin and belaboured her bottom with the poker.

'Disgusting wretch!' she exclaimed. 'Is no man safe in your errant hands?'

And as the poker smacked into her bottom, Henry quickly comforted the outraged Charlotte, pawing her hair and groping her breast, a certain sign that his affections were nonetheless affected by the wily whore who had served him thus.

'Lay them on well, misses,' said Charlotte, wriggling free from Henry and clambering up onto the coffin.

She sat on Olivia's back, rocking to and fro and squashing her breasts beneath. Henry was as quick to Olivia's head which hung over the edge of the coffin, and with Charlotte's back obscuring his mother from view, he whipped out his hardened member and thrust into her gasping mouth.

Olivia couldn't tell which pained her most; the poker racing in to her blazing cheeks, Charlotte bouncing the wind from her lungs, or the engorged organ she was obliged to suck. Breathing through her mouth was impossible, stuffed full as it was by that pulsating vegetable, and with Charlotte riding hard on the saddle, she had no recourse but to snort and grunt through her dilated nostrils.

'Oh, hark at the noise she makes,' exclaimed Charlotte, her legs now spread wide.

The grunting and snorting increased and the look of anguish on Olivia's blushing face had Henry eagerly thrusting to the back of her throat. She had given up sucking him, and with mouth stretched to its extremities, allowed his member to fulfil its ghastly function. And all the while Charlotte was fulfilling a function of her own, as was Mrs Reynolds; the latter assuaged her frustrations on Olivia's bare bottom by beating it to a jelly, and the former rode her back, legs spread and drawer-less.

Olivia, although so cruelly ravaged, realised now what form her life would take as maid of all work. Aside from her domestic duties, that grotesque family would use her as a plaything; Henry would go on with his attempted rapes until he had indeed finally penetrated her; Mrs Reynolds would make her life worse than a dog's; and Charlotte would do with her whatever Henry suggested.

Henry had again emptied into Olivia's mouth, and now stood back wiping his greasy organ in her hair. Charlotte had expended her passion all over her back and slithered back and forth uttering pitiful mews, as Mrs Reynolds continued to beat her bottom.

'I hope from now on we shall have no more of your licentious behaviour in this house!' she barked, out of breath and wiping sweat from her brow.

Olivia, as soon as Charlotte dismounted, swallowed Henry's sperm and stood painfully upright.

'You're evil, the whole lot of you,' Olivia sobbed, whereupon Mrs Reynolds broke into a flood of tears.

This left Henry no alternative but to punish Olivia further, eagerly egged on by Charlotte, who assisted him in escorting her into the yard to a kennel at the far end.

'I shall treat you as you deserve,' he said, throwing her to the floor.

He picked up a rusting length of chain that had once been used to tether an aged blood hound who had passed peacefully away some months before. Olivia was too shocked to resist the leather collar he slipped around her neck. The other end of the chain secured to the kennel would not allow her to stand fully erect, but only to sit or crawl about on all fours.

'This is how you will stay until you've learnt how to behave,' Henry announced, pulling the collar snugly round her throat.

'Quite right too,' added Charlotte. Then she gave Olivia a kick in the ribs.

'I'm not a dog,' Olivia protested, seizing a metal bowl and hurling it at Henry's face.

He dodged and it went spinning across the yard. 'Pity about that,' he said seriously. 'Now you will have to eat your meals off the floor.'

'You mean I was to eat out of that?!' she ejaculated.

'You were, and you will sleep in this kennel by night, and to get you used to the idea I shall leave you here for the whole of the coming day.'

There was method in his madness, for soon Mrs Reynolds and Charlotte would be off into the town to visit the haberdashers, and with Olivia tethered at the neck and unable to crawl very far, he was free to take her at will - doggy fashion, he mused. But his intentions were thwarted for an hour or two by Mrs Reynolds, who insisted he accompany both her and Charlotte by driving them in the cart. If he whipped up the horse on return he guessed that he would have sufficient time to enjoy Olivia before having to go back again to pick them up.

So off he went, leaving her alone in the yard, naked and chained and crawling around on all fours, feeling that whatever would befall her, nothing could be worse than this. In her shame and degradation she curled up beside the kennel and went to sleep, seeking what comfort lay there in a world of dreams.

It wasn't long before it happened; a hand passing lazily over her buttocks, trying to go between her legs. Olivia grunted and wearily opened her eyes.

'If you are going to assault me, you might at least have the good grace to take off this collar and stop treating me like an animal,' she muttered.

The hand was taken away and the collar slipped from her neck. Olivia rolled over and sat up.

'Who on earth are you?' she asked, covering her groin and breasts with her arms.

A handsome man in his late thirties, or perhaps verging on forty, gently lifted away the arm that concealed her nipples and leant forward to suck them.

'Who are you?' she repeated as his lips closed around her teat.

He made no reply but went on sucking, and Olivia let him do it. There was no will left to resist, perhaps this was all part of Henry's scheme, to allow her body to become the property of anyone who wished to use it. Any time now he would return and then both men would whip and prostitute her; have her naked here in the yard, taking it in turns to pleasure themselves in any manner they sought fit. And then she would be chained again and fed like a dog from a bowl, or if Henry did carry out his threat, from the bare floor like a scavenging beast.

'Turn over,' the stranger said softly, 'and lie on your belly.'

'Are you going to put it up my bottom?' she asked, assuming that was what he had in mind.

'Not at all. I'm going to slap you until you cry. Where would you like me to start? Your legs perhaps, or shall I go directly to your arse? You may choose.'

This was something of a novelty, being able to decide where she would be beaten.

'On my bottom, please,' she said, surrendering without a thought.

'And hard, I presume?'

'As hard as you would care.'

'Would you prefer I use a whip or will the flat of my hand suffice?'

Again she was given the choice. Why did he not simply abuse and ravage her as everyone else had done. Being unused to such thoughtfulness she was thrown into confusion. Usually those decisions were made for her, and now she found it difficult to reply.

'Well?'

'The flat of your hand, if that is to your liking, sir, and if it will not cause any discomfort to yourself.'

'You have learned obedience, girl, and to know your place - a change of heart from what I heard earlier in that shed.'

'I have learned my place, sir, and am aware that as long as I serve this household I shall be obliged to do whatever is required of me, however onerous or painful.'

'You welcome your punishment then?'

'If it is justly deserved, sir.'

'And is this justly deserved?' He picked up the dog chain and regarded it with seeming distaste.

Olivia remained silent. Perhaps it had all been her fault, for if she were not so good looking and curvaceous Henry would not choose to molest her, or Charlotte regard her as a threat. If she had borne it all in silence instead of protesting she might not now be in this position.

The stranger did not pursue the matter, but began slapping Olivia's bottom. Softly at first, but gradually increasing the slaps until they stung and made her cry. It was not a harsh slapping, there seemed to be an absence of brutality in the way his hand clapped around her buttocks, slapped the backs of her thighs and flanks.

He hit harder, piling up the blows one on top of the other, beating her flesh in the same place, a dozen, two dozen times, perhaps three. The slapping went on until, seeing her bottom and thighs turn a blazing red, he considered her adequately chastised, although, lying on her stomach revelling in the heat burning through her skin, Olivia still had no idea who he was or why he was beating her.

When he ordered her onto her back she complied without a murmur.

'Put your hands under your breasts, girl, and lift them. Bunch them together and ensure your thumbs are away from your teats.'

Olivia placed her palms where he instructed and raised her breasts from her chest, pushing them close together. Her nipples she left bare and erect.

He slapped her much harder than he had hitherto, landing the flat of his hand on the mountains of squeezed flesh, taking careful aim and striking all around her nipples, but as yet not striking them directly. Olivia looked down and saw her breasts begin to turn scarlet. She had stopped crying and exhibited only a series of short, gasping pants. Her legs moved involuntarily; the thighs opening and closing, her calves splayed outwards and heels digging into the earth. Then she began to groan and writhe, arching her back and lifting her breasts higher.

'Please hit my teats,' she begged, without knowing the reason.

'Is that what you want, to have your teats slapped?'

'Oh, God, yes. Please hit them hard, sir.'

The slaps put an end to her panting and had her groaning aloud, rolling her eyes and opening her mouth. Her legs spread wider and she was crying again, not from pain but from an unbearable tingling in her womb and slit. While he went on striking with one hand, beating the points of her aroused nipples, he slipped two fingers of the other inside her. Olivia nearly jolted from the floor and her hands flew from her breasts.

He ignored the clenched fists that beat on the ground and the heels that drummed, but went on with his wordless pleasuring of her womb, searching deeper inside, and driving her wild.

He let her climax and kissed her fully on the mouth.

'Please tell me who you are,' Olivia eventually panted.

'There is no time for that now. Go upstairs, wash quickly, and select one of the girl's dresses, and make haste if you are to escape.'

'Escape?' she asked dumbly.

'Do you wish to spend the rest of your life here?'

'But whither shall I go?'

'Anywhere you please, but if you take my advice, you will steer well clear of the town. Head across the meadows and by nightfall they'll have given up the search.'

He gave her a hard slap on the bottom that sent her running upstairs. In a trice she was back down again wearing one of Charlotte's dresses. He led her through a wicket gate and pointed to the distant horizon, indicating the way she should go.

'Why did you do that to me just now?' she asked, following him into the lane.

'Because I chose to, and it is not for you to question my motives.'

'No, sir,' she replied humbly. 'But what if they should come after me? I shall be whipped for days and made to live in that kennel.'

'Then in that case I suggest you make your move now, or do I have to whip your pretty backside all the way across that field?'

The stranger walked swiftly down the lane, turning occasionally to see how far Olivia had gone, and when she was but a distant speck of blue tearing across the far meadow, he entered the high road, climbed into an awaiting carriage, and rumbled away in the opposite direction.

CHAPTER SEVEN

Olivia, following the stranger's instructions, kept well clear of the high road, and headed across the meadows. Though she was nearly four miles away from the town, she ran alongside the hedgerows, keeping well out of sight, ducking and hiding like a criminal. The thought of being overtaken was too horrible to contemplate. On she went, not knowing whither she was going or what would become of her when she arrived.

She had acted on impulse, encouraged by the stranger who had almost driven her witless whilst smacking and fingering her, driving reason from her mind, leaving her breathless and panting. The ache was still there between her legs. She smiled at the thought of it and hurried on across the meadows towards a farmstead in the distance.

Why was it, she wondered, that men seemed always to be wanting to put their fingers into her, or smacking and whipping her bottom, or making her suck their organs, or threatening to seduce her at the first opportunity? There was nothing enjoyable in that as far as she could tell, except perhaps the aftermath of peace when they left her alone and, she had to admit, sometimes a peculiar tingling sensation that was not entirely untoward. The stranger had certainly achieved that, but had then set her on a path that she would never have dreamt of following. As the farmstead grew nearer she had an uncanny feeling she had not seen the last of him. She hoped it were true.

Olivia wondered what sort of reception she might receive if she knocked at the door for a slice of bread. In her minds eye she imagined a ferocious dog let loose on her, or worse, they might be acquainted with the Reynolds and thus drag her back there. It was not impossible that they might beat her and hand her over to the magistrate for a vagrant. At that moment a carriage thundered by, disappeared behind the buildings, and shortly came out again. Then she realised what had been troubling her; the place seemed oddly deserted, devoid of animals and all the impedimenta of a farm. There was not a beast or barn in sight. She moved closer, still keeping behind the hedgerows, watching and listening.

There was life of sorts; a couple more vehicles arrived in the yard, disgorged their cargo, and went the same way as the carriage had gone. Olivia stood up, and taking a few steps forward entered the farmyard, if indeed it was such. The men hurrying the crates into the building took little notice of her, apart from a polite good morning and a quick undisguised appraisal of her magnificent figure, which they couldn't help admiring under the thin, clinging cotton. She wished now that she'd chosen something more substantial that didn't reveal the swell of her breasts, or make it so obvious that underneath she was naked. How easy it would have been to lace on a corset or snatch up a pair of drawers. But what was done could not be rectified and, squaring her shoulders, she walked boldly into the building, ready to flee at the slightest bark or pair of hands that might grab at her.

Olivia thought, for a few terrifying moments, that she had strayed into hell. The whole building shook as if struck by an earthquake. Glass rattled and clouds of steam and soot poured through the open door. As it cleared she realised where she was, and stared in disbelief at the line of carriages grinding to a halt. The door directly in front of her opened and a man got out, took one look at Olivia and bowed her forward. She might have turned and ran, but for a voice which told her to hurry along, late already and no time to lose. All her life Olivia had responded to the voice of authority and half expected a whip to lash her buttocks into the bargain. She half danced her way across the platform and into the carriage. The door slammed, the carriage juddered, and slowly the station buildings began to move.

Olivia uttered a shriek of terror and collapsed onto the seat. The station vanished and she found herself in open countryside moving faster and faster. No sooner had she fixed her eyes on a tree or cottage it had disappeared from sight. It seemed as if the whole world was spinning round and round and carrying her away into oblivion.

'Your first time on a train?'

Olivia nearly wet herself. She hadn't seen the middle-aged man sat in the opposite corner leering at her over his newspaper. Her nipples, startled from shock, poked at the thin cotton, and to her chagrin it had also sucked uninvited into her bottom-cleft. From his wide-eyed grin she realised he knew there was nothing underneath that thin layer of material. Instinctively she huddled into a corner, crossing her legs and folding her arms over her unprotected breasts.

'London?' he enquired, dropping his paper.

Olivia didn't have a clue where she was going, so replied in the affirmative. It seemed the right thing to do.

'I hope you are more fairly treated there than you have been in this neighbourhood,' he replied kindly. 'When you got into the carriage I couldn't help but notice the evidence of a recent and severe whipping about your person, particularly around your hindquarters.'

'Is it your practice to notice such things?' Olivia said tartly.

'I could not help it ma'am, for if you were to reach under your rump you will discover a rather large and revealing tear in your dress, which not only bares your bottom, but also indicates that you are not wearing any drawers, or anything else for that matter.'

'How dare you sir,' she exclaimed, 'to be so forward.'

'There is a law which strictly forbids young women to travel on trains half naked and much to the consternation of fellow passengers,' he continued, 'and which leaves me wondering why you are travelling without luggage or a chaperone.'

'My luggage and chaperone have gone on ahead,' she replied, pleased with her quick and witted response.

'On the previous train, no doubt.'

Olivia replied that that was the case.

'Then your chaperone and luggage will be in some confusion, for the previous train has gone on to Dover, which leads me to the conclusion that you are a liar, and also dressed in clothes other than your own, which I am certain are stolen. In short, you are a penniless vagrant and will be handed over to the appropriate authorities as soon as the train arrives at Paddington.'

'The magistrate?' she asked fearfully.

'Indeed, unless you agree to take your punishment forthwith. And in your position that would seem the best alternative.'

'I suppose that means taking off my clothes and sucking your thing,' she said sullenly.

'No it does not,' he replied, genuinely shocked at her suggestion.

'I'm sorry, it's just that everyone else seems to demand it, that and being whipped as well.'

'You were made to do that?!'

'Frequently, and I don't mind saying that I'm beginning to think it's all I'm ever wanted for, to debase myself and indulge in such outrageous acts of lewdness.'

'Tell me what happened to you and I shall make it my business to see they are brought to justice.'

'Is buggery a capital offence?' she asked, intrigued.

'Not necessarily, but probably warrants penal servitude at the very least.'

'And what about sucking a man's thing?'

'If you were not a willing participant, possibly ten years in prison.'

She thought for a moment. Henry had treated her like a dog and deserved that. She might have to exaggerate a little, but the knowledge and pleasure of hearing him sentenced to ten years on a treadmill was worth it.

'Where would you like me to begin?' she asked, feeling a little excited at the prospect of being, at last, able to get her own back.

'At the beginning. But first, take off your clothes. I may need to see any evidence that will assist your case.'

Olivia willingly stripped and then sat naked in her corner, legs still crossed but arms by her sides resting on the seat; breasts bare and wobbling with the steady rocking of the carriage. Her nipples were erect from a draught that came through the open window, so the gentleman pulled on the strap and closed it, then seated himself beside her, his hand resting on her knee.

'Begin,' he said, giving an affectionate and encouraging squeeze.

'Reynolds, his name was, an undertaker by trade, and I had been sent there to work as a maid, but little did I suspect the real motives for my employment. On my very first day when I ought to have been polishing grates and such, he assaulted me in a fashion I dare not repeat.'

'I'm afraid you have to, if this Reynolds is to be brought to book.'

'It began in the storeroom where all the coffins were kept, a more dark and dismal place you could never imagine. And there I was all on my own a-polishing of the handles and lids. I was fair worn out when he came in all of a rage. "Is that all you've done?" he said, looking at the pile with utter contempt. I was furious, for all that morning I had worked my fingers to the bone.

'"I shall have to punish you for your laziness" he said, and then ordered me to take off all my clothes.'

'And did you?'

'What else could I do? He was twice the size of me and looked very sincere, what with taking off his belt and swinging it to and fro. So I took off my dress and stood there in my underwear, wondering what to do next. "And the rest" he said, "you have to be naked".

'Off came my corset and drawers, and there I stood without a stitch on, all of a tremble. "Put out your hands" he ordered, and then tied them behind my back with his cravat.'

'Are you sure you are telling me the truth?' the man asked suspiciously. 'He really did that to you?'

'Cross my heart and hope to die, sir, that's exactly what he did.'

'Show me. You can demonstrate with my tie. Do exactly as were ordered.'

Olivia stood up and put her hands behind her back, crossing her wrists and letting the man bind them. When he'd finished she sat down again in her corner.

'Very good. Now continue with your narrative, and be sure to leave nothing amiss.'

She thought for a moment. 'Then he led me to a pile of coffins and pushed me over them, and while I was helpless he made me spread my legs and tied my ankles wide apart to some benches that were there.'

'And you did not resist, even at this stage of the proceedings.'

'How could I with him holding me down with his hand on my back and pinching my poor, bare bottom?'

'I still find this rather difficult to credit. Perhaps you had better show me the exact position that you were in, then I can decide for myself'

'But there aren't any coffins,' Olivia said, as if it were the most obvious thing on earth.

'Then you can use my knee,' and seeing her hesitate he added irritably, 'oh, come along girl. If you want this man punished you must show me, or how am I to present your case?'

Olivia got to her feet, and while he shuffled to make room she lowered herself over his knees, her head almost touching the floor, legs bent feeling the vibration of the rails beneath.

'Now what happened next?' he asked, settling himself comfortably and resting his hands on her bottom.

'He whipped me of course, with his belt and then, after that he—'

'Go a trifle slower, miss. You state quite clearly that he whipped you. How many times? A dozen laid on hard, or was it perhaps a mere demonstration of his authority over you? A warning, so to speak.'

'I was whipped so hard that my bottom went red,' she replied indignantly.

The man reached for his portmanteau and opened it. Olivia gulped at its contents.

'Do you normally travel with such wares?' she asked, lifting her head and staring at the collection of whips that clattered to the floor.

'It's all part of my investigative procedure,' he replied, taking up a particularly nasty looking length of plaited leather and flexing it between his hands.

'Now I suppose you're going to whip me,' Olivia said dryly, as if she expected it.

'I don't have to, no.'

'But it would help me if you did?'

'Certainly.'

'Then you may continue, but when I tell you to stop you will do just that... understood?'

Unseen by Olivia, the man took a quick glance out of the window and did a mental calculation. In the distance were the beginnings of a city and he judged that there was time enough to give her a sound thrashing before the train heaved into Paddington.

Olivia clenched her teeth to fight the pain that seared through her bottom. He was whipping her hard; much harder than she could remember Henry having done. She saw the shadow of his arm rise and fall and felt a scorching welt spread across her cheeks. Her head jolted and hit the seat with a bump.

'Did you scream like that when this Roberts fellow lashed you?' he asked professionally.

'Reynolds,' she corrected. 'His name was Reynolds, and no, I did not.'

'Then don't do it now.'

He lashed her again, but on the backs of her thighs, shifting her further over his knee to get a more accurate aim. The next two strokes crisscrossed her shoulders and another caught her on the side of her flank. Henry had not whipped her quite like this, with such deadly precision, ensuring that each lash landed on an untouched part of her flesh, deliberately throwing her into studied confusion so that she didn't know where he would hit her next.

'I think I've had enough now,' she sobbed, trying not to scream any more.

'How many lashes did you receive originally when Reynards whipped you? It must have been a good couple of dozen, I'll be bound.'

Olivia fumed, would this stupid man never remember the right name? She tried to get up but he forced her back again, toppling her so that her bottom rested square across his knees, her weight thrown forward.

'Three dozen,' she snapped, not troubling herself to correct his earlier mistake. She would have to write it down later.

'Then three dozen you must have,' he said, lashing her back six times in quick succession.

'Must I really?'

'I'm afraid you must, unless you wish me to cease here and now and forget about any justice you wish to see done.'

'And what about all the other things he did to me, do we have to go through that as well?'

The train had slowed to a crawl and entered a passing loop waiting for the signal to proceed. It was possible that he could bugger her after he had finished with her bottom.

With that idea in mind he sent the plaits whistling into her buttocks, stinging her flesh and filling the compartment with wild shrieks.

'Cease your yelling!' he shouted at her. 'And behave yourself, or I shall be obliged to discontinue with my investigations!'

Olivia sensed a rage of anger well up inside her. She had done everything he had told her to do; had stripped off her clothes and permitted him to bind her, had submitted to a fearful whipping and was running the risk of being taken anally into the bargain. She wished now that she'd never mentioned the awful subject in the first place. Her teeth ground in anger and she kicked out like a pony, thumping the door and rattling the glass.

But the more she kicked the harder he lashed. Olivia simply couldn't believe that she had allowed all this to happen; putting herself willingly over a man's knee, a man she had never met, and was not only offering herself up for a beating, but was fully compliant, encouraging him to complete the punishment.

When the final lash fell it was on a pair of blazing cheeks that had lost all feeling. She had stopped grinding her teeth and snorting, and her legs lay lifeless and akimbo across the carriage floor.

'Were you untied when the next assault took place?' he ventured, 'or did you remain that way? Answer me girl, I have to know.'

'I was left tied,' she sobbed, 'but not like this.'

Her wrists were freed immediately and she found herself hauled upright and put back onto the seat. Her bottom sank into the upholstery and a wonderful feeling of relief went through her.

'So how were you tied?' he continued. 'Hands in front, or what?'

'Above my head,' she replied, thinking that having gone this far she might as well make the most of it and condemn Henry to death, or as close as possible.

'And you were whipped again?'

'Thoroughly.'

'And now I suppose you're going to tell me that you were taken down and he put it in your mouth with you kneeling in front, or did you go willingly to his bed?'

'I never entered his bed,' Olivia protested.

'So you were in the position I have just described?' Olivia gave a reluctant nod. 'And your hands were free to obey his instructions?'

'I can't remember,' she muttered, realizing what lay in store if she admitted as much.

'I think you have lied to me all along. This fellow Richards doesn't even exist, and because of that I shall report you to the authorities.'

'And I think you are not what you say you are. All of this was just an excuse to whip my behind.'

'Very well, I suggest we both return by the next available train and you shall have the opportunity to prove yourself. If what's his name does exist, I shall tender my apologies and leave you to pursue your own defence, assuming you can indeed prove these serious allegations.'

'Whatever you want with me,' she said sadly, and understanding the situation, 'just go and do it.'

'What do you think I ought to do with you?'

The train had moved out of the loop and was gathering speed. Out of the window the outer suburbs of London were coming into view. Then quite suddenly they were plunged into darkness. Olivia could just discern the bricks of the tunnel through the smoke.

The man had got behind her and forced her to the window, her bare breasts flattened against the glass, and she turned her head sideways to stop her nose and lips from doing likewise.

'Reach up and grab hold of the luggage racks,' he told her, guiding her hands upwards and outwards.

Olivia had to get up on her toes to obey his command. Her breasts glided up the glass and her navel and belly appeared above the lower part of the door.

'Higher,' he said, giving her bottom a vicious swipe with the whip.

Olivia jerked up and felt her pubic ridge and hair rise just above the frame.

'Oh, God, no!' she exclaimed, seeing the walls of the tunnel begin to lighten.

The train gave a shriek of its whistle and burst into the daylight. The man had evidently dropped his trousers and was pressing his erect organ into her bottom-cleft, keeping her up on her toes and compressing her against the window, so that no matter how great her struggles she could not escape. It became quite clear that from outside everyone would see her nakedness, but only a glimpse of the anonymous figure behind.

'We fit very nicely together,' he remarked, embedding his organ between her cheeks and using his hands on her buttocks to immerse it fully.

'Do we?' Olivia breathed, daring to angle her head slightly at the backs of rows of tenements coming into view.

'Were you really buggered?' he asked, starting to ride her.

Olivia winced as her hardened teats rubbed into the glass. She was so hard against it her breasts had squashed flat, giving the impression that they were huge - at least three, perhaps four times their real size.

The slaps she knew were coming landed on her flanks, for there was nowhere else he could hit her, pressed as she was.

'I don't have to suffer this,' she gasped, now that the train was entering the city proper and passing gangs of plate layers in the sidings.

'You haven't answered my question,' he replied, releasing his grip on her cheeks and softening the slaps.

'You refer to my being buggered, I presume.'

There was temporary relief when the carriage drew up alongside a goods train and she couldn't be seen. The tension in her bottom and legs subsided slightly. Her hands lessened their grip, but still she was up on her toes, held in check by his organ, which was poking uncomfortably close to her anus. A finger surreptitiously smoothed a cold cream into that shy opening.

'That's exactly what I'm referring to.'

'No... no never.'

She choked back a tear and then thrust her rump savagely backwards, almost affecting an escape from the window, but not quite managing it for the man was as quick on the return, and Olivia let out a whelp.

'You're having me!' she wailed, tensing her muscles and writhing her hips.

The man went brutally about his task, penetrating her with a forceful shove of his loins and pinning her hopelessly against the window. Olivia struggled and he slapped her sides repeatedly, beating her into submission, making the tears flow. Every time he withdrew and she thought her humiliation was ended, he speared her again, but more savagely, and kept on slapping her, and she screamed all the louder.

Now they were clear of the goods wagons and face to face with gangs of men working alongside the tracks - so close that dozens of shovels and hammers clattered to the ground as one - her humiliation descended to new depths. She screamed from revulsion and loathing as much as from his riding her. One of the men came boldly up to the window and flattened his rough hand on the glass, pretending to grope her breasts, making it go round and round in circles and mouthing audible obscenities.

It was the measure of her defeat that she had abandoned all resistance, and merely looked at the plate layer with half lowered eyes and drooping lips that said, yes I am being buggered, and if it pleases you, watch me - watch all you like.

Then, as suddenly as the man had penetrated her, he lifted her away from the window and pushed her to her knees. He wound his fists in her hair, and her mouth, open with surprise and shock, was abruptly filled to the hilt.

'Now suck!' he commanded. 'And be quick about it, you shameless trollop!'

And remarkably, Olivia obeyed.

Notwithstanding the acrid taste of her own bottom, she sucked his organ deep into her throat, and found her hand worming between his legs, clutching his fruits and bobbling them on her fingers. He stiffened at that, and Olivia worked her inexperienced mouth as if she were a seasoned whore; going up and down, sucking and blowing, nibbling at the plum, and all the while keeping her fingers manipulating and squeezing.

'A whore,' he exclaimed. 'I knew it from the start, and if I had the time I'd have you where you want it most.'

But time was not on his side. The train was easing its way from the sidings and the cacophony of lewd catcalls, and into the station itself. As Olivia brought him to his climax he bitterly regretted all the time he'd wasted trying to seduce her.

Olivia swallowed hard and took his organ out of her mouth. Then she spat a great gob of fluid across the compartment and burst into a flood of tears.

'I'm not a whore,' she protested. 'I did this because I thought you wanted to help me,' and she picked up Charlotte's dress and threw it over her head.

To her annoyance it got caught in folds around her breasts, and when she jerked it free she heard an ominous ripping sound.

'Now your arse really is bare,' he laughed. 'Look.'

Olivia stole a frightened glance at her reflection in the now darkened window. It was true. Her bottom bared itself completely, for the tear had ironically followed her crease and thus her buttocks were displayed from one side to the other.

'This is all your doing,' she protested, crying with the further humiliation she would now have to endure.

'If I were you,' he said solemnly, 'I'd wait here until nightfall. The train isn't going anywhere, so you have plenty of time to make whatever plans you have in mind.'

Then, to her utter amazement, he reached under his greatcoat and tossed her a shilling. She would have thrown it back but a warning voice told her to be more prudent. A shilling was better then none in a city as great as this.

'Am I supposed to be grateful?' she asked bitterly.

'You have a splendid bottom, miss,' he complimented, 'and if you take my advice you'll put it to good use. In your shoes I wouldn't ask anything less than half a crown.'

And before Olivia could utter an astonished reply he put on his hat and left her, quickly vanishing into the throng heading along the platform.

Chapter Eight

It was dark before Olivia ventured out of the compartment and onto the deserted platform. The tear in her dress seemed to have lengthened in its dimensions, and her whole bottom and upper thighs bared themselves to the cold night air.

The station, which she had hoped would be deserted at that hour, was still busy with porters loading things into vans, and officials scurrying to and fro waving bits of paper as a sign of their authority. Olivia made her way along the platform by dodging behind iron pillars, edging towards the entrance in the far distance. Her thoughts, like any other young woman in her position, although ready to point out her difficulties, were at a loss to suggest any solution, so she simply made a dash for an archway that seemed to lead out into the great wide world of London.

It was much smaller than she had imagined; an alleyway, narrow and cobbled, meandered into the fog which hung about her, swirling around her bare bottom and making her teeth chatter. She walked on, vainly tugging her bodice across her near naked breasts, for that too had ripped, not enough to expose them completely, but at the slightest heave they would burst loose.

At an intersection in the alley a half-starved mongrel jumped up and sniffed the join of her thighs. She aimed a kick at the filthy animal that promptly dodged behind her and placed its cold nose right into her bottom-cleft. When she started forward the brute ran off, taking with it the hem of her skirt, spinning Olivia round in a circle and leaving her completely naked from the waist down. Her hands flew to her join when a carriage rattled by. The driver yelled an obscenity and deftly lashed her thighs with his whip. A group of men trudging to work stopped to stare, thinking it was the gloomy light playing tricks with their eyes.

The suggestions they made indicated that if she were still there twelve hours from now, and if her private parts hadn't frozen over, they would give it to her good and proper. But Olivia had no intentions of standing there waiting to find out what that meant, and she bolted along the pavement ready to surrender to the first available magistrate. Everything had gone against her. She would approach the nearest person she saw and ask the way; a sound thrashing and six months hard labour could not be worse than this, she decided.

The alley opened onto a narrow street, and under a gas lamp she saw the vague outline of a woman leaning against its post. Now it was Olivia's turn to think she was delirious, for the woman's skirt was also ripped, and hung open to reveal a pair of bare legs which she was at pains to thrust at anyone who passed.

Olivia was about to cross the street, but suddenly a carriage drew up and the woman clambered in. The driver and horse stared straight ahead, quite oblivious of the squeaking springs and grunting that came from within. Then the carriage was gone, leaving the woman as before; looking up and down the pavement and hitching her skirts even higher. Olivia took a deep breath and walked up to her.

'Please,' she asked politely, 'I'm lost, and am in sore need of rescue. My clothes are in ribbons and I don't know where to turn. All this is new to me and—'

The young woman surveyed her with wild disbelief, and then interrupted Olivia's pleas with a wild shriek of laughter.

'God luv me!' she exclaimed, recovering slightly. 'For a moment you 'ad me fooled. Good line though,' she added seriously, 'must go down a treat.'

Olivia had to think about that, and in that brief interlude she observed the young woman much more closely She was about her own age with a pretty oval face and good legs, perhaps a little too thin but nevertheless very comely. Her waist was trim and her bottom pert. Her breasts high and firm, were exposed to the nipple.

'So how's trade?' the young woman asked. 'Been bug hunting 'ave yer?'

Olivia knitted her brows 'I'm sorry?'

'Bug hunting. You know, flicking drunks and cleaning 'em out'.

'I don't know what you are talking about I haven't been...' she couldn't bring herself to use that foul word, 'doing it with men, or doing any cleaning either I came to London to find gainful employment, and all I've had are assaults about my person by a man on a train who made me suck his thing and forced me naked out of the window and then left me, dress all ripped and like to be raped.'

'Dear, dear,' the young woman replied, with a great display of sympathy.

She was no longer laughing, but steered Olivia to a nearby cab-stand out of the freezing fog, which Olivia noticed didn't seem to bother her at all. She took off her shawl and wrapped it around Olivia's naked bottom.

'Got anywhere to stay?' she asked, knotting the shawl over Olivia's belly.

'No.'

'Money?'

'A shilling.'

'Hungry?'

'Starving.'

'Then I knows just the place.'

And so saying she marched quickly along the pavement, guiding Olivia with an arm around her waist, turning her into alleyways and through various courts until at length they halted outside a dilapidated inn. Olivia was considering whether all this was a good idea when the door opened and she found herself in a dark passage. A voice called from above and the young woman replied with more incomprehensible jargon, and up they went.

Olivia, groping her way with one hand, clung to the young woman's waist with the other. A door creaked open and Olivia was hurried over the threshold.

'Rita!' exclaimed several young women in unison.

Rita affected an extravagant bow and pushed Olivia forward. 'This is...'

Olivia whispered her name and was announced with equal flamboyance, whereupon the dozen or so young ladies introduced themselves in quick succession.

As they spoke, Olivia returned their wide and beaming smiles with horror-stricken eyes, for all of them were virtually naked, apart from those attired only in their drawers or corsets. She blushed at their nakedness and averted her eyes to the clothes hanging all around the walls.

'What is this place?' she asked, eyeing the strange collection of petticoats and frilly dresses.

'It's a kind of theatre,' a voice chirped, and the whole company fell into giggles.

'You're actresses?'

'When we're not flat on our backs.'

'Or up against a wall.'

'Or with our legs in the air.'

And they all laughed, slapping and poking each other. The laughing ceased abruptly when a middle-aged woman appeared from a back room and made straight for Olivia. She looked magnificent in black stockings, a black corset edged with scarlet lace, and with a figure that many women half her age would have killed for.

'A new girl, ma'am,' Rita said, introducing Olivia.

'Call me Euphemia, or Effie for short, and don't you pay any heed to these,' her arm swept the assembly, and as it returned led Olivia through a side door and into a room smelling strongly of cheroots and brandy.

'Take off your clothes and let's have a butchers,' she said, unlacing her own corset.

Olivia's tattered rags fell away. She didn't understand the term 'butchers', but assumed it was just another form of address, and she would just have to get used to it.

'Fine body,' Effie muttered, circling her, patting her bottom and prodding her midriff 'Fine form indeed, and tight between the fork. That'll go down well.'

She stood back to appraise her new arrival. 'Of course, I assume you've had your fair share of men in your time - what girl of your age hasn't? But what about women?'

Olivia's thoughts reverted to the advances of Flora, but she put that quickly from her mind.

'I've never been with either,' she replied, biting on her lower lip.

Effie recovered from her shock with surprising speed. 'But you could learn, or act as if you had, eh?'

'I suppose so, just as long as it didn't get out of hand.'

'It'll be in your hand for quite some time if I know my clients, or rather patrons, as we call them in the acting profession. Now don't tell me you haven't done that either - frigged a man, I mean.'

Olivia didn't understand that, so Effie demonstrated with a tossing motion of her hand.

Olivia blushed and shook her head.

'Well what have you done, in God's name?'

'I have been forced to put it in my mouth,' Olivia whispered, bemused as to why this woman was asking such personal questions, but anxious not to offend. 'And was made to suck until it went as hard as a rock and spurted a load of salty stuff down my throat. It was awful. Simply awful.'

'How many times?'

Olivia bowed her head in shame. 'Three,' she whispered.

Effie drew closer and very gently pinched Olivia's nipples, tweaking the teats until they hardened. Then she leaned over and kissed them in turn, licking at the areolae and slowly moving outwards, covering the breasts with her tongue.

'I want the truth,' she said softly and looked up. 'Are you still intact, down there?' and she raised her thigh and rubbed it between Olivia's legs, and kept on rubbing until Olivia reddened and started to pant.

'Are you really a virgin?' she asked, putting her arms around Olivia's shoulders and drawing her close.

Their bellies and nipples found contact and before Olivia could utter an astonished reply, Effie kissed her full on the mouth. But it was not like the strenuous advances of Flora. This was a real heartfelt kiss, soft, warm and gentle, accompanied with a deep purring from Effie's throat that had an almost hypnotic effect, as did the thigh pressing harder into her groin.

'Yes, I am a virgin,' Olivia breathed, allowing Effie to lay her on a nearby couch.

'And you've no objection if I prove that for myself? I have to know.'

Olivia shook her head and muttered, 'I suppose... if you really have to.'

'My, you are tight,' she heard Effie muse, as her fingers went up inside her, exploring carefully the tunnel walls and tickling the sensitive bud that the stranger at the undertakers had so willingly aroused.

Olivia's mind went back to that remarkable man who had set her forth on her journey, and she found herself in his arms dreaming dreams of knights in shining armour and being borne away on a white stallion. Her legs started to thrash and her hips began again that serpentine motion which lifted her bottom and thrust it hard against the fingers working inside her.

'Slap me... please,' Olivia begged. 'Slap me hard.'

Effie's eyebrows shot upwards. 'You want me to slap you?'

'Oh, God, yes.'

Effie obliged by driving the flat of her free hand into the sides of Olivia's thighs. Hard, uncompromising slaps that could be heard outside where the rest of the girls had assembled and were listening avidly to the proceedings. Effie, realising at once what was happening to Olivia, slapped her across the nipples and then bit them so hard that Olivia screamed. And she went on screaming and panting, jolting and heaving, until her juices seeped onto the couch.

Effie, herself in the throes of orgasm, left her, and with magnificent self-control went to a cupboard and came back with a whip.

'It seems that pain gives you pleasure,' she panted, rolling Olivia off the couch and onto her stomach.

The whip lashed into Olivia's buttocks, and when her legs shot outwards Effie sent another stroke whistling into her groin. The effect on Olivia surpassed Effie's wildest hopes, for Olivia writhed and thrashed in all directions, arching her back and tossing her head to and fro. The sight of those splendid legs and back, and those bottom-cheeks clenching and bouncing, sent Effie into spasms. Her own nipples were tingling as the whip lashed Olivia's virgin flesh, crossing her back and shoulders with thin red stripes. She was certain the girl was having another climax.

'Turn over!' she yelled, and hardly aware of what had possessed her, Olivia rapidly spun onto her back, throwing open her legs, hoping that Effie would lash her pouting mound.

She was not disappointed. The whip cut into her wetted slit, landing directly on her clitoris. Olivia lost all control and gave vent to a long, deep moan that had the girls in the passage nudging and winking at each other. She shrieked a lot louder when Effie sent the whip lashing over her nipples. Her bottom soared high in the air and returned with a crash of her hips. A yell, greater than those caused by the whip, reverberated around the room, for Olivia's head was thrown back, her mouth fully open and gasping for air.

Effie was down on her in a trice, sprawling between her legs and crushing mouth onto mouth, nipple to nipple, belly to belly.

'Don't stop now, I beg you!' Olivia gulped, suddenly throwing her legs over Effie's back.

She wriggled and squirmed, settling her hips and locking her heels together. Her arms flew around Effie's shoulders, nails scoring the skin. The door behind them had eased ajar and a dozen heads peered round.

Effie's muscular hinds bounded like a rutting mare between Olivia's thighs, which now glistened with trickling sweat. Above their gyrating limbs the air was thick and heavy with the scent of feminine, sexual odour. The onlookers could see clearly the way Olivia's nipples responded to the ministrations of Effie's searching tongue. Her hands had gripped her breasts and had forced them to a point, giving the teats greater prominence as she bit and sucked, not caring at all for the acute pain that Olivia was suffering.

Yet, strangely, the pain seemed delicious as its fiery darts shot through her breasts and belly and came together in one glorious cataclysm. Olivia thought a hot brand had been placed in her womb as Effie gnawed and chewed over her nipples. Her second orgasm climaxed simultaneously with Effie, who emitted a harsh grunt and slammed her pelvis into Olivia's hips. Effie lay there for a good ten minutes blowing and panting, feeling her juices flow into Olivia's drenched pubic triangle.

'I'm bleeding,' Olivia whimpered, letting her calves drop from Effie's back.

Effie heaved herself free and looked hard into Olivia's groin.

'You're not bleeding,' she said, knitting her brows. 'It's only... well smell for yourself,' and she placed her soaking palm over Olivia's mouth.

'What is it?' she asked, genuinely baffled.

'You are a virgin,' Effie said dryly, getting up and scattering the girls in the passage.

She settled back on her haunches between Olivia's thighs, resting her hands on top of them, feeling the sweating skin.

'The patrons are going to love you,' she remarked, 'and I have just the man in mind. But before that comes your training. I have no doubt that you'll make a good actress.' She laughed to herself. 'As if acting'll be really necessary! Have you been whipped like this before - I mean in all your secret places, and gone all wet like this?' Her hand went to Olivia's groin and rubbed.

'It would seem so,' Olivia replied, looking at Effie's arm going to and fro. Then she unwittingly let slip about the man on the train, and explained in great detail how he'd so rudely accosted her, and taken such dreadful liberties with her trusting nature.

Effie audibly sucked her breath. The hand stopped in midair and hovered uncertainly above Olivia's mound.

'Let me understand you aright,' she said, looking very intrigued. 'You've had it in your mouth and up your arse - both of which you permitted - but never here,' and she returned her hand, sliding her fingers inside Olivia's tunnel again.

'I suppose so,' Olivia grumbled.

'You suppose so. You didn't object when I put my fingers inside you.'

'You're a woman.'

'That makes not the slightest difference, apart from these,' and she put her free hand on Olivia's left breast and squeezed. 'And this here, I admit,' and she wiggled her fingers, watching Olivia's trembling lips.

'You've come to me a penniless trollop,' Effie continued, 'but when I've finished you shall be a fine actress, and rich into the bargain.'

'Please, have you finished now?' Olivia replied, shifting her bottom away from the clammy patch forming beneath.

'For the moment, yes. And after you've eaten I shall begin your education.' And with that startling piece of intelligence she hauled Olivia to her feet.

'What about my clothes?'

'What...? Oh, yes, clothes. I have just the thing in mind, but first we fill your belly, not literally of course, at least, not yet.'

Olivia, confused and not a little nervous, followed Effie into a kitchen where a plate laden with meat and vegetables already awaited her. The girls who had prepared it watched with some amazement as Olivia demolished its contents, then laughed when a loud and unexpected belch came from her rumbling belly. The pint pot of porter they placed on the table went the same way with equal ferocity, and another belch escaped her lips. But this time the girls didn't laugh.

After giving her time to digest they led her into a room that looked for all intents and purposes like the drawing room of a rich household. It put poor Olivia in mind of the governor's private quarters, and she shuddered.

'Sit on the sofa,' Effie said, now wearing an immaculate silk dress that must have cost a fortune. 'And watch closely while the girls perform, because afterwards you shall take part yourself.'

Olivia, a good deal restored and thankful that providence had sought fit to place her amongst such generous benefactors, reclined on the sofa, stretching her legs out in front of her. Her nipples still tingled and she wondered why it had been so important to undergo such rigorous examination, but then again, similar things were done in houses of correction and convents, and she was wise enough not to question it further. The memory of walking bare bottomed through a railway station was not one she cared to repeat.

'Watch closely now,' Effie repeated, seating herself in an armchair and lighting an extraordinarily long cheroot.

A curtain was drawn aside, but instead of a window a stage revealed itself and Olivia, uttering a cry of shock, curled up into a ball. The man who had taken its centre was dressed like the headmaster of a school, and in front of him sat four of the girls, appropriately decked out as his pupils. Olivia only just recognised Rita and her companions, now wearing knee length frocks, their hair in ringlets and faces chalked and rouged.

The girls were hard at work scribbling on their slates, until someone in the wings rang a bell and the headmaster briefly left the stage. No sooner had he left when the girl seated on the end rose from her bench and, taking up the chalk, executed a perfect outline of a hugely erect phallus. Olivia gasped in shock and shrank deeper into the sofa. The girl returned to her bench and again took up her slate. A few seconds later the headmaster returned and affected unconvincing horror at the obscenity drawn on the blackboard.

'And who is the author of this outrage?!' he roared, moving aside so that any audience present could not fail to notice it.

None of the girls spoke, but fidgeted nervously with their hair and tugged at the hems of their skirts. They did indeed give a very real impression of appearing terrified.

'If you do not own up I shall have no recourse but to flog every one of you!' the headmaster roared again, and he opened his desk drawer and laid a cane across its top. Then he folded his arms and waited for the culprit to declare herself.

Silence, and then greater shuffling of bottoms on the bench. 'What shall be done with them?' the headmaster asked, as if addressing an imaginary audience.

Olivia glanced first at Effie, and then at the other girls not taking part but who had come in unnoticed and were sitting around the room.

'Beat them,' Effie said coldly, and in her eyes Olivia saw a peculiar sparkle.

'What say you?' the headmaster asked, directing his gaze at Olivia, who visibly squirmed.

'Beat them,' she muttered, wondering just what sort of pantomime this was turning out to be.

'What did you say? Come, speak up.'

'Beat them,' she repeated in a louder voice which betrayed considerable reluctance.

'You heard,' he said to the girls. 'Now get yourselves over your desks.'

They all rose as one and bent over their respective desks, taking their weight on their arms and letting their heads fall forward in shame.

'You,' exclaimed the headmaster, pointing his cane at Olivia, 'step forward and assist me, if you please.'

Olivia swallowed. Surely he was not seriously suggesting that she carry out the punishment? She glanced quickly at Effie, who motioned her to the stage. Up she went and stood naked in front of the headmaster.

'Lift their skirts,' he ordered.

Olivia went behind them and did his bidding, folding their skirts neatly over their backs, revealing four pairs of red knickers, voluminous at the waist but gathered tightly at the knee just above their white, calf-length cotton stockings. That done, Olivia stood aside awaiting his next command, which to her great relief ordered her off the stage. Another girl quickly took her place, and with obvious relish slipped her fingers under the knickers of the nearest unfortunate and very slowly drew them downward.

Olivia watched in horror as the girl's buttocks came into view, then the length of her thighs. Her knickers were left caught around her knees while the girl undressing them moved on to the next. Soon four bare bottoms shone under the gas lamps, side by side, and touching at the hips.

'Twenty strokes apiece,' the headmaster announced. 'And on their bare bottoms. The first to cry out or soil herself will receive an extra six. I shall begin with you.' And he glared menacingly into the face of the nearest girl, whom Olivia could see was genuinely shaking.

Not for one moment did Olivia think that they would be caned for real, but as the first stroke sliced down she quickly altered her opinion.

The girl's head jolted and her right hand flew to her welted bottom. The girl beside her sobbed even though she had not yet been struck.

'Put your hand back where it was,' the headmaster ordered brusquely.

She put it back and the cane whistled into her flanks. Olivia heard her catch her breath and saw how tightly she gripped the edge of the desk. He lashed her again with his full strength, and the girl jolted forward bumping her knees, which had the onlookers rocking in their seats. The repeated strokes fell progressively downward, slashing the backs of her thighs and then by degrees, returning to her blazing bottom. When he had finished on the first he went quickly to the second, sweeping his arm with fearful whistles and landing the cane with the sickening sound that Olivia knew all too well.

'Ah ha!' he exclaimed joyfully. 'This wretch has wet herself!'

The girls in the audience craned their necks and Olivia, following their example, saw how the red material had indeed discoloured.

'You shall have another six after I have dealt with these other miserable offenders,' he announced brightly.

Olivia thought that very cruel, for the poor girl had not uttered a cry, but had borne her welts bravely with not even so much as a flinch.

The headmaster lashed the girl next to her, cutting into her thighs and cheeks like a madman. But to no avail; she neither wetted nor screamed - unlike the last, however.

What a weakling, Olivia thought as the first stroke brought forth a shriek. He lashed her again, slicing into the fat of her bottom just above the thigh. At that she tried to make her escape, which delighted the audience but had the headmaster positively seething. His left hand bore down on her back while he lashed her with the right. Her legs kicked out, and so he struck them for good measure, catching her across the backs of her stiffened calves, producing tears in her stockings, and going on until they were reduced to tatters.

'Let that be a lesson to you,' he said, somewhat out of breath, to the two girls who had not earned another six. 'Pull up your drawers and get back behind your desks.'

With groans of pain they reached behind and slowly obeyed, sliding their underwear up their thighs and deliberately stretching them over their burning bottoms.

'And now we return to you two miscreants,' he said to the two girls who did, in his considered opinion, deserve a further six strokes. He abandoned the cane and simultaneously took hold of their hair with both hands.

He lifted their heads and turned them around to display their tear-streaked faces to the audience. Olivia was astonished to see that it was Rita who had cried out so easily.

'Where shall they take their punishment?' he inquired of the audience.

Several suggestions were made, and he settled for the last. Upon his instruction Rita and her companion unbuttoned their fronts and drew aside the lapels of their dresses.

'Take them off?' he roared, and then suddenly ripped them clean down the front.

Their bare breasts fell forward, and without being told they placed their hands beneath them, lifting them upwards and at the same time squaring their shoulders.

'Turn and face each other,' he ordered, pushing them between the shoulder blades until their nipples touched.

Olivia stared with bated breath at the breasts now so close to one another the flesh pushed and squashed, making them appear larger than they were, and also presenting a target he couldn't fail to miss, especially as he had now exchanged the cane for a thick leather belt.

Olivia had never seen such artistry in the deliverance of a flogging. Each searing swipe was delivered at an angle, hitting the left breast of one and the right of the other, When he landed it vertically it caught them both across the nipples, which now had risen sharply and with the teats just touching.

'Stand still, you disgusting bitches,' he roared, and went on roaring, allowing his terms of address to get more filthy with every utterance.

He gave them a lot more than their allotted amount, and kept on hitting them until Olivia thought they would faint dead away. He would have finished at the final lash, but changed his mind and told them to take off their knickers and stand only in their socks and shoes, facing each other, arms around their waists and hugging closely.

Effie leaned forward in her chair and watched with avid interest while he continued anew, belabouring their bottoms, thighs and calves. The girls' heads had slumped forward and were touching at their foreheads; indeed their bodies were touching all the way down, particularly at the belly and thighs. Every lash was carefully aimed to make them jolt and rub against each other, and very soon Olivia guessed the reason.

Far from screaming they were panting, blasting their hot, excited breath into open mouths and onto flushed cheeks. They managed, despite the distracting calls and equally aroused pants from the audience, to climax simultaneously, after which they did collapse into a tangled, gasping heap.

'Well?' Effie asked, seating herself beside Olivia. 'Do you think you could act as well as that?'

'Is this performed in public?' Olivia replied, watching Rita and her exhausted companion struggle to their feet.

'Not exactly, more in front of select audiences who pay very handsomely for the privilege, and usually in drawing rooms rather akin to the one in which you are now seated.'

'They pay handsomely to watch girls being whipped and showing their bottoms?' Olivia asked agog. 'But doesn't it hurt?'

'Not as a rule, unless they are invited to participate.'

Olivia thought for a moment. 'No, I meant for the actresses. It certainly looked real enough to me.'

Effie smiled to herself in the manner of an adult having difficulty explaining something to a small child and finding charm in its naivety. 'Of course it hurts;

the skill lies in not minding that it does. Pleasurable pains, if you like.'

Olivia didn't like. She didn't like the idea at all.

'What else do you perform, apart from grown women dressed up like little girls and having their bottoms whipped?'

'Our repertoire is wide and varied,' Effie replied grandly. 'That display was as much for your benefit as for those taking part. It was, how shall I say, a dress rehearsal, learning the ropes.'

'And when will I learn my ropes?' Olivia asked.

'As soon as the stage is made ready, which will not be long. And if you perform well, which I have no doubt you will, you shall be given a fine set of clothes, a hot bath, and all the gin you can drink.'

With that Effie left her in the tender care of Rita, who seated herself on the sofa and put her arm lovingly around Olivia's shoulders.

'Effie's very kind to us girls,' she began, 'takes care of everythink, does Effie. We don't have to worry about nothink, all we have to do is act up for the genelman and give 'em wot they want,' and she gave Olivia a sly nudge of her elbow, as if that in itself made the situation crystal clear.

Olivia would have liked to interrogate Rita further on just exactly what it was the 'genelman' wanted, but instead found herself ushered into the room where all the costumes were stored, along with the 'props' as Rita called them.

She was not entirely surprised to see cupboards and drawers full of whips, chains, manacles, and costumes that had obviously been designed to display a woman's figure to the best advantage.

'This is pretty,' she remarked, holding up a costume that might have belonged to a young shepherdess.

She put on a straw hat and tied its pink ribbons under her chin.

'Lovely,' complimented Penny, a voluptuous redhead who was busy applying a dark coloured dye to her nipples, exaggerating their size, and producing a sort of shine on the pimpled areolae.

'You'll get your woolly flock disturbed all right,' laughed Dora, rubbing a darker dye into her pubic hair.

'All night, more like,' rejoined Penny, twisting and turning in front of a looking glass.

'Do you have real sheep on stage?' Olivia inquired, taking off the hat.

The girls stopped whatever they were doing and laughed uproariously.

'Only when we're asked,' said Dora, clutching her stomach, 'which ain't often, I'm happy to say.'

'Tush, tush, girls,' Rita interjected, herding them away from Olivia and leading her to a cupboard.

'You won't need to black up,' she said, running Olivia's raven hair through her fingers, 'or down there either by the looks of things,' and she ran her fingertips lightly over Olivia's pubic mound.

'What am I supposed to be?' she asked, seeing Penny and Dora fitting themselves with enormous black wigs. 'Conkerbines, you know, them wot lived in harems.'

Olivia was none the wiser, but stood erect while Rita passed a gleaming brass collar around her neck with a large ring at the front and a hasp behind which was fastened with a click. She passed a much larger band around her waist, again fitted with rings behind and in front.

'Hold your arms out,' said Rita, manacling Olivia's wrists with what frighteningly resembled the handcuffs she had worn in the van that had transported her to the House of Correction. A chain extending from the handcuffs was fed through the ring at the front of her waist and throat and pulled tight enough to draw her hands upwards until they stopped just beneath her breasts. Then Rita, with the assistance of Penny, manacled her ankles and fed another chain through the same waist ring, passed it beneath her legs, threaded it through the ring above her buttocks, and finally secured it at the nape of her neck. When it pulled taut the chain went into her slit and bottom-cleft, and Olivia suddenly took fright.

'Am I going to be hung up and flogged?' she asked fearfully, recalling her encounter with Flora in the mill.

'Flogged, maybe. Hung, definitely not,' said Rita, fastening more chains to the waist rings.

As Olivia let out a sigh of relief the door opened and behind her she heard the voice of a woman, rich and melodious, a smooth drawl whose resonance seemed to fill the room. Olivia turned. She had never seen a black woman and for a moment stared rudely at her, marvelling at the darkness of her skin. Without any hesitation the woman stripped off her clothes and went straightway to the cupboard, selecting various chains and an enormous wig that suited her naturally.

'Sappho,' said Rita, by way of an introduction, and having finished bedecking Olivia she went off to see how things were progressing on stage.

Olivia watched spellbound as Sappho broke into a splendid gyration of her buttocks, passing the chains under her legs, twisting her hips and swaying her breasts, and fastening the chains with lightning speed and agility. She left her hands free and, picking up a bottle of lavender oil, rubbed it all over body, particularly around her breasts, belly, and the dense mass of curls between her legs. When she had finished she shone like polished ebony, much to the obvious admiration of Penny and Dora.

'You new here?' Sappho asked Olivia, giving the bottle a fervent shake.

Olivia, replying that she was and forgetting that she was manacled, went to shake her hand. Sappho overlooked that and tipped the contents of the bottle over Olivia's chest. It ran between her breasts in a river, which Sappho caught and began greasing back up the cleft. Round and round her hand went, making the breasts gleam. She used the tip of her forefinger to polish the nipples and remarked favourably at the reaction. Her own nipples were huge in comparison, as were the orbs themselves, quite the largest Olivia had seen.

'Hand reared,' Sappho smirked, 'makes 'em bigger, and the buttons.'

Olivia found herself wondering how such an exotic personage came to be in a backstreet theatre in London, whereupon Sappho broke into an exciting narrative of how she had come over on a clipper as a plaything of the captain and crew and, because of her insatiable sexual appetite and energetic prowess in bed, had been set free and had been found wandering through the fog and rescued by none other than Effie herself. It seemed to Olivia that everyone in the place had been found wandering at some time or other, and likewise had been brought to this establishment.

'Did you really go to bed with all those men?' Olivia asked, as Sappho went behind her and proceeded to rub the oil into her buttocks.

'I took 'em all on,' she replied in her husky voice whilst passing her broad palm under Olivia's legs.

'How many of them were there?'

'Thirty or so, but I couldn't take on more than twenty a day, 'cause the cap'n wanted 'em fresh for work.'

Olivia gathered her thoughts. 'How long were you at sea?'

'Sixty-five days in all.' And she tipped another dollop over Olivia's back.

'So that means you had...'

'About fifteen hundred cocks,' replied Sappho, saving her the effort of working it out for herself. 'Give or take a couple of hundred, I suppose.'

'Did they ever put it up your bottom?'

Sappho shrugged. 'Not that I recall, but I did take on two at once.' Seeing Olivia balk she added with a wide grin, 'they both shot me at the same time, and didn't I like that, God luv me!'

'And I suppose they put it in your mouth as well?'

'Not two at a time,' she laughed. 'I'm a one cock girl when it comes to that. Now come over here and let me chain you.'

She led the astonished Olivia to where Dora was putting the finishing touches to her nipples and lifted the chain dangling from her waist. This she fastened to the ring at Dora's rear, then as Penny went behind Olivia she repeated the performance, chaining them in line, bottom to belly. When Rita returned, announcing the stage was ready and waiting, she took her place at the front with Dora behind. Sappho fastened the chains, and then as if she had suddenly remembered an important task, went quickly to the cupboard and fetched a stick of chalk.

'Why are you writing numbers on our bottoms?' Olivia asked, beginning to feel rather like a beast at auction, and not realizing just how close she was to the truth.

"Cause I'm the only slave with her hands free.'

'We're supposed to be slaves?' Olivia cried. And before anyone could think of a ribald answer, Rita led the procession along the passage and through a pair of doubled doors held open by the beautifully costumed Effie.

CHAPTER NINE

When Olivia stepped onto the stage she wasn't sure whether it was outrage or embarrassment that brought a burning flush to her cheeks. What she assumed was a rehearsal in which she would 'learn the ropes' as Effie described it, had turned into a full performance in front a male audience.

While the bejewelled Effie went through her introduction, Olivia stared at the floor not daring to look at the wide and rolling eyes gazing into her groin. She would have liked to cover it but the chains artfully prevented that. Neither could she cover her breasts, but could only stand, naked and chained, a veritable feast for the hungry eyes already devouring her.

Sappho, who was behind Olivia wielding a whip that had magically appeared from nowhere, caught hold of her hair and jerked her head upright. Then, for no reason other than to punctuate Effie's speech, she whipped all four of the linked girls across their buttocks. Not a playful lash, but delivered with the full swing of her hips, designed to make the slaves jolt and rattle their chains, which had the audience sweating in their seats.

Effie was getting near the end of her speech in which she had let it be understood that the slaves were indeed for sale, and to the bidder or bidders who guessed aright the amounts of money chalked on the girls' behinds. While the men debated amongst themselves, Sappho went from slave to slave, making a great play of fondling their breasts and then standing behind them and sliding her hand under their legs, rubbing it to and fro, producing gasps and sighs and wrenching of chains. If any of the slaves did not respond enthusiastically she whipped them, as Olivia soon found out. She gave her three on her bottom and another two on the backs of her thighs.

'Now pant, you stupid cow!' she hissed in her peculiar blend of Creole and Cockney.

She slid her hand beneath Olivia's legs and she responded with a barrage of fast, energetic gasps, which made her breasts bounce and nipples tingle.

'That's good,' Sappho whispered. 'Now lower your eyelids and keep your lips parted - breathe deeply.'

Olivia obeyed, this time her chest rose and fell with great heaves, and she saw the immediate effect it had on the men sitting in the front row. At another command from Sappho she resumed her panting and gasping, getting louder as she went.

Sappho left the stage and began a slow swing of her hips along the front row, flicking her whip into the men's hardened pillars which raised the fronts of their trousers, and then fondling them with her hand. Olivia had a mental picture of her taking them all on at once, and wondered if her story were true. Seeing the way she now deftly manipulated her fingers she thought it probably was.

Her thoughts were rudely interrupted as the bidding began. Olivia assumed that when her price was accurately guessed she would have to perform some light-hearted entertainment, such as offering herself up for a severe flogging, or having to bend over and display her wares while they too were chastised.

Dora was the first to be released from the stage, and as no less than five of the participants had guessed correctly the amount chalked on her bottom, it was they who led her away still chained hand and foot.

'What are they going to do with her?' she managed to whisper above the deafening shouts.

Penny ceased snaking her shoulders. 'Anything they like, we're slaves remember, we're here to obey.'

'But what if we refuse?'

'Then Sappho will have you.'

Penny had but finished her warning when her price was called, and beaming a compliant smile she waited until the chains binding her to Olivia were released and hopped off the stage. Only three men this time, Olivia noticed, hoping that the odds would keep on shortening in her favour.

By now the place was heady and thick with smoke from numerous cigars and cheroots, and it was difficult to see who was bidding for her. The price, set at ten guineas, was called out more than once, she was certain of that, because the man in the front row who had called first turned round to see who else had rivalled him.

Effie gave Olivia an encouraging slap on the bottom and she stepped down. The man in the front row leapt from his seat and, taking up the chain hanging from her neck, led her along as if he were a farmer leading a prize cow from market. In the smoky shadows there came the rumble of chair legs and hazy figures picking their way towards her.

'Four of you!' she said aghast, as the chain tugged her through a pair of curtains and into a dimly lit chamber.

'You've been let off lightly,' one of them remarked. 'At the previous auction the redhead took on a dozen. No wonder the poor bitch was bow legged for a month!'

At that piece of intelligence the men broke into wild guffaws and scrabbled to remove the chains that fell away with surprising ease, which of course they were designed to do. 'Am I to be raped?' Olivia asked, sniffing back a tear.

'That would depend very much on your definition of the word,' replied another.

'Forcing me to do something I don't wish to do is rape.'

'Perhaps we should seek the advice of the darkie - let her decide whether you're to be raped or not.'

'Oh, please, don't call Sappho, she'll kill me,' Olivia blurted.

'In that case shut up and do as you're told.'

One of the men who had not spoken came forward and gently squeezed her breast, thumbing the nipple as he did so.

'Now, now, gentlemen. That is no way to address a lady. Why, you have frightened her, and as she is so obviously a novice, perhaps we ought to treat her with a little respect. Hmmm?'

'Yes please,' Olivia sobbed.

'You shall not be raped,' he assured her. 'Indeed, our actions shall be guided by your consent.'

'Then I am not to be ravished?'

'Not here,' he replied, whisking his hand between her thighs. 'Effie has given strict instructions on that score.'

'I don't understand you,' Olivia said, feeling herself goose bump.

'You will consent to open both your mouth and your behind,' interrupted a more forceful tone. 'And in deference to my learned colleague, you are free to choose who goes where.'

They were already taking off their trousers before Olivia could even come to a conclusion. But one thing she was certain about, that if she failed in her duty and gave cause for complaint, Sappho and/or Effie would punish her, and very heavily.

And, she thought, she ought not to appear ungrateful; after all, Effie had seen fit to safeguard her virginity. The reason for this consideration never entered her head as she knelt compliantly to the floor.

'I think that you have misunderstood, miss,' spoke the kindly man. 'You see, we intend to take you both ends at once, so to speak. So I would advise you to position yourself thus.'

'Get down on all fours,' came an abrupt command.

A belt that had been surreptitiously swinging behind her sailed across her shoulders. Olivia jerked and fell forward, landing appropriately on her palms. A pair of hands placed themselves on the insides of her knees and slid them open. She knew that one of the men had knelt between them, and she gasped as a finger rubbed some ointment into her bottom-cleft.

On either side of her face the plums of two male organs smoothed into her cheeks, going in small circles and getting ever closer to the outer extremities of her startled lips. They met in the middle, hovering under her nose, impatient to be sucked.

'I can't do both at once,' she protested, then she remembered Sappho's earlier observation and repeated it verbatim.

'So, you're a one cock girl, are you?' the left hand organ said, giving her a cuff.

By way of reply, Olivia grunted as the first man at her rear entered his plum. His companion seized her waist and held her rigid while the entire shaft relentlessly filled her. He let go and leaned over her back, placing his hands on the halves of her bottom and prising them open. She heard a throaty sigh of satisfaction and the intruder slid in another inch.

Olivia let out her own sigh of relief and immediately the two plums jabbed into the corners of her mouth. Instinctively her jaw gaped, dropping open, lips stretched wide.

'Methinks the lady has a big mouth,' the right hand organ observed, edging tentatively forward.

'Room enough for the both of us, I should think,' uttered the left organ, thrusting a little deeper.

Olivia steadied herself on one hand and cautiously lifted the other to encompass the organs threatening to choke her. With a skill she was unaware existed her fingers closed around the shafts and pressed them together until the plums were in line at the centre of her mouth. Then, taking a deep a breath as possible, she rocked forward and puckered her lips over the plums, and kept up her rocking motion until she felt them slip into the grooves.

'Excellent,' the right organ complimented, as Olivia took her hand away and put it back on the floor.

'See if you can fire off both barrels with the same trigger,' the left organ suggested.

That was much easier said then sucked, for the man at her rear was pounding her buttocks without the slightest regard for his companions bulging Olivia's cheeks. His method of reaching his climax and also to obtain the maximum pleasure from Olivia's bottom was to penetrate her in a corkscrew fashion, by twisting his hips in as wide a circle as could be managed.

The method was not lost on Olivia who clearly felt every turn, and it seemed to her that he was splitting her apart by degrees, forcing her buttocks away from the cleft, opening her up wider than the mouth of a bucket. She squinted her already closed eyes and tried to concentrate on the plums jabbing slowly to her throat. Another irrational fear gripped her imagination; what if they did fire both barrels at once, she would be inundated with sperm and like to drown.

Get a grip, she told herself, you have done this before, just use your tongue and get the filthy business over and done with. That too was not as easy as she imagined it would be. Her mouth was filled to capacity. Not since childhood when she had stuffed her mouth with real plums had she been so engulfed. But she had been able to grind them to pulp between her teeth; try that now and she would surely suffer the consequences.

Gingerly, she eased her tongue under the probing plums and, finding the grooves, wiggled it back and forth. She was learning from experience which parts to tease and would be most likely to produce the desired results. Unfortunately, the men on the other end of the organs were not quite as forthcoming as she hoped. They were well versed in the noble art of fellatio and could hold back for as long as they sought fit; hours if necessary, depending on the whore who pleasured them. And Olivia, they decided, was worth prolonging.

While she struggled with her tongue the man at her rear had emptied himself and had slid out of her with a loud groan, and while her bottom hole remained stretched open his companion quickly filled it. His manner of entry was completely different. Instead of corkscrewing her, he took her with frantic and violent stabs as if he were as eager as she to get it over, which in fact, he was.

He had seen how Olivia's mouth was performing and the ecstatic expressions on the faces of her recipients, and now longed to feel the same.

The man who had spent himself reached under Olivia's body and began amusing himself with her breasts, squeezing and pulling on them, trying in his own evil way to cause her as much pain as possible. He overdid it when he pinched her nipples and Olivia bit on the soft flesh inside her mouth.

'You clumsy cow!' one of the organs cursed, and rewarded her with a slap on the side of her head, which was soon followed by another on the opposite side.

She would have apologised but could only utter a mumble that was taken as a protest, and would therefore be justly punished.

'Use the belt on her,' an organ suggested. 'Give her back a jolly good leathering.'

Olivia shook her head as if to say that was the last thing she needed. It simply wasn't fair. She was doing her very best and getting very little thanks in return. Slowly she was forming the opinion that the whole of the male sex were downright selfish and very inconsiderate.

The man who had been milking her teats took up the belt and whipped her without compromise. He had his own theory that the more a woman was whipped, the greater her sexual appetite, not entirely dissimilar to that of Effie, who for her part had discovered that long ago when she also had spent six months in gaol, flogged morn, noon and night.

The story that Sappho had told Olivia was only true in part; she had flicked her way to England on a ship and had got through the entire crew, but on arrival had been employed as a housemaid and had been seen by Effie during one of her working visits to the master of the house. Tall black voluptuous women were something of a novelty in England, and Effie had made up her mind straight away that she must have her. A considerable sum had changed hands, and Sappho very soon became one of her most sought after actresses.

But today both she and Effie were not involved with the clients, and had retired to their own quarters at the top of the building.

'What do you think of the new girl?' asked Effie, slipping out of her costume and folding it neatly into a cupboard. 'Green,' was Sappho's dull reply. 'And I suspect, a virgin.'

She slipped off her chains and tossed them into a heap.

'That's why I gave strict instructions that she is not to be deflowered. Whipped yes, buggered probably, fucked no.'

Sappho opened a drawer and took out two long thick strips of leather, one of which she handed to Effie.

'What you going to do with her?' she asked, cracking the strip onto the seat of a chair.

Through the cloud of dust that rose from it Effie flexed her own strap, testing its strength.

'I'm keeping her for them that likes little girls, and when the time comes I'll have her scrubbed and painted. I should say she'll fetch at least twenty-five guineas. With luck she'll pass as a virgin for a year or two.'

They came towards each other, straps swinging by their sides.

'Until her cunt is too well trafficked,' observed Sappho, gathering her strap ready to strike.

They lashed each other simultaneously, slashing into their buttocks, but for the present standing apart and still, gradually increasing the velocity of the blows, whipping up their blood. They always began in that manner until, as if an understanding had been reached, they judged themselves sufficiently aroused, when they would slash at their respective bodies with the fury of the demented.

Occasionally selected clients would be invited to watch the two women circling round each other like female gladiators poised to kill. A blazing fire brought them out in a sweat. It ran off them in rivulets, over their bouncing breasts and buttocks, lending their thighs a polished sheen, and dripping from between their legs. The shrieks of pain and pants of longing were genuine as they landed the straps with unerring accuracy into the forks of their opened legs. Sappho, who by far sported the largest breasts, took a fearful whipping across her jet black, pointed nipples. Effie, in return, took her own whipping across her bottom as Sappho circled round her with leaps of her long, agile legs.

Watching them striping their flesh with countless livid welts, whipping their slits to a froth, one would never have guessed that they were lovers and this was but a prelude to their frenzied coupling. It was a trial of strength, a contest of powerful thighs and sturdy frames, of arms and shoulders tireless in their delivery. Lash after lash landed on their taut, quivering buttocks, and down the whole length of their backs and thighs. Snarling at each other they closed in near enough to start slapping with their free hands, usually at the breasts or sides of their faces, and if one of them lost her footing and fell the other would fall on top of her and continue the slapping, hitting to the point of exhaustion.

Arousing though it was, the administering of pain was not enough to deliver the complete and final satisfaction that they needed. If there were men present they would take them one after the other - but alone they solved the problem in their own way.

Sappho, who had tumbled Effie to the floor, sat astride her pinching and punching her breasts, squeezing the nipples until tears flowed.

'Yes, now!' Effie breathed, and Sappho went speedily to the cupboard and fetched out the phallus.

When it was fitted, rising proudly up from her groin, she slithered between Effie's outstretched legs and plunged into her.

Locked together with arms and legs and clinging like limpets they rolled over and over, back and forth across the carpet, Sappho riding Effie with powerful thrusts of her shining, ebony hips, and Effie in return with her hands on Sappho's buttocks, pulling her in deeper. They became as animals, a tigress and a serpent; Effie, coiling her legs and arms around Sappho's back, holding her in a death like grip while Sappho bit, tore and scratched. They wriggled and writhed, desperately trying to escape the gnashing teeth and crushing thighs, yet longing for it to continue. At each thrust Effie threw back her head and moaned aloud as if she were being burnt with hot tongs, for inside her whole sex was on fire. The phallus that Sappho pumped into her was piercing the very base of her womb, stretching open her lips until they ached.

Sappho achieved her own climax by inflicting as much pain as time would allow. In addition to riding Effie she tormented her lover's thighs and breasts with savage bites. Her arms had gone under Effie's knees and raised them high over her chest, offering a long length of creamy thigh, which she bit without respite. Effie reached her climax before Sappho, and now on her back she bounded and jerked her hips, and it was all Sappho could do to remain mounted. As the climax died its death Sappho pumped her hips desperate to reach her own orgasm before Effie's strength wilted.

Rocking over Effie's satiated body she drew up her knees, positioning them close to Effie's soaking buttocks, then with a sweep of her forearms lifted them from the floor. Effie hung suspended on the phallus while Sappho broke into a wild jerking of her loins. In the paroxysm of her climax, Sappho did not feel the sharp talons that sank deep into her buttocks. The tiny streams of blood that flowed into her groin were lost in the violent outpouring of her juices...

'About the new girl,' Sappho eventually panted, lying exhausted between Effie's thighs. 'Will I get the chance to have her?'

'Of course,' Effie murmured blissfully, 'but not until she can no longer pose as a virgin. I intend to put her to work as soon as possible.'

If Olivia had heard that she would have felt greatly insulted. She had never worked so hard in all her life. Her jaws ached from so much sucking, her back had been leathered numb, and her bottom felt as if it had been penetrated by an organ of equestrian proportions.

'Please, I'd like to rest awhile,' she begged, after her bottom and mouth had fulfilled their purposes.

'You can rest when we have finished with you,' said the man who had been belabouring her back.

Olivia, who had collapsed on the rug, looked up at his now pulsating erection.

'You will wash before you put that in my mouth, won't you?' she asked plaintively.

'Your tongue will suffice,' he replied tartly.

'But it's just been up my bottom,' she said askance.

'Are you refusing to go about your duty?'

'It's not my duty to do such things,' she protested.

'Poppycock. Now tell me loud and clear that you will be a good, obedient girl and suck my pego, and that of my friend, and also receive the other gentlemen up your backside.'

Olivia wiped away a tear and muttered, 'I will be good and obedient... and suck your pego.'

'And?'

'And... and have your friends up my bottom.'

'Good. Now that you have stopped shilly-shallying and have willingly consented, we can resume where we left off. Back on all fours, if you would be so kind.'

Muttering silent curses, Olivia obeyed. Again she felt herself obliged to have both men in her mouth at once while being cruelly pounded at her rear.

'Ever tasted your own arse?' one of her tormentors joked, wriggling his plum into her cheek.

Olivia gulped heavily as the second plum entered her mouth. The taste was not quite as repugnant as she thought it might be, and to avert her mind from the awful task she was performing, she repeated the same exercise with her tongue that she had practised earlier.

She furled it into the grooves, and after probing this way and that, slid it between them and licked up and around the sides. In response the organs began to move in and out, withdrawing to the edge of her lips and gliding back in again, pushing into her cheeks and savouring the hardness of her teeth. Unlike their companions who did manage to fire both barrels simultaneously, these fired one after the other, the interlude being long enough for Olivia to swallow one inundation before receiving the next.

She held the final spurt in her mouth in preparation to spitting it out, but the man who was still rogering her bottom gave her a hard slap on the back. Olivia's head jolted and she swallowed suddenly.

'Have you all quite finished?' she asked bitterly, licking the remainder from her lips as the last man withdrew from her back passage.

She sat up, resting her sore bottom on the backs of her calves, surrounded by a quartet of flaccid organs.

'We have, but you have not,' the man with bushy side-whiskers announced.

'What more do I have to do?' she wailed.

'Listen to her!' he exclaimed. 'Again her defiance rises to the fore. Did you ever encounter a more recalcitrant bitch in all your lives?'

They shook their heads in mock disbelief and went into a huddle, deciding which would be the most humiliating act they could make her perform. When Olivia was informed of their decision she threw her arms around the legs of the nearest man, shaking uncontrollably.

'Oh please, don't make me do that! You can play with my bosom if you want to, or smack my bottom, but don't I beg you make me put my—!'

'Stop snivelling, girl, and just count yourself fortunate that Effie has spared your cunt!'

'My what?' she asked, pulling away.

'That piece of meat between your thighs,' came a sharp reply.

Now that they had drawn attention to that delightful morsel, she covered it with both hands and blushed.

'Your hands are in the wrong place, miss,' said the nearest man. 'Kindly obey your instructions.'

Olivia, knowing that it was useless to offer up any further protestations, rose off her haunches and placed her right hand on her bottom, her index finger at the entrance. She looked up hoping that, by some miracle, they might change their minds, or someone would come into the room and rescue her. But she hoped in vain, they were adamant and no one would come.

She gave a shove of her wrist and was rewarded with a cheer.

'All the way up, if you please,' said the clean-shaven one with a sadistic leer.

Olivia pushed again and her finger went in to the knuckle. She blushed so hot that her cheeks burned.

'Now move it about, let's see your wrist turn.'

Olivia screwed her wrist back and forth, worming her finger deep into her bottom. She was still wet inside from her rogering. 'You know what to do next,' said the side-whiskers. Olivia retrieved her finger, hesitated, and then plunged it into her mouth.

'Suck on it, there's a good girl.'

She didn't know who said that, for her eyes were closed in shame, unable to bear the leers of her tormentors, who it seemed, were thoroughly enjoying the spectacle of seeing a captive young woman debase herself.

When she had sucked her finger clean she took it out of her mouth and placed her hands back into her lap, covering her embarrassment.

There was still some time left, so to amuse themselves further they made her wash their organs with her wetted tongue, going to each in turn, taking in the respective plum and cleaning it until it shone.

'Have I done my duty now?' she asked acidly.

The men were too busy dressing to bother with an answer, and one by one they trailed out of the room leaving her sobbing and wishing that she had the courage to get up and run.

It was quite a while before Effie came to find her. She had fallen asleep in Sappho's arms as she often did after a bout of whipping and lovemaking.

'Come along,' she said softly, 'and join the other girls in the parlour.'

'I did my duty,' Olivia said defensively, as she trotted beside her. 'Will I get some clothes now?'

'All in good time,' Effie replied, ushering her into the crowded parlour.

The girls lay in various stages of post coital abandonment, legs and arms akimbo, and hair tumbling over their faces. Most of them were already stupefied from gin and the heavy inhalation of tobacco.

'You did well,' Effie complimented, seating Olivia on a sofa and pouring herself a glass. 'My clients, that is the patrons, were well pleased with your performance.'

'They didn't appear so at the time,' Olivia retorted. 'From their manner in dealing with me I had the impression that they were most dissatisfied.'

'Probably because they had strict instructions not to deflower you.'

'What sort of theatre are you running here, exactly?' asked Olivia, glancing around at the doped women, now falling into each others arms.

'Don't you like it here?'

'I certainly did not expect that my person would be so shamefully abused. If you knew the things I had to do I'm sure you would agree that—'

'Yes, yes,' interrupted Effie, growing impatient. 'That was an exercise to see how well you could perform, throwing you in at the deep end, so to speak.'

'Thank you very much,' Olivia said bluntly. 'Next time I am to be thrown in the deep end I would appreciate a little warning.'

'We don't as a rule perform here. As I said earlier, we are what is termed, 'strolling players', but instead of travelling from town to town we go from house to house. Not all of the actresses perform in one place, some are virtuosos in their own right and perform singly.'

'I performed singly in there,' Olivia remarked, rubbing her bottom with exaggerated gestures.

'And you shall perform singly again, but not in front of so many men - in fact only one. A gentleman who is kindly disposed to ladies of our particular calling. But before that happy event arrives, there is just a little more preparation that you have to undergo.'

'I think I'm prepared enough already.'

'Not quite. But no more of this now. You have more than earned your rest, and tomorrow I shall begin your education proper.'

Effie showed Olivia to a bedroom, her own room where, for the first time in living memory, she slept soundly on a sprung mattress, her head on a feathered pillow, sucking her thumb, which normally she never did.

Chapter Ten

'Are these my clothes?'

Olivia held out the costume that Effie had presented her with. She could see at a glance that the dress was about three sizes too small.

'Try it on,' Effie said encouragingly.

Olivia struggled into the red velvet dress that came halfway up her thigh and only just buttoned over her cleavage, leaving the greater part of it exposed. The white stockings fitted a little better but reached only above her knee, displaying a generous area of thigh between the tops and the hem. Her hair had been washed that morning and was tied in bunches at the side of her head. The sleeves came to mid upper arm but were loose enough to allow movement. Her feet were shod in child's shoes but had obviously been made to fit a grown woman.

'I can't go abroad looking like this,' said Olivia, looking sideways into a full-length mirror.

'You're not going anywhere,' Effie replied firmly, 'until I'm satisfied that you've thoroughly learnt your craft.'

'But last night you said I did very well, and the patrons were pleased with my performance.'

'True. Very true. But any fool can suck a man's pego or have it up her arse. The other girls do that for a pastime. It takes great skill to behave as if you really don't want it, but all the while actually longing for a good rogering.'

'I don't want a good rogering,' Olivia retorted. 'All I want is to earn an honest living without getting involved in prostituting myself'

'And you shall earn an honest living, the most noble there is, by bringing comfort and solace to those far less fortunate than yourself. Or have you forgotten what you were before I took you in; a penniless beggar fleeing from her employer.'

Olivia wished she had kept her mouth shut about all that.

'I'm sorry,' she apologised, hanging her head and staring at the gloss on her shoes. 'I am grateful, please believe me.'

'I'm not sure that I do, so it will be up to you to convince me otherwise.'

'What do I have to do?' she asked, eager to prove herself.

'If you care to follow me, I'll show you.'

They went into the room where the stage stood, but instead of looking like a schoolroom it had been got up to look like a child's nursery, complete with rocking-horse and boxes of toys scattered hither and thither. Rita and Dora were already in situ, dressed very similar to herself and twiddling with some skipping-ropes and rattles. Olivia stifled a laugh as she mounted the stage and took the doll that Rita handed her.

Effie clapped her hands, at which Rita began skipping and Dora swinging her rattle. Olivia quickly grasped the situation and made a pretence of patting the doll's head and fiddling with its clothes. But very soon this harmless situation descended into total anarchy. Rita's skipping rope became hopelessly tangled with Dora's rattle, which spun round and smacked into the side of Olivia's head. A fight broke out and the props were used to batter each other, and in the process their clothes suffered numerous rips and tears. In a matter of minutes all three participants were virtually stripped naked. The dress that Olivia thought must have cost a shilling or two was ripped from her back. She stumbled and fell, and on the way it was rapidly taken from her altogether.

When she regained her feet it was too find that both Dora and Rita were down to their stockings and shoes, and nothing else. The melee ceased abruptly when the door of the nursery flew open and the man who had played the headmaster the night before came in masquerading as an outraged father.

'Fine goings-on here!' he roared, slamming the door behind him and marching into the centre of the nursery.

Olivia took one glance at the ferocious bulge in his trousers and cowered in the corner along with the other two.

'Which one of you is the ringleader?' he asked, hands on hips and glowering at each in turn.

Olivia was well aware that this part of the charade had taken a serious turn, and the cane that he brandished was not there for effect.

'If the guilty one does not own up I shall whip all three of you,' he promised, swishing the cane through the air and smacking it onto the saddle of the rocking horse.

Olivia looked at Rita, expecting that as she was the principle player she would take the lead. But she said nothing and hung her head.

Dora spoke first and blamed Olivia, who went weak at the knees. Then Rita accused Dora.

'I shall whip all three of you,' he said, 'and in particular, you,' and he aimed a swipe at Olivia's bottom.

'Why me?!' she gasped.

'Because you are the eldest and led on the younger ones.'

'But they are older than I!' Olivia returned desperately, forgetting that reality had been turned on its head.

'Liar!' shrieked Rita.

'Always lying!' rejoined Dora, looking forward to seeing how Olivia would get out of this.

'You deserve a sound thrashing,' spoke the father, 'for telling such dreadful lies.'

'But I'm innocent,' Olivia exclaimed, on the verge of tears.

'Innocent, my foot,' Dora broke in. 'Why father, did you know your eldest daughter, who is supposed to set an example, goes around sucking men's pegos?'

'And has them up her bum,' Rita confirmed.

The look of horror on father's face was very convincing, as it was on Olivia's.

'Is this true, child?'

'Yes... yes it is,' Olivia replied miserably.

'Once a whore, always a whore,' said Dora.

Olivia's reaction startled them all. She swung suddenly and slapped Dora straight in the mouth, and then recovering, landed another on Rita's ear. No playacting this, but serious intent. The father retreated to the side of the stage to see what would happen next.

Dora, with the speed of a cobra, snatched one of Olivia's bunches and came perilously close to ripping it off her head. At the same time Rita punched her hard on her left breast, to which Olivia responded by kicking her in the groin. Then all three fell to the floor punching and slapping. The father, unsure whether this was supposed to happen or not, looked on with interest at the spread legs and thrashing thighs. Olivia, either by accident or design, took hold of Dora's pubic hair and wrenched a clump from her mound, sending her out of the fray sobbing and swearing.

Rita, who had fallen across Olivia, suddenly yelped in pain. Her bare back was a sight too good to resist and the father lashed it. As Olivia's naked thighs were in close proximity he lashed them into the bargain.

'Hold still, the pair of you!' he snarled.

His voice, acting though it was, had the desired effect and both of them froze in mid-tangle. Rita's middle rested on Olivia's stomach and she could feel the pubic fleece rubbing to and fro with every lash that cut into her back. When the father changed target and began striping Rita's bottom she moved much faster.

'Luv me, I'm goin' to come,' she panted, and she twisted her head and begged to be beaten much harder.

Father also had gone hard and, master of his craft and familiar with the peculiarities of every girl's arousal, he went on caning until the pants reached fever pitch. Dora, quick to grasp his intention sidled round him and, seizing Rita by the ankles, dragged them wide across the floor.

'She wants it,' Dora observed, rather unnecessarily, as by now Rita's opened slit was weeping the first drops of her longing.

The cane whistled into the slit and Rita's bottom bounced off Olivia's belly.

'Give it to her!'

Father turned round and saw Effie watching the proceedings from the wings. Not one to argue he reached down and gripped under Rita's hips and lifted her bottom high enough to penetrate. Still lying on her back, Olivia watched with intense fascination as his organ slipped into Rita's lips. She forgot about the throbbing pain in her thighs, the dull ache in her breasts, and the blatant absurdity of the situation, but concentrated instead on watching everything that was taking place at Rita's fork.

She had known for quite some time the purpose of the slit between her legs, and had gathered that men seemed always to want to immerse their organs there, but had never actually seen it done. She was also astute enough to know that her mouth and bottom were substitutes for the same and wondered, at that rather inappropriate moment, why Dora had seen fit to fondle the fruits she saw swinging beneath Rita's tuft.

She soon learned the reason. Father went wild when Dora squeezed them, and she could see how much bigger his organ had swelled. Neither was it to her liking. It looked horrible; the throbbing trunk with its gnarled blue veins sticking out like creepers, and Rita's lips slavering around its perimeter, making sucking noises and expelling juice which dripped onto her stomach.

'Urgh!' she grunted, trying to wriggle free from the pool that was collecting in her navel.

As father rose to his release Dora artfully relaxed her grip and began bobbling his fruits on her fingertips. The organ turned almost purple, and in the next instant fired its charge hot into Rita's flowing tunnel.

Rita emitted a loud shriek and collapsed over Olivia's stomach. A second barrage of spurting globules spattered up her back, and with a groan father slid out of her and back into Dora's outspread legs.

Effie gave a derisively slow clap of her hands and hauled Rita away from Olivia. A kick on her bottom sent her flying across the stage.

'You are supposed to be schooling the new girl,' she said tartly, glowering at father, who struggled to extricate himself from Dora's wandering hands.

'She slapped me in the mouth,' Dora told her.

'You did?' Effie asked of Olivia, sounding surprised that the girl was capable of defending herself.

'She called me a liar.'

'So you clocked her.'

'If you mean I hit her, yes.'

Effie wrapped a thought in a smile and dismissed Dora. 'I will not have my girls slapping each other,' she said seriously. 'Unless it happens to be under my direction, d'you hear?'

'But they blamed me for it all.' Olivia exclaimed indignantly.

'They were following my instructions. After this shambles, father was supposed to comfort you.' She cast a dull look at the man. 'But I see he has taken comfort with someone else.'

'We can still go through with it,' he suggested, eyeing Olivia's naked body.

'Will someone explain just what is going on?' Olivia asked, totally confused.

Effie's patience snapped. The client that Olivia was supposed to visit was expecting her that very evening and had paid handsomely in advance, the price for deflowering a virgin being suddenly raised to twenty-five guineas. But if Olivia responded in the like manner in which she had just dealt with her companions he would more than likely demand a refund, and Erie's reputation as a supplier of fresh young virgins would be in ruins.

'The explanation is a simple one,' Effie began, putting her arm around Olivia's shoulders and leading her out of earshot. 'You possess extraordinary talents, which I am most anxious to explore, and with a little cooperation on your part there can be no doubt of your rising to the top of your profession...'

'As an actress?' Olivia beamed.

'As an actress,' Effie repeated, wondering how the girl could possibly be so dim as not to grasp her meaning. 'Tonight, your hidden talents shall be explored in the arms of one of my most respected patrons. You have already proved your worth, and now it is time to go a little further, do you understand?'

'I am to perform in my own right?' she replied, overjoyed at the prospect.

'God, I hope so,' Effie muttered.

'You may rest assured,' Olivia said, squaring her shoulders, 'that I shall not disappoint you, and that the gentleman will be most pleased. What do I have to do?'

Effie wondered whether to explain it directly or leave everything to providence. Perhaps, after she had been plied with a generous imbibing of gin, she might drop both her drawers and her defences. If she did not, then she would have to be taken by force.

'Do everything that the gentleman requires of you,' she said with a sigh.

'I presume that entails doing everything that I have done before,' Olivia replied dryly, 'whilst I have to dress up like a little girl.'

'Remember that in truth, under all those frills and bows, you are a big girl, and will be expected to act as one, so help us.'

Olivia promised to remember that as she took the dress that Effie handed her. It was very similar to the red velvet one that had been shredded during the fracas, and Olivia gasped at what all this must cost. The acting profession, she decided, was definitely a lucrative one.

The carriage set off away from the grimy streets and alleys of Paddington towards the more affluent areas of Grosvenor. Olivia reflected, as it passed through Hyde Park, that the only vehicles she had ever travelled in were prison vans or dog carts. This was the height of luxury. She sank back in the seat and adjusted the silk bows floating around her ample bosom. After all she had been through, acting like a young girl and pandering to some lonely old man would be easy. In her mind's eye she imagined having to sit on his knee and call him grandpapa, and every now and then break into fits of giggles and let him smother her with doting kisses. It would be nice to be pampered like that for a change.

The equipage swung round Hyde Park Corner and along Piccadilly, gathering speed as it passed Green Park and into the Circus. It swung into Regent Street, where hordes of brightly painted women were patrolling the pavements and calling out lewd suggestions to passing coaches. If a coach stopped a whole gaggle rushed towards it, one of them would be invited in and the coach would set off again, rocking furiously on its axles. Olivia's driver followed one of them into Conduit Street, where it drew up outside a particularly splendid mansion.

In the interlude while they waited behind the coach, she was sure there was something vaguely familiar about the ragged looking woman pacing up and down the pavement. How could she ever mistake that profile that had appeared in the prison dormitory and later had her mercilessly whipped?

'Flora!' she called, but Flora could not have heard her, for the driver had pulled away and was thundering across New Bond Street and into Berkeley Square.

Olivia didn't have time to wonder what she was doing there. The driver escorted her up a flight of steps and waited until the door had been answered; seeing her safely into the hallway, he vanished into the fog.

'This way, miss,' said the maid, not at all surprised at Olivia's peculiar attire.

The old gentleman was not as old as she had imagined. She put his age at mid to late forties, and curtsied low when he rose to greet her. He quickly dismissed the maid and motioned Olivia to a richly upholstered couch. Doing what she thought she was supposed to do, she sat upright, hands folded in her lap, knees close together, head bowed; a perfect picture of humility.

'I am sorry to hear that my ward has been so disobedient,' the gentleman said, 'and that I have, yet again, cause to chastise you.'

Olivia's knees shook. She had a sinking feeling that whatever he had in mind would not bring forth fits of giggles or doting kisses. Instinctively, she looked around the room for any signs of whips or birches, but there was nothing, just shelves full of books and a writing table with nothing more harmful on it than what appeared to be a ledger of some sort.

'Your governess informs me,' he continued, folding his arms over his chest, 'that instead of paying attention to your lessons, you performed an act of gross indecency.'

'I did?' Olivia replied nonplussed, wondering what to say next.

'Do you deny that you went to that very window and displayed yourself to the son of my next door neighbour?'

'No sir,' she said miserably, 'I do not deny it.'

'Then what shall I do with you?' he said sadly, shaking his head, which Olivia had to admit was rather handsome, as was his strong physique.

It was quite plain that all this was leading up to a thrashing, and that acting the part of a wilful young girl added to his thrill.

Rising to the occasion she said sorrowfully, 'I deserve a beating, sir.' Her head bowed lower and she choked back a convincing sob.

'A beating, indeed?' he said. 'But with what and where, I wonder?'

'A strap across my bottom,' she replied.

'Your bare bottom?' he said with emphasis.

'My bare bottom,' she agreed.

'But first, show me how you revealed yourself to the young master.'

Olivia got off the couch and lifted her skirt, high enough to display her white silk pantaloons.

'Is that all you did?' he asked speculatively.

'I took them off,' she whispered.

'And what else did you remove? Go on tell me, leave nothing out.'

'I took off my drawers and my dress.'

'You mean to say that you stood in that window naked?'

'I had my stockings and shoes on,' she said.

'But nothing else?'

'Not a stitch,' she assured him.

'Show me, let me see how you disgraced my good name.'

Olivia slipped her fingers under the strings of her pantaloons and wriggled them over her bottom. Then with a graceful bending of her knees, she slid them down her calves and stepped out, one foot at a time. She reached behind her and untied the bow of her sash and let it float to the floor. The dress came off with awkward jerks of her shoulders and hips. She pulled it over her head and cast it away with a flourish, then curtsied.

'This is how you were?' he asked licking his lower lip, and clutching the edge of the desk.

'I was like this,' she confirmed, legs together and hands over her bushy triangle.

'And why didn't you take off your stockings and shoes?'

'Because he told me to leave them on,' she said stupidly.

'I don't believe you. I think you were naked. If you were prepared to go that far in your disgusting behaviour, I see no reason why you would have stopped there.'

'I was naked,' she muttered, realizing that was how he wanted her.

And without waiting for any further instruction she bent over and loosed the buckles. After discarding her shoes she rolled down her stockings, very slowly, revealing the contours of her calves an inch at a time. When they had drifted to the carpet she stood up with her hands behind her back, shoulders thrust backward, breasts pushed out.

Under the subdued light of a solitary oil lamp he came tentatively towards her, eyes riveted on her body. His hand slipped around her waist and began feeling her bottom, exploring its curves and cleft, lifting the globes of her buttocks, testing their firmness and squeezing the taut flesh.

'T'will be a pity to beat such a splendid piece of work such as this,' he conceded.

'Is it necessary?' she whispered.

'I'm afraid it is. There is nothing more gratifying on this earth than to whip the behind of a beautiful young female, and roger her afterwards. The way she squirms when her blazing bottom chaffs against the carpet brings a man off to perfection. Don't you agree?'

'Oh, indeed,' Olivia replied. 'If the woman is disposed to be rogered.'

'That we shall discover later,' he promised her, 'after your hinds have been well served. Shall we say, three dozen strokes?'

'I deserve that,' Olivia agreed, 'for being such a naughty girl.'

'And, I have no doubt, a very promiscuous one. If you were willing to bare your body, I am quite sure you are not slow in putting it to good use elsewhere.'

The theme had been taken up again and Olivia responded. 'I have put it to good use,' she volunteered. 'And am anxious to please my master in that quarter.'

Assuming that she had understood his meaning he went to the table and swiftly fetched over a belt, much stouter and thicker than any that Olivia had previously tasted.

'Put your hands on your head,' he instructed her; 'and keep very still.'

He moved behind her and ran his hand lightly over her buttocks, patting them as he did so. When he came round to her front, his eyes had a curious look in them; a flash of recognition.

'I cannot but help but think that we have met before,' he said mysteriously.

'I am your ward, sir.'

He quickly recovered. 'Yes, of course, and a very naughty one at that. Three dozen on your bottom and a dozen across your breasts.'

Olivia caught her breath. 'If you please, master.'

He ordered her into the centre of the room and positioned her before a footstool beneath a bar, on either end of which hung two unlit lamps.

'That ought to take your weight,' he mused. 'Reach up and catch hold of it.'

Olivia stood on tiptoe on the footstool and grabbed the bar at the middle, where it was supported from the ceiling by a chain. It creaked under her weight but didn't give. She was right on the very tips of her toes when the belt came whistling into her bare bottom. The shock of the blow sent her feet flying forward, and as she clung on for dear life he hit her again, catching her on the return swing.

'Do you have to strike so hard?' she wailed, recoiling under another lash that caught her across the front of her thighs. 'You said you deserved it,' he reminded her, lashing the small of her back.

Olivia swayed gently to and fro, clinging by her fingertips, just managing to hold on. Her toes dragged across the velvet stool, bringing her to a halt.

'Are your fingers hurting you?' he inquired thoughtfully.

Olivia choked back a sob and nodded, whereupon he put his hand under her legs and lifted her up so that her hands went right around the bar. Her feet lifted a half-inch from the stool, swinging her clear.

'Better?'

'Much, thank you, sir.'

The next blow was so violent her whole body twisted at the hips. She was sure something had cricked in her spine.

'Keep still,' he advised her, 'or you may do yourself a permanent injury.'

He stood slightly to her left and swung the belt upwards, smacking it into the lower part of her buttocks immediately above the crease of her thighs. A sharp bolt of pain shot through her legs and she screamed. Before he could deliver another blow into her bottom-cleft the maid came in bearing a tray of glasses and a decanter.

'Put it on the table,' he directed her, 'and then come over here.'

The maid set down the tray and padded dutifully across the room, standing behind Olivia but looking directly at her master.

'Please take hold of my ward's legs and hold her still,' he said calmly, 'the wretch is leaping about like an ape.'

'I am not an ape,' Olivia sobbed, over her shoulder.

Master and maid ignored that and Olivia felt a pair of cold hands grab her ankles and hold them close together; a grip that would indeed have done credit to the creature that had been named in reference to herself.

The maid ducked as the belt sailed across her head and cracked into Olivia's bottom. She visibly winced when the shock reverberated down Olivia's calves.

'I think her arse has taken enough,' the master remarked, after reddening it with another dozen swings of his arm. 'Perhaps the backs of her thighs need a little chastisement, eh, Helena?'

The maid nodded and ground the bones of Olivia's ankles harder together, knowing that when the belt landed there she would jerk and twist much more violently.

She was correct in her assumption, for as soon as the first welt cut the flesh, Olivia's knees buckled with such force her ankles tore free from Helena's grip and compassed outwards.

The master quickly responded by lashing between her legs, striking her twice before her knees and ankles cracked together.

'You didn't say you were going to hit me there!' Olivia complained.

'I shall strike where I please,' he replied, noticing that the blows had induced a trickle from her slit.

He laid aside the belt and licked the inside of her thigh, savouring the sweet, earth taste of her juice. He licked her all the way up and into the join of her thighs, tracing it to its source. He was certain now that he and Olivia had met before.

'Helena, part her legs,' he commanded, and the maid took hold of Olivia's knees and spread them outward, stretching her own arms wide.

The belt could not but fail to lash into Olivia's slit, striking the outer lips, lashing the lower regions of her abdomen, making Olivia howl and squirm. He gave her a half-dozen, one on top of the other, deliberately punishing her mound, bringing forth a fresh outpouring, which he at once sucked noisily from her slit.

He might have let it go at that, but not one to go back on his word, he ordered her down from the bar and told her to lie over the writing table, on her back, hands over her head, pulling her breasts taut and allowing the maid to seize her wrists.

'We did agree that your breasts would be suitably punished, did we not?'

Olivia nodded and threw her head back, awaiting the onslaught.

'Her teats respond well,' Helena observed, watching the nipples rise up from the shock of the first blow.

And in between the lashes, she left off holding Olivia's wrists and amused herself by pinching the dark, bruised nipples, rolling them under her fingers, squeezing hard to inflict as much pain as possible.

'They do indeed,' the master replied, flicking the end of the belt hard on to the very tops of the teats, watching how they hardened and how the pimpled discs spread wider.

'Have your teats always been as dark as this?' he asked suddenly.

Olivia, released by the maid, struggled onto her elbows. Her breasts were covered with bright red blotches, the nipples standing proud and erect.

'Ever since I can remember,' she answered, wondering why the colour should interest him so.

'And your slit, has it always been so generous in dimension, even before you grew your fleece?'

'So I believe, sir. But in truth it has been my undoing, for every man I meet wishes to put his thing there, and although I am well versed in sucking them and having it up my bottom, I intend to remain a virgin until I am wed.'

'Very commendable I'm sure, but how do I know that you are telling the truth? Any woman can glibly say that she sucks men, but doing it is something else.'

'I am telling the truth, sir.'

He left her and marched over to the bookshelves and retrieved a large tome; an album of photographs which he spread open on the writing table now vacated by the obedient Olivia.

'I am a photographer by profession,' he told her, 'and my speciality is life studies, women in particular.'

He directed Olivia's gaze to the album. The first pictures were innocent studies of fully clothed women posing beside props of various sorts. But as the pages turned their clothes gradually came off until they were naked. A few more pages revealed poses that made her clasp her hand to her mouth.

'Oh, my,' she exclaimed, staring at a photograph of a young woman bending over a couch and about to be penetrated by a man dressed as a monk. The more the pages turned the more filthy and outrageous the pictures became

There was one in which a man sat on a chaise longue with a young woman sucking him. She was naked, and beside her another young woman was being treated the same by a man. Her legs were open and Olivia could clearly see his tongue licking her open slit, which the woman actually held apart with her fingers.

'If you claim to have done these things why are you so shocked?' the gentleman asked.

'Because I've never seen what it really looks like,' she replied, wringing her hands, and realizing that the woman sucking the man was the maid, Helena.

'I don't think you've ever done anything like this,' he said sceptically. 'So much for Effie's promises.'

'I have done it,' Olivia protested. 'And if you doubt my word, I'll show you.' And with that she dropped to her knees and wrestled open his fly buttons. Much to her surprise, he left her to her own devices instead of forcing her head to the root and making her swallow it all. He went on turning the pages of the album as if searching for a particular photograph. Olivia went on sucking.

Helena, who had been watching the proceedings with great interest, stripped off her uniform and knelt beside Olivia, taking her master's organ and joining in.

'Take his balls in your mouth,' she instructed Olivia as she closed her own lips over the shining, throbbing plum.

Olivia angled her head into his groin and carefully coaxed them into her mouth. They were much larger than she anticipated, and filled her cheeks to capacity.

'We'll take it in turns,' Helena suggested, 'and then he can have us both.'

He's not having me at all, thought Olivia, manipulating his swollen fruits from one side of her mouth to the other.

As she went on rolling them over her tongue, Helena put her hand between Olivia's legs and started rubbing her mound until it was wet enough to slip her fingers inside the excited slit. Olivia jolted, expelling the fruits and sitting upright.

'Why have you stopped?' said the photographer, leaving the album open at the place he wanted and staring hard at Olivia.

'Because she's doing it to me,' she protested.

He had been close to shooting his bolt when Olivia had drawn back, and that made him angry. What ought to have fired into Helena's hot and willing mouth now remained churning in the shaft. The maid popped the plum from her lips and sank back on her haunches, giving Olivia a bewildered stare.

The photographer glanced at the album and then at Olivia. He was certain that his instincts were right, but had to be sure before he declared himself.

'You see this picture,' he exclaimed, hauling Olivia up by the hair.

Olivia looked at it. A woman was kneeling on the floor, her arms above her head suspended with chains, her knees were wide spread and held open with an iron rod between them. Around the woman's neck was a collar from whence came a length of chain held by another woman, who was in the act of beating her with a birch. The chained woman's head was in profile, mouth open in agony as the whipper prepared to land another stroke on her already bruised bottom.

'Yes, I see it,' Olivia remarked dryly.

'Then you know what is demanded of you.'

In the very same studio Olivia obediently knelt and raised her arms while Helena fastened her wrists to the customary chains hanging from the ceiling. She pulled on them until Olivia's knees lifted just clear of the floor, then she fetched a broad leather collar and fitted it around her neck. When she pulled on the chain, Olivia's head was jerked backwards at a side angle, imitating the woman in the photograph.

'Are you proposing to take my picture?' Olivia asked, wincing from the pain in her wrists and arms.

'Certainly. And at the point where your suffering is greatest. Lay on the stripes, Helena, on her bottom, if you please. You know what you have to do with that chain.'

Olivia summoned all her resolve as Helena tugged on the chain again, arching her head, neck and back, sending fresh spasms of pain down her spine.

The birch hummed through the air and burned into her taut buttocks like a shower of hot coals. For a rather slim and slightly built girl, Helena's strength was prodigious. Olivia's suspended body shot forward accompanied by a howl of agony.

A vicious tug on the chain brought her back again, swaying her knees to and fro, chaffing her toes and feet as they bore the whole weight of her body.

Olivia quickly understood the method of this particular punishment. She had a choice to either remain still from the heavy blows and endure the searing pain in her whipped buttocks, or to jolt naturally forward and run the terrible risk of having her neck snapped.

'How much more of this am I to suffer?' she choked, as Helena whistled the twigs into her bottom.

It was impossible to avoid the sudden jolt of her back, evading the excruciating tide of pain that rose through her soft flesh. Helena had whipped her buttocks to perfection, landing each stroke just above and below the other, until the cheeks were a mass of throbbing welts.

The photographer eyed Olivia's blazing rear through the lens and nodded appreciatively. 'You will suffer it until I am ready, miss,' he said, fiddling with a lever on the side of the camera.

With steady deliberation Helena went on whipping her, now slowly working her way towards her shoulders. The higher she went the more Olivia's hips twisted and the more severe the pull of the chain. Her head hung forward, no longer in profile as the photographer instructed, but gazing numbly at the floor.

'Turn her head back again,' he said, now ready to take the desired picture.

Helena took Olivia's head in her hands and twisted it sideways.

'Now stay there,' she said impatiently.

Knowing that her agonies were almost at an end, Olivia steeled herself to remain still while Helena commenced whipping the backs of her thighs. This she did with greater vehemence than that which had seared Olivia's bottom. She started at the top, just beneath the crescents of her bottom-cheeks, and was not a quarter way down when a bright flash filled the room.

'Have you finished?' Olivia sobbed.

The photographer slid a plate from the camera. 'Oh, indeed. But as it will take a little while to develop, I suggest that Helena continue with her whipping until I return.'

Helena curtsied and took up where she had left off, thrashing the backs of Olivia's thighs. When she had finished she would have filled in the time by starting on her front, but the sudden and excited entry of her master spared Olivia further pain. He ordered her release and had her brought back into the drawing room, where he placed the photograph he had just taken next to the one in the album.

Olivia, despite the pain in her whipped flesh, could not help but wonder at the remarkable likeness between the images. It was as if she appeared in both, so similar were the profiles, the contours of the bodies, the shapes of buttocks and thighs.

'I had to be certain,' said the photographer, 'which is why I had you chained and whipped exactly as the woman in the original. She was my sister-in-law and my favourite model, as well as my lover. She died shortly after this picture was taken, my brother having already deserted her for a whore in the town where she lived. What became of her daughter I know not, except that she was taken into care by the parish.'

'What was your sister-in-law's name, sir?' Olivia asked, ashen-faced.

'Judith Holland.'

'And I am Olivia Holland, brought up in a workhouse, and latterly a penniless beggar.'

His hand went around her back and lovingly patted her bottom. The other fondly squeezed her breast. Then he kissed her aroused nipple.

'Welcome home,' he said, patting her other cheek. 'Welcome home, my long lost niece.'

CHAPTER ELEVEN

The very same night that Olivia was recognised by her uncle and invited to remain under his roof until such time as she found a suitable husband, there travelled by train to London two persons with whom Olivia had already become acquainted.

Henry Reynolds, deciding that after all the undertaking profession brought little reward, settled himself in the corner of a first-class compartment and lit a cheroot, eagerly awaiting his new adventures in the great metropolis.

Charlotte had dutifully followed her lord and master and was ensconced in the open trucks of the third class. Beside her was the heavy baggage that she had lovingly borne on her sweltering back across the meadows, following, more or less, the same path that Olivia had taken. In her purse were the contents of the safe that she had robbed on Henry's behalf, and which he had left with her for safekeeping.

Her bosom had swelled with pride when she had clambered into the draughty, wind swept truck, the gold laden purse secured in her drawers. But there was method in his madness; if they had been pursued and caught crossing the meadows, the money would have been found on her, which would leave him free to assert his innocence, and escape ten years in gaol. Charlotte, who was too dim-witted to work this out for herself, lovingly agreed to offer her services to any fellow passengers who might further enhance their store. But alas there were none, and so as soon as they trudged off through the grimy back-alleys of Paddington, Henry set her to work at once, walking the streets while he awaited her return, lazing in an armchair and smoking a cigar.

It was just on the stroke of midnight when Charlotte returned dishevelled, and her clothes in tatters. She staggered through the door and collapsed sobbing on the hearthrug.

Henry regarded her with some amazement.

'I've been whipped!' she blurted. 'Cruelly whipped about my person!'

'Were you paid?' he replied suspiciously.

Charlotte handed over a half-crown and resumed her sobbing.

'Well, tell me what happened,' said Henry, pocketing the coin.

'I was walking up and down the street, like you told me to, and asking gentlemen if they fancied a bit of slap 'n' tickle, and then all of a sudden a carriage draws up and a man leans out and asks me if I wanted a ride. So in I gets and there's three other men in there, and being as there's no room, I sits on the knee of the man nearest the winder, and off we goes.

'Afore long they took off all my clothes...'

'Everything?' asked Henry, leaning forward with considerable interest.

'They made me strip naked and threw my drawers and corset in a heap. Then I was made to bend over the knee of the man I had been sitting on and they took turns in slapping my bottom, and they didn't stop slapping me until we reached a big house by the river, and in we all went.'

'You were still naked?'

'I was, but they moved so fast I was through the door in no time and found myself in a drawing room. There was a woman there, the like of which I've never seen.'

'Describe her.'

'A tall woman as black as coal and built like a navvy. You wouldn't believe the size of her tits, big as pumpkins, and thighs that could crush a man to pulp.'

Henry felt his palms go sweaty and poured himself a large tumbler of whiskey.

'Then what happened, with the men and you and the black woman?'

'I was made to stand in the middle of the room, with my legs open and hands behind me. The black woman fetched a pair of handcuffs and put them on my wrists. While she was fastening them, the men started feeling me all over, putting their fingers in me and squeezing my breasts, pinching my bum and my thighs, like I was a piece of meat. Then the black woman joined in, and she was worse than the men, biting my nipples and kneeling in front of me, burying her 'ead in my bush and sucking me.

'In no time I was as wet as could be. Her tongue went right up inside, licking places I never thought were there. She didn't stop until I nearly swooned, then I was dragged to the floor and someone fetched a whip. There was nothing I could do but lie there groaning, twisting and shrieking, begging them to stop. But they kept on whipping me and rolling me over and over, not stopping until my poor bottom and thighs were covered with lashes, and my fork drenched.

'While all this was going on, the black woman sometimes sat on my face, moving her mighty bum to and fro until she too was all wet. The smell from her fork was overwhelming, as was the juice that ran from her.

'"Lick me out, you dirty bitch" she says, riding her bottom faster and faster, and moaning and groaning all the while.

'I had no choice but to do her bidding, and while the men went on thrashing me I went on licking and sucking in her slit, swallowing the thick juices that poured from her hot, steamy lips.

'After I had performed that disgusting task and she had rolled off me, rubbing herself between her sweating thighs, she knelt at my head holding me still with her thighs, and her hands on my chest.'

'And the men, what were they doing?' Henry asked, leaning ever closer.

'I was coming to that. To begin with, nothing more harmful than sitting on me and making me suck their cocks.'

'Did they make you swallow it?'

'Just as I felt it about to shoot they whipped it out and spurted all over the black woman's thighs and breasts, and kept on doing it until she was soaked. It was running off her in streams and I heard her panting and snorting behind me like a horse. Then when that was done she got off me and made me lick her clean, all the while slapping my back and bottom.

'I hadn't been properly taken as yet and thought that was all they wanted me for, just to lick their stuff from the black woman's body. Never was I more mistook.'

'They took you then, after you finished cleaning up the woman.'

'No they did not. I was up on my feet and the chains taken from my wrists. I stood there rubbing away the pain and feeling where they'd whipped me, when the black woman announced that the entertainment was about to begin and that the men should seat themselves on the sofas.

'I thought they'd had enough entertainment for one night, what with whipping and fondling me and such, but the black woman had other ideas. There we were, both naked, facing each other, while one of the men who had not yet taken his place fetched some more chains. I watched in horror while he knelt at her feet and fastened a pair or iron rings to her ankles, with just enough length of chain between them so she could move her legs freely. Then I was shackled in the like manner.

'The next set of rings went around our left wrists with another length of chain between them, so we was bounded together with our right arms still free.

'"Now fetch the crops", the black woman says, and into our free hands were placed a riding crop apiece. Still baffled by all this I wondered what was coming next, when the bitch sent hers lashing into my bottom.

'I screamed and leapt into the air, and was as quickly pulled back again by a pull on the wrist chain. She circled round me like a huge cat, smacking her lips and flexing the muscles of her thighs and arms. I watched them ripple in the lamplight and saw how her teats had gone all hard, and she was wet again between her legs.'

'It was a contest then?' Henry suggested. 'You had to whip each other while you were still chained?'

'I soon worked that out, and I thought I'd give her the same as she was about to give me.'

'And did you?'

'To begin with, yes. I caught her unawares and landed my crop on the side of her flanks, and then another on her arse. She howled and snorted, much to the delight of the men, who were partly on my side as I was new to all this. Then she pulled on the chain and I fell forward, and as I did so she whipped the tops of my thighs, six strokes in all, one after the other. I was hopping about all over the place, and then she caught me across my teats, a real swinger. Now it was my turn to yell, and didn't I just.

'I was furious, and returned another stroke on her back, and then I caught her on her teats. I couldn't really miss 'cos of the size of them. Her big black tits wobbled to and fro, and she clutched one of them and rolled it round and round under her hand. The men loved that, and then I realised the true nature of this contest. One look in her eyes told me that she enjoyed being whipped as much as she enjoyed whipping me. So I gave her another, an upward cut that sliced into her fork and had her hopping about like a rabbit.

'She let go of her tit and came charging towards me, eyes rolling and tits shaking. I saw the way she was dripping between her legs and knew I'd found her weak spot. If I could but lash her there I might win the contest. But she was as agile as a panther, and somehow got behind me and started lashing the backs of my legs, making them buckle at the knees and burn at the thighs. My bare bum was all ablaze she hit me so much.

'But her keenness to cripple me was her undoing, 'cos while I stood there shrieking and yelling, I worked out a plan to cripple her. I spun round and tugged on the chain, and with a cry she tripped and fell, dragging me after her.'

'You fell on top of her?'

'I landed between her open legs, and quick as a flash her powerful thighs went round my back.'

Henry mopped the sweat from his brow and adjusted the organ prodding at his breeches. He could just imagine the effect all of this must have had on the men watching from the sofas; two naked women, their bodies drenched in sweat, slithering about like a pair of eels, reeking of the odour that only women seem to produce.

'It was over then, I presume.'

'It certainly was not. Her heels locked and her thighs closed in like a great sweaty vice. I felt my ribs crack and my mouth go dry. Then to my utter amazement she kissed me, a long slobbering kiss that went on for ages.'

'Good God. And what did you do?'

'Kissed her in return. What else could I do, held as I was between those solid walls of muscle threatening to crush the life out of me? Our tongues went right into our mouths, wiggling into our cheeks and to the backs of our throats. Our breath was so hot after all that leaping and whipping, as were our slits. Our breasts and teats were swollen and gleaming, striped with dozens of welts that made it worse. Suddenly I was panting and snorting too, and the men, seeing the state we were in, suddenly leapt off the sofas and dived on us all at once.'

'Did they separate you from your chains?'

Charlotte paused to search her memory and take a swig from the whiskey bottle.

'They did, but instead of letting us get up they took us right there, side by side, our knees up to our chests, thighs and shoulders touching. Can you imagine that?'

'Easily. Go on.'

'The dirty devils took turns on us. Each of their cocks was still wet from the other when they plunged back in. Imagine how I felt, knowing her juices were mingling with mine. They rode the pair of us for ages, changing from one to the next as was their will. Those who'd just shot their bolts in one dripping slit shoved their cocks into the mouth of the other of us, so as well as having her juices in my tunnel, I was obliged to swallow them into the bargain.'

'Just as you did when she sat on your face.'

'I suppose so,' she said grudgingly. 'When they'd rogered themselves dry and we were sore and aching, they dragged us to our feet, although she wasn't nearly as exhausted as I was and seemed ready for any amount more. But seeing the state I was in they took pity on me and took to thrashing our backsides instead.

'I think it was another contest to see which of us would expire first, and I was determined to prove my worth. After I'd taken a full score of welts from the crop I was turned over, as was the black woman, and saw to my dismay they had all gone hard again, from the thrill of lashing us, I suppose.

'She whispered something in their ears and they all glanced at me, whereupon she rested her head on my stomach, and lying on her side, lifted her thigh so she could be had in that fashion. One of the men got behind her and slipped in. I saw and felt her head jolt with the pleasure of it, and then of course it was my turn.

'I thought she was just using my belly as a pillow, but soon discovered otherwise. After riding me for sometime, the man at my fork withdrew and put it straight into her mouth. She sucked it for quite a while, then back into me it went, hot once again from her devious tongue.'

'Were you obliged to return the compliment?'

'No, I wasn't. But they did make us do it with each other. I was too tired to resist, and besides, I knew that I was doing it all for you, and that every penny I was earning would help us.'

'Very thoughtful,' said Henry, polishing off the remainder of the whiskey.

'Well anyway, there we were, atop of each other, our forks in each other's faces and licking for all we were worth. I emptied out before she did; she was so good at it. Her thumbs pressed into my lips and opened them right up, stretching them so wide I knew I was baring my all. Her long tongue went deep inside me and I wriggled from the shock of it. It was in that deep I could feel it tickling my sides, and all the while her lips were pressed against my own, trying to eat me, it seemed.'

'What were the men doing while you were eating each other?'

'They stood over us and tossed their hands about their cocks, showering us with their spurtings. I felt it spotting all over my back and bottom, and the black woman, being underneath me, took hers on the thighs and all in her hair. It didn't bother her in the least; she just kept on pushing her head harder and harder into my fork.

'Her teeth went nibbling all around my petals making me gasp and pant between her dark thighs. My own head was well in them and I was nibbling at her hair. She was quite a size down there, and my face fitted easily in her gaping cavern.'

'You sound jealous, my dear. Are you sure you're not exaggerating her blessings?'

'Cross my heart and hope to die. It was as big as the slit on that girl what run away.'

Henry did not wish to be reminded of that. He had seriously considered getting rid of Charlotte and replacing her with Olivia after whipping her into obedience and half starving her into submission. His mother, who owned the business, had threatened to reduce his allowance after Olivia's escape. She would have made a hard working slave for many a year.

'And you went on nibbling while she was searching into your cunt?' Henry said rudely.

'I did, but not as clever as she. Her teeth went on nibbling until my juices flowed and I heard her lapping them up, her lips and tongue drinking from my fork like there was no tomorrow. I had to keep on going until I'd done my job, which weren't easy, 'cos she took such a long time in coming.

'When she did her legs rose off the floor and started waving about all over the place. Her thighs rubbed into the side of my 'ead and I thought I'd suffocate. Everything went black.' She paused and laughed at her own joke, but Henry wasn't laughing. The more Charlotte continued the greater his desire to meet the woman. There was no doubt in his mind that she would be worth a half-sovereign of the takings, even for half what Charlotte had experienced.

Charlotte, seeing the serious look on his face, guessed what he was thinking and quickly ended her delivery.

'I found her bud and nibbled that, then with a cry to wake the dead her arse shook and she came as well. I could hear her tunnel making sucking noises as well as the lips slapping into the sides of my face. Disgusting. Horrible. I wouldn't want to meet her again for all the tea in China, even if she does want to meet me.'

Henry sat bolt upright. 'What did you say?'

'Nothing.'

Henry slapped the side of her face very hard. 'You said that she wanted to meet you again. Don't deny it. I heard you.'

'If you really want me to meet her, I will,' she said, grovelling at his feet and reaching for the bulge in his breeches which was bigger than she had ever seen.

'Did she tell you where this meeting was to take place?'

'The same spot as where the carriage drew up, and tomorrow night if it pleases me.'

'It will please you,' he said sternly. 'And if you're offered employment in that quarter you will take it, d'you hear? You did well tonight, and shall do so again with as many as pleases. The more men you have the better for us both.'

'I only want to please you,' she said, releasing his organ and rubbing it between her fingers.

'You did that right enough,' he said, smiling artfully. 'Indeed, I should like to meet this woman. For your protection, you understand.'

'And so you shall,' Charlotte replied. 'If I am to be set to work, I should want you with me.'

'And what if I should have to chain and beat you? How would you like that?'

'I would be honoured, Henry.'

'And you wouldn't care at all how many men you had to have?'

'As many as it takes to make you happy.'

With that she took his organ into her mouth and started sucking for all her worth.

'You're a dirty girl,' he complimented, 'and will make me - us a fortune. The dirtier you are, the richer my purse. What good fortune when you got your fat arse into that carriage.'

Charlotte didn't hear him. Her mouth was working hard, unlike her brain, which almost ceased to function the second Henry's organ stiffened in front of her.

CHAPTER TWELVE

All the trials and tribulations of Olivia's former life began to fade from her mind as she revelled in her new found happiness. She had been in her uncle's house for a week and was slowly becoming accustomed to his peculiar foibles and quirks. She didn't mind in the least the young women who arrived there at night, sitting on the mattress and doing nothing more untoward than feasting his eyes on her beauty, reminding himself perhaps, of the days spent with her mother, which he told her had been the happiest of his life.

Quite suddenly he announced that they were going to visit an old friend of the family, who for the present wished to remain incognito, but was desirous of making her acquaintance. Olivia rode in the carriage alone on the short journey that brought her to his door. She was shown into a small, dimly lit, but comfortably furnished drawing room, and left alone while the maid went off to inform her master of Olivia's arrival.

While she waited she amused herself by looking at the photographs on the wall, hoping to find a clue as to his identity, but there was none. Most of them she recognised as her uncle's handiwork; women in various stages of undress, baring their bottoms and in the process of receiving a flogging. She was so absorbed that when a strong pair of hands gripped her from behind she nearly passed out with fright.

'Don't move,' he told her, and in the next instant slipped a mask over her eyes.

She was spun round, blinded, with the man so close that she could smell his cologne drifting into her nostrils.

'Who are you?' she asked.

'It is not necessary that you know my identity, only that you do exactly as you are told. Do you understand?'

She nodded and told herself that there was nothing to fear. She as sure that this was a game her uncle was playing, and soon he would reveal himself much to the amusement of the participants.

'You will now remove your clothes. Your underwear you will leave for the present,' the stranger said, and she heard him step back from her, giving her room to undress.

'Does my Uncle Walter know I have to do this?' she asked, thinking that this sort of game was not entirely to her liking.

'That does not concern you. Your obedience is all that matters here; obedience without question.'

The timbre of his voice left Olivia in no doubt that any disobedience on her part would be very foolish.

'I will obey,' she said reluctantly, reaching behind her.

She loosed the tiny pearl buttons of her dress and slowly drew it away from her shoulders, constantly aware that, although she was in darkness, he was watching her every move. The jacket slipped from her arms and fell to the carpet with a sad plop.

'Now your skirt,' he said. 'Take that off, and when you have done that, stand up straight, hands by your sides.'

Olivia tutted to herself and wriggled the skirt to her knees. It fell of its own accord to her feet and she clumsily stepped out of it and kicked it away. Then she stood upright in the position he had demanded.

Suddenly she felt very vulnerable, standing in her underwear, blindfolded, and in front of a perfect stranger. From behind her mask she could feel his eyes boring into her, studying her figure, going all over her stockinged calves and the bare area of chest above her corset.

'Now your petticoats.'

Olivia tutted louder, which he ignored and watched with great interest as the five layers of cotton came off, one at a time, forming a pink and yellow heap over her already discarded dress.

'I have a right to know just what you are going to do with me,' she said abruptly.

'You consented to obey without question, so why now are you making these demands? If you were lawfully married would you question your husband, or disobey his will?'

'You are not my husband,' she retorted.

'But if I were you would obey me, would you not?'

'Without question, sir,' she said suddenly, as if the power of his voice had transformed her into an obedient and willing wife.

'Then remove your corset.'

'And my drawers?' she asked dumbly.

'Just do as you're told.'

Olivia struggled with the strings, fumbling with knots and trying desperately to do his bidding. She heard him walk across the room, open a drawer and return softly, standing directly in front of her. A length of cold steel slipped under the string nearest her waist and tugged sharply upwards. Olivia caught her breath. No one had ever used a knife blade to cut away her corset, much less so close to her bare skin!

She stood rigid while the strings broke away up her belly and over her breasts, where because of the tension, they suddenly flew apart and her breasts burst forth, naked and proud.

'Now you can remove your drawers,' he said, clattering the blade on a table.

Olivia bent over and slid them down her legs, knowing that her breasts were swaying to and fro as her shoulders hunched forward and each knee was raised and then lowered. She stood up again, attired only in a pair of black thigh length stockings and high-heeled boots. It was a miracle that she had not lost her balance during the proceedings.

'Are you going to whip me?' she asked fretfully.

The mysterious gentleman made no answer, but placed his hands on her hips. They drew slowly upwards into the curve of her waist, pinched it for a while, and then continued up her sides, not stopping until they rested at the outward swell of her breasts.

'Touch your nipples,' he whispered close in her ear.

They rose immediately, partly from the resonance of his command, and partly from a fear that she could not quite readily understand. A cold chill rippled through her belly when, at his next instruction, she gathered the full weight of her breasts and lifted them high in the air, still teasing the teats with her thumbs. She kept up her fondling until he told her to take her hands away and lie herself on the floor, legs open.

Groping in the darkness, she lowered herself to the carpet in front of the fire, whose heat now radiated through her back and thighs. Awkwardly she shuffled away from the crackling flames and the sparks that now and then, with a loud crack, fired onto the hearthrug.

'A while ago,' he began, 'you allowed a stranger to put his hand inside of you, an action which you did not resist, and indeed found most pleasing.'

Olivia had to think about that. Quite a few strangers had put their hands inside of her of late, but none, to the best of her memory, had actually pleased her.

'At the undertakers,' he reminded her, 'where you were chained like a dog.'

'I do remember,' she faltered. 'But how...?'

'Your uncle has told me everything,' he said, 'and now I wish to see it for myself. But from the ministrations of your own hand.'

'I'd rather I was whipped!' she replied, turning her knees inwards and obscuring her slit from his gaze.

'That will come later,' he assured her, 'after you have obeyed this command, and to my satisfaction. Or do you dare risk disobeying me?'

Dumbly obedient, Olivia let her knees fall open and stretched her hand down into her groin. Under the mask her eyes were tightly closed as she recalled how the stranger had put his fingers inside her; had aroused the chill in her belly and made her go wet and dizzy. A feeling she had not encountered since with anyone.

The mask served its purpose as her fingers encountered the quivering slit between her parted fleece. Others had touched her there, in her most private place, but then it had been under sufferance and almost always against her will; something she suffered because she had too. Occasionally she had fingered herself, but in aspect of curiosity, and always in the furtive privacy of her bed, well away from prying eyes. Now she was expected to do it herself in front of a stranger, but the mask at least spared her blushes.

She wondered, as her fingertips searched around the perimeter of her lips, why he was making her perform such an act. Perhaps it was mere curiosity, but that could not be true, being as he was obviously a mature man who doubtless had had many women, or was it because they were related and, like her, he did not wish to look into the eyes of one engaged in what was, after all, her private affair?

As her fingers slipped in through the wetted portals of her slit, Olivia recalled an incident from childhood; one that she had forgotten until now. She had been gone into the nursery and seen her cousin, Adele, stretched out on a couch, one leg draped over the edge, her head thrown back moaning, her hand rubbing her fork. Olivia had watched her face redden, and had seen the look of undisguised pleasure on her face when she had reached her climax.

Olivia's own fingers now penetrated to the knuckle, and slowly she worked them to and fro, feeling them get wetter and wetter. Her mouth opened and she heard herself beginning to pant, the breath starting to come in short, urgent gasps as if she were running. A bead of sweat formed on her brow and trickled across her temples.

Adele had told her that when she worked as a governess she had felt the urge to rub herself, and in the schoolroom, when she was alone, had laid across the desks and put her fingers inside her. Her employer had heard the noise and caught her in the throes of her climax. When Olivia had asked if she had been dismissed or confined to a madhouse, Adele had laughed and replied that he had ordered her to take off her drawers and continue with the exercise. When she was again panting and blushing he had entered her, and many times after that, it seemed.

Olivia wondered, as she recalled how disgusted she had felt, whether the same would now happen to her. She knew the man was sitting close by, possibly between her open legs watching every move of her wrist. Was this what he meant by obedience, doing everything she was told? He could hardly accuse her of not obeying him, for now her fingers were moving faster and the heels of her boots digging deeper and deeper into the carpet.

'Is this what you want?' she panted, opening her eyes and finding herself still in darkness.

His silence unnerved her, only his unseen presence willed her on. Her back arched high off the carpet. Her bottom lifted, supported by straining thighs and bent, trembling knees. Using her heels as levers, and with the back of her head pressed hard into the floor, her whole body lifted, exposing her dripping slit and a hand that moved so fast it blurred before his eyes. Suddenly the room seemed to spin, and it felt as if her whole life's blood were draining from her fork. She let out a piercing shriek and went rigid. Drenched in sweat, her body crashed to the floor and she lay still. Only her head moved, lolling gently from side to side.

The gentleman waited until Olivia's chest resumed its normal breathing, and then ordered her up on her feet. She reached out for his hand but no help came. In the dark she struggled onto her haunches, then her knees, and finally tottered on her heels to wherever he was leading her.

She followed blindly, bumping her knees against the furniture, until she found herself positioned against a wall.

'Put up your arms,' he commanded, and Olivia obeyed without question, without thinking, without offering the slightest resistance.

She knew that the rings being fitted around her wrists were another test of her obedience, as would be the whipping she knew would not be long in coming.

'What will you use on me?' she asked, her body flattened into the wooden panelling.

He made no answer, but lifted the chain that bound the rings and slipped it over a hook, thus suspending her up on her toes.

'You choose. Which method of punishment causes you the greatest pain?'

'The cat o' nine tails,' she murmured.

In the interlude when he went off to fetch the required instrument, Olivia wondered why she had so willingly complied, and not had the good sense to mention a cane or strap that would hurt far less.

He came back and she heard, or thought she heard, the clanking of metal.

'While you were in the House of Correction, you were fitted with an iron belt, were you not? One that penetrated you from beneath.'

Olivia nodded. 'A belt with an iron spike, that went up inside me.'

'I cannot vouch for the pedigree of that particular fitment, probably a relic from the Inquisition. I can however explain the history of this, which you will find equally as painful, but as you are flogged will give you considerable pleasure. Please open your legs.'

Olivia shuffled her soles across the floor until her weight was taken on the tips of her boots. Her knees caved in and touched the panels and seemed to hold there.

'It was used on slaves,' he told her, 'by the Sultans of Turkey, when the girl in question was less than forthcoming.'

Olivia's buttocks went taut as he slid a long cylindrical, metal tube into her vagina. At the end of the tube, appearing from between her parted lips, was a key which he slowly turned. Against the wall of her tunnel she felt a curious tingle which grew more painful with every turn. The spikes coming from the tube were not honed to points, but nevertheless were sharp enough to make her catch her breath as he went on turning.

'It is designed to open you up,' he said, 'and would, had you been in the harem, open you wider, day after day, usually for a month, or until the slave begged for release and consented to whatever her master had in mind.'

'I have consented,' Olivia protested. 'I will do anything that you require of me.'

'My requirements are that you should wear this while you are being flogged, and that you demonstrate your obedience by having it willingly inside you.'

'I am having it.'

'But willingly?'

'Yes, willingly. I want you to put it in me.'

He gave the key another turn and Olivia emitted a painful groan.

'Even if it hurts?'

'Especially if it hurts.'

The key had reached its extremity and would turn no more. Inside, Olivia felt the spikes pushing against her walls, holding her wide open. At its base was a ring that had gradually expanded at the same time as the spikes had advanced from the cylinder. It was there to open her labia much wider than the spikes had her tunnel, and to prevent her from closing her legs.

'It will hurt a lot more when you are flogged,' he said, 'unless you are capable of keeping your bottom totally relaxed, which you know from experience is impossible.'

He took up the cat o' nine tails and flicked it playfully across her haunches, noticing with evident satisfaction how her buttocks immediately responded. The globes tightened against the crease forming deep hollows on their sides, whereupon Olivia uttered a faint cry of pain.

He flicked her again, a little harder on the backs of her upper thighs, sending the tails of the lashes licking against her stretched lips. The cry of pain grew louder and louder still when he flipped the lashes directly across her taut buttocks, hitting her at half strength.

She knew that soon the lashes would fall thick and fast, and her hips and buttocks would writhe. It would require great strength of will to resist the mounting pain burning through her bottom.

He went on lashing her buttocks and flanks, gradually increasing the pressure with every fresh stroke. And every time it landed her hips jerked back and forth, moving her vaginal walls against the spikes. The belt she had worn in the House of Correction had been designed as a punishment, one that would cause her humiliation. But this was not a punishment, neither did she feel humiliated, for there was no one to witness it, no one to mock and jeer at her discomfort; only the man lashing her bottom and the sensation of mounting fire welling within her slit.

It grew at every lash now falling at full strength. The wriggling of her hips and flexing of her buttocks, although themselves on fire, were producing the same inexplicable and delicious feeling she had felt when she had fingered herself. She could hear her own screams of pain slowly subside into low, harsh moans of pleasure. The urgent writhing of her hips surrendered to a graceful gyration as again her juices started to flow.

'Now you understand why you have the implement inside you,' he said, lashing the apex of her fork.

Olivia could not reply; she was panting faster, oblivious to anything but the tingling of her belly and the dull ache of the ring pressing against her lips. At the moment of her climax she let out a great cry of despair. This whipping was unlike any other she had experienced. True, the pain was as excruciating as ever, but inside she felt nothing but the heat of her orgasm, the now welcoming caresses of the spikes, and the ring stretching her open.

The final stroke fell and Olivia hung lifeless, her legs buckled against the panels. The gentleman reached between her fork and began turning the key. The spikes and ring slackened. The cylinder slid from her tunnel and was taken away.

'Quite an achievement,' he complimented, lifting her wrist chain from the hook.

Olivia collapsed in his arms and was surprised to find herself lowered gently to the hearthrug.

'Has my obedience satisfied you?' she whimpered.

'It has more than satisfied me. I have found out everything I needed to know. Now it only remains for me to take you, and for you to swear your loyalty to me.'

'How can I swear loyalty to a man I do not even know, or have never seen?'

'You have seen me, but in circumstances less propitious than these. There is no need for further questions; all that is required is your total and unswerving obedience. Allow me therefore to take possession of your bottom, your other place I shall spare for the time being. No doubt you are somewhat sore.'

Olivia allowed herself to be prostrated over the arm of a chair while he spread open her legs. Involuntarily she reached behind and parted her cheeks while he smoothed a warm ointment into her rear entrance.

'Your assistance is most touching,' he said, thrusting into her with a shudder of his loins. 'No doubt you are well used to having men up your backside.'

While he took her his hands carefully explored her body, running over her flanks and bottom, the curve of her hips, and reaching under to gently squeeze her breasts. His touch was unlike any other she had experienced, as if he were a connoisseur of the female form and appreciated beauty when he saw it.

Inside, he seemed to fill her to the core, thrusting at her as if he wished to touch her heart. Olivia orgasmed with a quick succession of climaxes, grunting and drooling, giving vent to harsh groans of wanting, hoping he would never stop. As her bottom squirmed and wriggled hard against his organ he reached his own climax, emptying into her with shuddering jolts, filling her with hot, liquid fire.

'Why won't you let me see your face?' she asked, when he withdrew and seated her on the sofa, still panting.

'After you have sworn loyalty to me and no other, you shall see me. Perhaps in a week or so. Now, please open your legs and prepare yourself for some considerable pain.'

Olivia obeyed, stretching her ankles as wide as she could. She heard him moving away from her and in a short while returning, positioning himself somewhere near the fire.

'What are you going to do with me?' she asked, breaking into a fearful sweat.

'As a token of your betrothal you shall wear my ring,' he replied, shuffling between her open legs.

'We are to be engaged?' she gasped.

'Yes, but not in the usual way. The ring I shall give you, and you will wear, no man will see except myself when I undress you, and when you in turn offer yourself to me.'

'Are you going to put it where I think you are?'

His hands were between her legs and thumbing apart her labia. 'That would very much depend on where you think I am going to fit it.'

'Between my legs,' she replied on a rush of air.

'Precisely.'

'But why not on my finger, as is usual in such circumstances?'

'Dear girl, a woman may sport a dozen rings on her fingers, but that does not prevent her from bestowing her favours on anyone she pleases. Neither does a wedding ring for that matter.'

'I am not an adulteress,' Olivia protested. 'My word shall be my bond.'

'I don't doubt it, but with a body as beautiful as yours you are fresh meat to any ravenous male that seeks to appease his appetite. This particular ring will make them seek their meat elsewhere. Now kindly brace yourself.'

Olivia clenched her teeth and gripped the arms of the sofa. The ring was a circle of metal, one end fashioned to a sharp needlepoint that fitted into the hollow of the other half, and once in situ could not be removed.

'Before the ring is fitted through your lips,' he explained, 'it will be necessary to pierce them, rather as if it were your ears. A sharp, short pain which will soon be over.'

The excruciating pain was indeed sharp but certainly not short. The needle that he used to pierce her lips was about half the diameter of her little finger, and heated until white in the coals of the fire. Olivia shrieked when it was forced through the first of her lips and slowly drawn through, allowing the heated metal to scorch and sear her tender flesh. The length of needle was pulled free, and then reinserted and allowed to rest there while he prepared the first half of the ring.

Olivia's thighs quivered their whole length, as did her labia and belly.

'Hush now, t'will not be long,' he soothed, planting a kiss on her navel.

'You're treating me as if I were an animal,' she whimpered. 'I wonder that you don't fit a chain to me.'

'That will not be necessary, after all, now that you are residing at your uncle's I doubt that you shall stray far.'

'Then why are you ringing me like this?'

'Insurance,' he muttered, leaving her somewhat baffled.

The needle was withdrawn and the first half of the ring slipped through the hole in her labia. To Olivia's great relief the metal was cold and did to some extent relieve the agonizing pain shooting through her groin. Her mouth opened and breathed in deeply. She choked back a sob and wiped her nose with the back of her hand.

'Now the other,' she heard him say, and felt the heat of the needle approaching her upper thigh.

She screamed aloud and went rigid, her legs as stiff as ramrods drummed into the carpet. She was sure the heat was much greater and the needle much longer. Again he pushed it through the pouting lip, now discoloured from pink to scarlet and swelling all the while.

'You should be proud of such gorgeous attributes,' he complimented her. 'There are many women who would give a fortune to possess such magnificence.'

'They won't look magnificent when you've finished,' she sobbed.

'I can assure you that you will look just as splendid, perhaps even more so.'

The other half of the ring slipped through and was locked into place. Then he turned it through the holes in her labia, positioning it so that the join of the ring had disappeared under her skin.

'Now that you are thus locked t'will be unlikely that anyone will try to roger you, and even if they do the effort of getting past that ring will hopefully outweigh the delight of coming in you.'

'No one has ever "come in me" as you so crudely put it,' Olivia said bitterly, running her fingers blindly over the ring.

'And nor will they until your wedding night, when it shall be removed.'

'And how shall that be?' she inquired, giving the ring a gentle tug and wincing from the pain of her newly burned flesh.

'Only I know the answer to that, and so shall you when the time comes.'

With that he left her naked and sprawling on the sofa, still rubbing her burning groin.

'Your carriage will be here shortly, miss.'

The voice was female. The maid, Olivia assumed. 'May I take off this awful mask?' she asked irritably.

The maid removed it for her and Olivia blinked in the light. Looking between her parted legs she gasped at the sight of the ring. It was larger than it had felt, and she winced when she tried to close her legs. The ring had been strategically placed about a third of the way up her labia, rendering it almost impossible for any man to penetrate her.

She blushed red and hurried on her drawers. God knows what her uncle would think or say if he ever found out what had gone on here. She would have to dream up a good excuse not to sit on his knee and let him fondle her as he always insisted on doing.

Perhaps, she thought, he might already know of the ring, and from henceforth, with luck, everyone would leave her alone; would stop putting their organs up her bottom, and making her suck them and then whip her from head to toe. Only her husband would be allowed to do that.

As the carriage rattled off into the night she put her hand between her legs and felt the ring, longing for the day when the same hand would unlock it. Hopefully it would not be long in coming.

CHAPTER THIRTEEN

When Olivia did not return, Effie was beside herself with rage. The carriage that had been sent to collect her had been turned away empty, and the driver given to understand that Olivia had now taken up permanent residence with the gentleman.

'I want her brought back!' Effie rasped, glaring at Rita and Dora as if they were directly responsible for her disappearance. 'She can't stay in that house forever! She has to go abroad sometime, and when she does, you'll fetch her here! Fail me and I'll have you flogged day in and day out!'

So Rita and Dora took up their stations either end of the street where Olivia was now living, and waited and waited and waited. For three days they guarded the street, relieved only at nightfall when they were permitted a few hours sleep in a nearby lodging house. When at last Olivia emerged they sighed with relief and, keeping out of sight, followed her into Berkeley Street, seemingly heading towards the crowded throng of Piccadilly.

Her errand was not a long one, merely a visit to a haberdashers to purchase a pair of white stockings, which her uncle enjoyed removing as she sat on his knee.

'Olivia, our dear sister!'

Olivia spun round and came face to face with Dora, who immediately linked arms with her. She might have struggled free if it were not for Rita who took her other arm and proclaimed to all and sundry how Olivia had run away from a good home and how, after being driven out of their minds with worry, her sisters had at length found the ungrateful wretch.

There was little sympathy from the onlookers, who shook their heads as Olivia was propelled into the nearest hackney carriage. A dose of chloroform subdued her cries as the horse gathered speed, galloping towards Paddington.

'Strip,' Effie said flatly, as soon as a bottle of smelling salts had revived Olivia.

'At least she's brought us some good togs,' Rita remarked, already half stupefied from the gin Effie had given her.

Olivia stood in front of the assembly and took off all her clothes. In her confusion and anger she had completely forgotten about the engagement ring that encircled her labia.

'What on earth is this?' Effie proclaimed, eyeing the shining metal.

'I am engaged,' Olivia replied proudly.

When the shrieking and guffawing had abated, Effie slipped her forefinger through the ring and half dragged Olivia into her private quarters.

'Engaged to whom?' she asked, intrigued.

'The man who wishes my hand,' she replied stupidly, whereupon Effie slapped her face.

'His name, you halfwit!'

'Don't know.'

Effie groaned. 'Well what does he look like?'

'I was blindfolded and never saw his face.' Seeing the incredulous look Effie shot her she added defensively, 'It's the truth, I was blindfolded the whole time.'

'Even when he fitted that?!' she exclaimed, bending low to inspect the ring.

Olivia said nothing but stood stock still while Effie turned it in her fingers wondering how it had been secured.

'Your suitor has done me a good service,' she mused, standing upright again.

Then without any more ado she stripped off her own clothes and fetched a cane from her cupboard.

'Touch your toes,' she said, flexing the cane in her hands.

'You have no right to treat me thus,' Olivia protested. 'I was brought here against my will, and my suitor will see that you are justly punished.'

The cane whistled into Olivia's bare rump. 'If your suitor has found you so desirable to ring your cunt, I daresay he will pay handsomely to have you safely back. Punishing me will not be uppermost in his mind I can assure you. Now bend over!'

Olivia had no will to resist. She knew that sooner or later her bottom would taste the fury of Effie's cane, a just punishment for having betrayed her generosity. She gave Olivia two-dozen strokes in quick succession on and all around her bottom, hitting her with the full strength of her arm, slicing into her succulent cheeks, landing the strokes side by side, not stopping until Olivia was reduced to a blubbering wreck.

'Now, about this ring,' she said, laying aside the cane. 'What use can we find for that, I wonder.'

Olivia wished now that the wretched thing had never been fitted, for there was no doubt in her mind that Effie would make good use of it, and in a way calculated to cause the maximum of pain and humiliation.

She tugged on a bell-pull and Rita entered, her face flushed and thighs still damp with sweat. 'Bring me every length of chain in the building, and whatever else that is employed along with them,' Effie said darkly.

Rita was gone in a hurry, and soon returned bowed under the weight of yards of chain of various lengths and sizes. She dumped them on the floor, and after some considerable time returned with a host of weights and other fearsome looking objects.

'These we keep for our more imaginative patrons,' Effie said gaily. 'And sometimes when the girls are less than imaginative themselves.' She kicked over the pile of chains and metal objects, stroking her chin as she did so.

'What would be most appropriate to use on you, d'you think?'

Olivia eyed the objects with a shudder as Effie scooped up a length of chain and threaded one end through the ring.

'Open your legs,' she commanded, letting the chain hang between them while she sorted out a small brass padlock.

This she secured to the ring and the chain and locked it into place. When that was done the length was wrapped around each ankle and given to Olivia to hold while she rummaged through the pile of objects.

'This will do nicely,' she remarked, selecting an iron collar.

'Please don't put that on me,' Olivia begged, as Effie stepped up behind her.

Ignoring her pleas, Effie slipped the collar around Olivia's neck and fastened it at the back with a hasp. All the way around its circumference were a collection of other rings about the same size as the one which pierced Olivia's labia. Going back to the pile of chains, Effie retrieved a half-dozen lengths, and one by one threaded them through the collar rings. On the end of each length were either manacles or hasps.

'These will fit around your wrists,' she said, taking up two of the manacles.

The manacles did not reach to where Olivia was holding the length of chain that had already passed around her ankles, so Effie told her to lift her hands and place them between her breasts. Two of the lengths projecting from the sides of her neck were drawn to her clasped hands and tightly fixed.

The chain that Olivia was still holding pulled tight, and she felt a momentary wince of pain as the ring in her labia jolted downwards.

'When your hands are pulled up to your neck,' Effie began explaining, 'the chain you are holding will slid around your ankles and put greater pressure on the ring in your cunt. Quite clever when you consider that I've only just thought of this.'

And to demonstrate her meaning, she took a length of chain from the pile and secured it to the bracelets on Olivia's wrists. This she laid over Olivia's shoulder and then drew down her back. As the chain pulled her hands further up her chest, Olivia understood what was being done to her. The more pressure exerted on her hands, the higher they lifted, and in so doing she could not but help lift the chain that had been padlocked to her labial ring, which, because it had been passed around her ankles in the first place, in turn exerted downward pressure on her labia. All in all it was quite ingenious, that as her hands lifted, the ring in her labia should tug in the opposite direction.

Effie pulled on the chain she was holding and passed it under Olivia's open legs. She pulled it so tightly that Olivia's hands were forced almost to her shoulders. Then, regardless of the cries of pain, Effie secured it to the labial ring with the aid of another padlock.

'Now I shall fix the chain you are holding,' and with that, Effie relieved Olivia of her burden and fixed the chain to the rings in her collar.

'Every time you move either your hands or feet you will be reminded of your mysterious suitor,' Effie chuckled. 'You see, the slightest movement will pull on that ring between your legs, so every step will make your eyes water, not to mention the rest of your punishment.'

'Isn't this enough?!' Olivia cried. 'Look at me, trussed up like a convict, and naked into the bargain.'

'That's just how the patrons like our girls - chained and naked. Whoever chooses to take you will find entering your cunt quite a challenge, I should imagine.'

'Is that the rest of my punishment?' Olivia asked bitterly.

'Not at all. Dora and Rita will draw lots to see which of them will whip you. You have put them both to a great inconvenience, watching that house day and night, out in all weathers, simply because you chose to stay in the lap of luxury instead of returning home to your friends, eh?'

Effie rang the bell-pull, and in answer to her summons, not only did Dora and Rita enter the room, but Sappho, who went wide-eyed at seeing Olivia chained and unable to move.

'Show her your engagement ring,' Effie taunted.

Olivia parted her legs and Sappho stepped forward and lifted it with her fingers.

'Never in my life have I seen such devotion,' she laughed, and then pulled it, causing Olivia further pain.

Effie took three tapers from a pot on the mantelpiece and, breaking one in half, held them in her hand, bidding the three girls make their choice. Sappho selected the shortest.

'Take her into the back parlour, she's yours to do as you wish,' Effie said, almost without interest.

'We shall help her,' Dora quickly rejoined as Sappho seized Olivia by the hair.

'Whip her across the belly,' suggested Rita, when they were safely in the parlour. She lifted a strap hanging from the wall and thrashed it onto the table.

'I want to inspect the manner of these chains,' Sappho said, going behind Olivia and intently studying the way Effie had bound her. She tested the chain running down her back, and quickly realised if it was pulled downwards Olivia's hands lifted, making the ring tug on her labia. Sappho's lips broke into a twisted grin and she cast her eyes about her.

'I have an idea that will make you scream and beg for mercy,' she said, bending down to retrieve a heavy poker from the hearth.

She slid it under the chain, just above Olivia's buttocks at the point where it disappeared into her crease. When it was balanced at the centre of its shaft she ordered Dora to take it in both hands at either end. Then she told Rita to position herself in front of Olivia in readiness to ply the strap.

At the first stroke Olivia let out a cry of pain, but it was nothing to what was happening behind her back. As Rita gathered the strap for a fresh strike, Dora gave the poker a half turn. Olivia felt the chain suddenly tighten. Her hands drew upwards towards her shoulders and she screamed all the louder. The ring in her labia bit hard into the tender mound, stretching the outer lips downwards.

'Six more lashes and six more turns of the poker,' Sappho said sternly, and both girls willingly obeyed.

Rita began by hitting Olivia with deliberate slowness allowing her to feel the burning welts in her belly and the gradual twisting of the chain. It seemed that the pain was coming from everywhere at once; under her legs and in the crease of her buttocks, across her belly and all over her labia.

'Beat her faster,' Sappho remarked. 'And harder. I want to see her suffer.'

The strap fell thick and fast and the poker twisted round and round until Olivia thought the chain would saw her in half. Her cries and muted sobs gave way to ear piercing shrieks and a wild shaking of her head.

'Only a few dozen more,' Sappho said kindly, caressing Olivia's cheek and then kissing her full on the lips.

'Please stop,' Olivia begged, hardly aware that Sappho was tenderly squeezing her nipples and biting the hollow of her neck.

'I'm sure you can take another thirty or so, then your punishment will end. You can go on screaming and yelling for another hour, just one hour that's all, and in that time you will be wet between your legs, so wet that my fingers and tongue will slip in you easily.'

Rita lashed Olivia's belly from the outer fringes of her pubic hair, up over her navel and across her stomach. From behind Dora had wound the poker so tight that the chain passing under Olivia's legs almost lifted her from the floor. Her labia felt as if it would tear from her groin.

'Your punishment is over,' Sappho eventually smiled, as the final lash seared into Olivia's belly. 'Now thank me for being so generous in your chastisement, and also my assistants.'

Olivia thanked them between her choking sobs, but was more thankful that it had ended. As the poker was unwound and the chain slackened its awful progress, the pain subsided remarkably. The sawing under her legs and in her bottom-cleft suddenly ceased, and her stretched lips desisted their burning.

'Oh thank God,' she breathed. 'Thank God it's all over.'

If ever there were a pleasant aspect of being cruelly tortured it was when it ended. The relief was overwhelming, her gratitude genuine; she did not resist Sappho's tongue searching inside her open mouth or the hand that rubbed her groin, neither the fingers that rolled and pinched her nipples. If anything, her most sensual parts seemed more responsive to tongues and fingers after her body had undergone grievous torments. The greater the torment the more eager her response. In truth, she almost wished the ring had not been fitted, thereby allowing Sappho complete access to her most intimate places.

Seeing the glazed look in her eyes, Sappho told her companions to get out at once. She wanted Olivia all to herself

'These chains, shall I remove them for the time being?' she asked. 'It will leave your hands free to explore my body, if you so wish.'

Olivia nodded. She already had a good idea that Sappho intended to take her, and that the chains would hinder her advances.

'Are you going to finger me?' she asked innocently.

Sappho loosed the padlock between her legs and slid the chain from the ring. 'Would you prefer I used something else? The poker, for example.'

'I couldn't take all of it,' she gasped.

Sappho slapped her face playfully. 'I was jesting, you fool. However, I do intend to use my own favourite method of taking you, and as flicking you in the normal place is out of the question, I shall have to resort to your bottom.'

She unwrapped the chain from Olivia's ankles and then went to work on the shackles around her wrists

'I shall have to chain you up again when I've finished with you,' she said, freeing Olivia's hands and letting the chain slid over her shoulder. 'Effie wants you permanently chained to make sure you don't run away again. The collar I shall leave on. No sense in taking that off, is there?'

'Does this mean I am to be chained like an animal?' Olivia asked.

'Only until you've learned your lesson. No one ever leaves here unless Effie decides to sell them to another establishment.'

'Sell them?' Olivia gasped. 'You make us sound like slaves or something.'

'You poor, simple girl,' Sappho replied, bringing Olivia to her knees. 'That's exactly what we are. Men's playthings, to be used as they see fit, and to do whatever they command. Why d'you think Effie took you in?'

'I thought it was because I was going to be an actress and learn a useful profession, instead of being treated like a... like a prostitute,' she blurted.

'You're not a prostitute exactly,' Sappho said, taking her by the shoulders and guiding her to rest her forearms on the padded seat of a chaise longue. 'More a piece of property. You belong here, and as long as you're here, you'll do as you're told. Now grip your cheeks and spread them nice and wide. I shall finger your bottom hole first, just to loosen you up.'

'Then what are you going to do?' Olivia asked, resting her flushed forehead on the seat and already fearing the answer.

Sappho aimed her index finger into Olivia's bottom and gave a vigorous thrust. Olivia jolted forward with a grunt.

'Ride you, of course. Effie permits that. She'll probably have you herself after I've finished with you, then I think will come the final part of your punishment.'

'What?'

But Sappho made no reply. Her finger had sunk in to the knuckle and was turning back and forth, going in and out, forcing Olivia's bottom hole to open wider at the entrance. The interior muscles were already beginning to slacken.

'What punishment?' Olivia asked again in between grunting and moaning from Sappho's deeply probing finger.

And again she made no reply, but when she deemed Olivia's anus sufficiently ready, she withdrew and crawled to a chest of drawers, opened a drawer and took out her favourite weapon.

'It's a man's cock,' she said from behind Olivia. 'Much bigger than they ordinarily are, but then it needs to be when you consider how much cock you and everybody else has already had. Rita for example, has had so many that she's hard pressed to be satisfied these days, poor girl.'

'You're disgusting,' Olivia retorted.

'I see little trouble in taking you,' Sappho chuckled.

'Would it make any difference if I did otherwise?'

'None at all, except for the pleasure of raping you.'

'And have you raped any other poor, unfortunate girl?'

'Oh plenty,' she grinned, strapping the cock to her groin and tying its strings behind her. 'Why, only a couple of days ago I buggered a girl fresh from the country, while her master watched on. She squealed like a stuck pig and wriggled like an eel, but I think, after an hour or so, she quite liked it.'

'Then I suppose you had her master while she watched on,' Olivia replied sarcastically.

'No I didn't,' and she wormed the enormous plum of her cock into Olivia's hole.

Holding Olivia by the shoulders, she moved her hips in a beautiful side-to-side motion and pressed firmly forward. Olivia jerked as the shaft slowly filled her, sliding in an inch at a time.

'It is big,' she gasped, feeling it stretch the walls of her bottom.

'And long,' Sappho whispered hoarsely.

Her black hips and buttocks broke into a sweat as she began to ride in earnest. She was powerfully built and had earned a just reputation as being a woman of exceptional prowess. It was a rare man who could stay the course with her, and when she had tired them all it was to the girls she turned to slake her uncontrollable lust. Olivia, she decided, had a particularly inviting bottom. She wondered, as she pushed deeper in, how difficult it would be to remove that ring. But that, she would think of later.

She rode into Olivia without mercy, arching her back and thrusting her pelvis, at the same time pulling her back and forth by the shoulders. Between her legs the strap that held her cock bit deep into her slit. Sappho had discovered that there was as much satisfaction to be had from the strap as there was from riding her victims. If she angled her groin correctly the strap teased against her clitoris and soon she was panting towards her climax.

Olivia's bottom began to respond with ecstatic wriggling, for inside of her anus was a sensitive place which, when touched by finger or cock, brought her to her own orgasm. Her labia tingled where it had been ringed, she could feel the mound starting to swell.

'You're coming,' Sappho exclaimed, listening to Olivia's groans as the cock rode harder into her bottom.

'I can't help it,' Olivia apologised. 'It's that thing you're pushing into me.'

'And what about your teats, how do they feel?'

Before Olivia could even think or reply, Sappho reached under her and grabbed both her swinging breasts. Her hands were large enough to encompass both globes and she rolled them flat against Olivia's chest, taking care to ensure the nipples received a hard pinching. The feel of the aroused, pointed buds had Sappho pumping her pelvis and loins faster and faster.

Olivia gasped for breath as the whole length of the cock penetrated her bottom, going in right to its base, slamming against her cheeks and then gliding back out to the plum. Sappho let it hover at the open hole, teasing it up and down the crease and around the cheeks. Olivia's buttocks had turned bright red and were covered with a fine glisten of sweat that slowly trickled into the cleft.

Sappho paused to run her forefinger under Olivia's legs, gathering up a globule of vaginal nectar.

'You taste so sweet,' she remarked, sucking her forefinger. 'Has anyone ever told you that?'

'Many times,' Olivia replied, catching her breath, grateful that Sappho had temporarily halted her mad thrusting.

'I think you should taste yourself now,' Sappho observed, running her finger over the pouting pudenda. 'It seems this ring has excited you,' she said, poking the swollen halves. 'Why, you're twice your normal size, and your hair...'

Olivia was well aware how her pubic hair had bristled at the touch and how her lips had become puffy and swollen.

'It's not only the ring,' she said defensively, her breath resuming its normal pace.

'Is it my cock?' asked Sappho hopefully.

'When it touches a place inside me I go all of a tremble,' Olivia replied, the shaking in her voice betraying the truth of her admission.

A bead of sweat appeared between Sappho's enormous ebony breasts. Her nipples had become so erect they ached. She looked down at them, watching the hardened buds swelling even larger. Suddenly she extracted the cock from its snug sanctuary, reached under Olivia's armpits and hoisted her back onto her haunches, spinning her round and aiming her head directly between her breasts.

'Now suck!' she commanded, her voice deep and husky.

Olivia dumbly obeyed, discovering at once a remarkable, exotic taste that seemed to come from the nipple itself. The harder she sucked the stronger and sweeter the essence on her tongue. The nipples were huge, as large as ripened strawberries.

Sappho put her hands behind Olivia's head and squeezed her hard to her breasts.

Olivia, without being instructed, found her tongue sweeping around Sappho's mountainous orbs, licking every inch of glistening flesh.

'You're coming on well,' Sappho breathed, placing her hands on either globe and burying Olivia's head between them.

The cock still strapped to Sappho's groin reared up, the plum nudged invitingly into Olivia's belly, making a slight crease in the plump flesh.

'What a pity that ring prevents me from taking you with my cock,' she said sadly. 'But there is always your willing mouth, is there not.'

Olivia's mouth was not quite as willing as Sappho assumed. She looked down and balked, not only at the size of it, but at the juices of her own bottom which still covered it.

'I'd like to wipe it first, please,' she said softly.

'You will take it as it is,' Sappho rasped, and she fell backwards, dragging Olivia's head after her.

Olivia took a deep breath and opened her mouth wide. Her lips barely went round the shining plum. A jerk of Sappho's hands forced it into her mouth and she nearly choked.

'Take all of it,' Sappho grunted. 'The whole length, and put your hands on my tits. Play with my nipples, or so help me I'll whip you raw.'

Olivia relaxed her tightened throat and lowered her head, letting the cock slide further into her mouth. Clumsily she groped for Sappho's breasts and began fingering the nipples.

'Go deeper,' she heard Sappho command, accompanied with an upward thrust of her hips.

Abruptly, the cock nudged to the back of Olivia's throat, and her nostrils suddenly filled with the rich and earthy smell of Sappho's groin.

The sight of Olivia's head bobbing up and down, and the feel of her fingers teasing her nipples, had Sappho panting and heaving. Soon the small parlour was filled with the sounds of her climax. Her hands fell away from the back of Olivia's head and thrashed against the floor. Her long, silky legs went rigid, the muscles contracting as hard as iron.

'Oh God help me!' she groaned in her deep, harsh voice, and her hands beat against Olivia's back, a hollow, thumping tattoo of sweating, pulsating pleasure.

Olivia pulled back and saw how thoroughly her mouth had cleaned the cock. The taste of Sappho's orgasm lingered on her tongue. 'Have we finished now?' she asked, wiping her lips with her fingers.

Sappho could not answer for several minutes. Her orgasm had all but drained her. She lay bathed in sweat, her forearm resting across her forehead, her legs spread wide, dripping at the groin.

'Lick me,' she whispered. 'Lick my cunt.'

Olivia, knowing she had little choice, crouched between her legs, and lifting away the cock, placed her head into Sappho's fork. While she licked at the quivering lips she involuntarily kept her hand around the shaft and began tossing it as if it were flesh and blood that throbbed in her palm.

'You like that?' Sappho asked, watching the long, slender fingers caressing the length.

Immediately Olivia ceased and looked up, her face horror-stricken. 'I didn't realise I was doing it,' she gasped.

Her task between Sappho's legs was complete and she recoiled away from the spread legs, and in particular the cock.

'You had it up your bottom, so why worry about holding it?'

125

'I had it because you made me. I don't have to hold it of my own free will.'

'But you said yourself it gave you pleasure. That place in your bottom that made your cheeks go all red and sweaty. Don't come the innocent. I saw it with my own eyes.'

'Every woman has some part of her that gets excited now and then,' Olivia retorted. 'It's only natural.'

'It's natural to have it in your cunt, but so far you've been remarkably clever in avoiding that. But not for much longer, I can assure you.'

'What do you mean?'

'Sooner or later that ring will be sawed off you, and when it has been you'll be fucked from here into next week, and the week after that. So much that you'll walk about here bow-legged.'

'Never!'

Sappho stood up and untied the cock, and with Olivia still kneeling in front of her she rubbed the head of the plum up and down her cheek and around her lips. Olivia's mouth opened slightly and Sappho stuffed it into her mouth.

'We had a girl here before you who ran away, and do you know what her punishment was?' Olivia shook her head. 'She was trussed up like a chicken and had this very cock stuffed into her mouth for a week. That made her think twice. Effie, however, has something else in mind for you. Hark, here she comes.'

'Have you finished with her?' Effie asked, standing over Olivia and eyeing her darkly.

'She's yours,' Sappho said dully, as if Olivia were little more than an old rag.

'Put the chains back on her and bring her into the kitchen,' Effie said bluntly.

Sappho refitted the chains, but not nearly as expertly as Effie had done. She slid the longest length through the ring, padlocked it and fastened it to the shackles around Olivia's wrists. These she fastened in turn to the ring at the front of her collar. Her ankles were left free. Olivia could not move her hands away from her chest without either pulling on the collar or the ring in her labia. But it was a relief not to have the chains biting into her bottom crease or shackling her legs.

'What's going to happen to me now?' she asked as she trotted alongside Sappho towards the kitchen.

Sappho made no reply, but led her through the door into the stifling heat. In the grate a fire blazed like a furnace, and every so often Dora increased the heat by pumping on a pair of bellows.

'Position her against the wall,' Effie said. 'Tightly if you please.'

Olivia was placed flat against the brickwork while Sappho took a set of ropes from a cupboard and passed them around Olivia's waist and thighs. These she tied to two hooks apparently placed at just the right height. Effie stepped up behind her and patted her bottom, remarking on its beauty and saying that it was such a shame to mark it.

Behind her, Olivia heard the rush of air from the bellows and a sudden roar of flame. Even though she was on the other side of the room the heat warmed her back. She caught a clanking of metal and a muffled stirring of the coals. Suddenly she started to wriggle and pull at the ropes.

'Not that!' she shrieked, tearing her body away from the wall.

Effie picked up a cane and lashed the small of her back. 'Be still!' she shouted.

Olivia froze. Over her shoulder the bellows were breathing like a monster in a cave. The heat in the room rose to tropical proportions. Sweat gathered on her skin and started to trickle downwards in rivulets.

'T'will all be over before you know it,' said Effie, again patting her bottom. She looked at Rita who was sitting beside the fire smoking, apparently oblivious to the goings-on.

'Open her cheeks,' she said, giving Rita an encouraging slap on the face.

Rita arose sluggishly and drifted to where Olivia was standing. She placed her hands on Olivia's bottom, her fingertips well into the crease, and then prised them open. Someone, Olivia couldn't see who, was stirring the fire, and then came a cascade of hot ashes tumbling onto the hearth.

'Oh, please no!' Olivia begged with a sob.

Then came a hiss of flame and the smell of scorching flesh. As if she had been struck by a bolt of lightning Olivia writhed and screamed, and all the while Sappho counted the seconds. It seemed as if the hot iron was burning Olivia to the bone, she was sure it had remained there for an hour.

'Four... five... six...' counted Sappho triumphantly.

An unseen hand took away the iron, leaving in its wake a pattern two inches long and half that in width. The mark slowly turned a dark brown colour and a finger traced its outline. The indentation between Olivia's buttocks was a quarter of an inch deep.

'Now you belong to me,' Effie said flatly.

She stood back to admire the scorching imprint, and as Rita took away her fingers, Olivia's buttocks wobbled back into place.

'I'm not sure about that,' Effie mused. 'The brand is not quite as clear as I'd hoped. We shall have to give her another, where it stands out much more clearly. I'm sorry Olivia; I seem to have made a mistake. Please accept my sincerest apologies.'

And the iron was placed back into the coals to the sound of the creaking bellows.

Olivia clenched her teeth and waited.

'On her bottom this time. Her left cheek.'

Effie patted the exact place where Olivia was to be burned for the second time, in the centre of her buttock where the flesh was fattest and at its most full.

'Ten seconds should burn her well,' Effie remarked, as the iron was judged sufficiently hot enough to leave its mark.

Another hiss of hot iron on flesh abruptly followed, and Olivia shrieked so loud that the cups on the dresser rattled in their saucers. Again Sappho counted, but Olivia never heard anything past six. She hung against the wall like one dead, and as the iron was taken away and the ropes loosed she crumpled to the floor in a lifeless heap.

On her cheek was emblazoned the imprint of an erect phallus, burned deep into her flesh; the mark of a whore to be used and abused as any man saw fit; a symbol of her calling that would remain with her until her dying day.

Chapter Fourteen

'There is a woman to see you, sir,' Helena curtsied.

Walter Holland looked up from his desk, his face still grief stricken. In front of him lay the album open at the photograph of Olivia's mother.

'A woman?' he asked absently.

'Says she wishes to speak with a Miss Olivia.'

Walter's eyes lit up. 'Show her in!'

The woman dropped a half-hearted curtsey, and as she did so he could not help but admire her voluptuous frame and high, rounded breasts that blossomed above her dress. As she righted herself the acrid odour of unwashed flesh wafted into his nostrils.

'Who are you, and what do you want with my niece?'

The woman appeared shocked at this intelligence, and for a moment or two glanced warily around the room, obviously intimidated by its sumptuous surroundings.

'My name is Flora,' she began, brushing her dirty hair from her brow. 'I have been in London for a month with no hope of a position, save that of a vagrant. I know no one here, and am at my wit's end with not a soul to turn to. Indeed, I thought of ending it all.' She wiped a tear from her eye and fiddled with the trimming around her cleavage.

Seeing that the gentleman was unmoved, she continued. 'I would have thrown myself under a carriage that very night, but then I saw Olivia and knew I would be saved.'

'You presume much,' he replied sadly. 'She is not here, but I fear has been abducted into the place from whence she came.'

Flora's hand flew to her mouth. 'The House of Correction?'

His head shook speculatively and motioned her to a chair. 'Tell me what you know of her.'

Flora recounted her life and that of Olivia when they had been inmates, and how she herself had been released and walked to London and had ever since been a beggar.

Throughout her delivery, Walter studied her closely. The woman was still in good condition, even if somewhat ragged and starved; nothing that a hot bath and a good meal wouldn't cure.

'Take off your clothes,' he said, when her babbling came to an end.

'What for?' she asked, intrigued at such an odd request.

'Because if I am satisfied with what I see, you shall help to retrieve Olivia, and in so doing also save yourself.'

None the wiser, but sensing something greatly to her own advantage, Flora stripped off her rags and stood naked before him, hands clasped over her pubic mound and head bowed as she had done many times before when men chose to inspect her.

'Splendid,' he remarked, running his eyes up and down her sturdy legs and hips. 'Effie will find you irresistible.'

'Who's Effie?'

'I shall reveal that after you have been washed,' and he summoned Helena, giving instructions that Flora was to be taken to his bathroom and scrubbed clean.

The bath was as big as a rowing boat; a shining enamel affair with brass taps at one end and a dozen more at the other, all in a line progressing up the wall and sporting levers on either side. Helena turned one of the brass taps and a gurgling started up in the pipes. It got louder and louder and then suddenly a torrent of scalding water cascaded into the bath. In no time at all the room filled with steam so dense that Flora could hardly see the maid turning the other tap. Cold water rushed from the spout and Helena swirled it round and round until the tub was almost full.

'Get in,' she said, standing aside.

Flora clambered over the rim and lowered herself into the water. It was so deep that her body floated on the surface. When she let herself sink it lapped around the curves of her breasts, exaggerating their size and shape. The maid ignored the erect nipples that peeped up at her and tossed Flora a bar of soap. Then she left as silent as a ghost.

Flora played the soap around her cleavage, lifting each breast in turn and lathering them until the skin shone. She let the soap drift to the bottom of the tub and began teasing her nipples, letting them slip between her fingers, squeezing and pinching until they tingled. She lifted her left leg out of the water and rested her foot on the end of the bath, admiring the sheen of her thigh and calf. Her hand smoothed the side of her flank and then idly strayed to the join of her legs. It reminded her of the laundry where the inmates had made love to each other, feeling their secret places, rubbing themselves tightly together, making each other climax. She wondered if Olivia would remember her when they met. But then, how could she have forgotten?

Flora felt her heart jump at the remembrance of Olivia chained in the mill, flogged raw, her body twisting to and fro as the whip slashed her back, belly and bottom. Grateful for the help that was coming her way, she would gladly submit herself to any flogging that Olivia cared to deliver.

She stroked her clitoris, closing her eyes to concentrate on its arousal; the way the bud swelled and poked from its protective petals, hardened and became unbearable to the touch. Would Olivia dare suck her there? She hoped, drifting into a preorgasmic daze.

'Dear God, the girl's swooned!'

Flora sat up with a start, whipping her hand away from her fork. Walter and his maid had come into the bathroom and were standing over her, regarding as they might a specimen under a microscope.

'I'm sorry,' she apologised, crashing her leg back into the water and splashing their clothes.

'Now I'm all wet,' Helena complained, and began undoing her uniform.

In the clearing steam Flora watched aghast as she stripped herself completely naked, seemingly not troubled by the presence of her master. When her stockings had been peeled from her thin legs she went to where the taps protruded from the wall and stared rudely at Flora's bare and gleaming breasts. Flora covered them with her arms.

'The task I have in mind will require great fortitude on your part,' Walter said, seating himself on the edge of the tub and gently taking away her hands. 'Are you averse to a beating on your bare bottom?'

'I don't understand,' Flora replied, feeling her flesh goose bump beneath the water.

'Olivia is being held prisoner, I am sure of it, and your task will be to rescue her. Do you think you can manage that?'

'Held where?' Flora asked, shifting uneasily.

'In a brothel,' Helena interjected.

'A brothel? How on earth...?'

'Never mind that,' Walter blurted. 'The point is that you have to get yourself in there, find out where Olivia is being held, and bring her to me. A very dangerous task, I know, but are you up to it? Can you stand being whipped and more than likely taken by men?'

Flora swallowed hard. 'I'm not frightened of either,' she boasted. 'But it depends what's in it for me.'

'A good rogering and a sound thrashing,' Walter assured her.

'No, I meant after that, when I bring her back.'

'A place in my own household, a regular wage and all the food you can eat, as well as my own company, which you will find most rewarding.'

'For that I don't care how much cock or cane I have.'

'Listen to her,' Helena exclaimed. 'How so bold she is.'

'We shall have to put your boldness to the test, young madam,' replied Walter, getting off the tub and rolling up his shirtsleeves.

'Stand up in your tub and reach for those taps,' Helena said, as if she were mistress of the household.

Flora heaved herself out of the water and stood upright, her body running and dripping from every curve and crevice. Walter eyed her erect nipples lasciviously and couldn't resist thumbing them. Flora shivered, shaking her breasts and fleshy thighs. When she stepped forward, Walter gave her bottom a slap, not particularly hard but enough to echo around the room and leave a faint, tingling imprint.

Flora bent over and put her hands on top of the taps, crooking her fingers around the spindles and clutching them tightly.

'Bind her wrists,' Walter said to Helena.

'I don't need binding,' Flora protested with a hint of a sneer.

'Nevertheless, bound you shall be. And we'll see if your bottom is as bold as your mouth.'

Helena used a length of sash cord to tie Flora's wrists to the taps. She wrapped it around the brass shaft and then around the outstretched wrists, tying them with great skill, knotting them so securely that Flora was held fast. Then she went off to fetch a cane from the hallway, the one her master used on her and took with him on long walks through the park.

Flora gulped when she saw it. Not an ordinary cane, it seemed, but a stout Malacca, as thick as her middle finger, springy as a whip and well polished from regular use. The first stroke would be enough to cut her.

'First we need to soak it,' said Walter, immersing it in the water.

'It hurts much more when it's wet,' Helena grinned, patting Flora's bottom. 'And it cuts,' she added gleefully.

Walter let the cane soak for a full ten minutes while he contented himself to run his hands all over Flora's body, kneading her flesh and testing the prowess of her muscles.

'Built like an Amazon,' he complimented. 'Shall we say at least two dozen strokes?'

'Oh, make it three,' Helena added.

Flora blushed. 'Why not make it four?' she said sarcastically, her hair tumbling into her eyes as she jerked from Walter's probing fingers.

'Then four it shall be,' he said, lifting the cane from the water.

'I didn't mean it!' she cried.

'Then you should not have opened your mouth so readily, madam.'

'She has got a big mouth,' Helena observed.

'And equally as generous under her arse,' Walter replied, touching the tip of the cane into Flora's dripping tuft.

He took the cane away and raised it high above his head. Flora heard it whistle through the air and land on her bare rump with a sickening smack.

'Aaaaaoow!' she howled, jolting her body forward and bumping her head on the tiles.

Helena had been right about the wetted cane. It hurt much more than if it were dry and warm. A hot, searing pain shot through Flora's buttocks that left her trembling and shaking her head in despair.

'What price your pride now?' she heard Walter say, as he lifted the cane again.

Flora knew that however hard she was whipped, her mouth had been her own undoing. She would have to endure it, even if only to save face, especially against the maid, whom she was beginning to dislike intensely. When the time came she would show her what a real caning was.

The second stroke cut upward under the fat of her buttocks; a much louder smack than the first, and far more furious in its delivery. Helena laughed when the force of the blow lifted Flora from the floor of the tub. Her wrists pulled on the cords and her breasts wobbled, slapping into each other.

Hardly had they settled back into place when the third stroke caught her square across her bottom, welting the cheeks with a savage hiss. This stroke did cut her and the welt turned a livid red, threatening to bleed. Another half dozen descended in quick succession on the backs of her thighs, and the pain was so acute and unexpected that poor Flora howled all the louder.

'Not so easy as you thought, eh, girl?' Walter chuckled, dropping the cane back into the tub.

Flora was mouthing silent obscenities. In her desperation not to scream she had clenched her teeth and could only breath through flaring nostrils, which snorted and grunted at every stroke. When the maid took hold of Flora's hair and lifted her head, it was to see a face begrimed with snot, slime and dribble.

'Throw some water over her,' Walter said, in return to her exclamation of disgust.

Helena willingly complied and fetched a pail from the storeroom, which she deliberately filled from one of the taps at the other end of the bath. Flora shrieked when a wall of freezing water hit her full in the face. She shivered from the shock, shaking her head and shoulders, muttering obscenities much more profane than the last.

'Your language is revolting in the extreme,' said Walter, genuinely taken aback.

'She called me a treacherous cunt,' rejoined Helena.

'Filthy trollop,' remarked Walter, slicing the cane into Flora's bottom.

'I'm not a trollop,' she winced, still shivering from the cold water that dripped from her hair.

'But I daresay that your arse has had many a visitor. Has it not?'

'A few,' mumbled Flora, drawing her legs together.

'As I thought, a regular whore, a gutter queen seeking to inveigle her way into my home, no doubt to steal anything within reach. Friend of my niece, indeed!'

And with that he sent the cane singing across Flora's flanks, making her hop up and down in the tub, sobbing and wailing her innocence.

'If you can take the rest of your punishment, I may consider that you are telling the truth, but only after I have laddered your back and bottom.'

Walter was true to his word and lashed the cane across her shoulders, crossing the welts from blade to blade and then steadily progressing downwards, leaving a deadly succession of dark blue parallel lines that gradually turned to red and purple. When he struck her bottom the cane had been freshly wetted, and she writhed her hips from side to side, trying to counter the blows as they fell.

Flora felt each one as if it were the first, the pain brought tears to her eyes, but now her mouth was open and no sound came. She was determined not to utter any more filthy oaths, or give the maid any further cause to abuse her. Only a muted sob warbled from her throat from each stroke, for by now the punishment was almost at an end. Walter was caning the crown of her bottom, and soon the final strokes would land where they had begun. He gave her four hard lashes on the crease of thigh and buttock, and tossed the cane into the tub.

'You are indeed telling the truth,' he said, marvelling at her striped body. 'A remarkable young woman, is she not, Helena?'

'Indeed she is, sir,' and she made to untie the cords. 'Leave her for a while and wash away the blood from her back,' he told her.

The maid climbed into the tub and stood directly behind Flora, wetting a sponge from the taps and squeezing the water over the ripening welts. She washed every strip from shoulder to waist, and paid ever greater attention to the buttocks and thighs. A fully loaded sponge went under Flora's legs and soaked her pouting mound, wiping it clean of the sweat and blood that had gathered there.

'Master likes his women fresh in their parts,' Helena advised, ringing the sponge.

'Surely he's not going to take me here?' Flora gasped.

'Where else?'

'But I'm still tied to these taps, and my poor backside aches so.'

'All the better. That's how he likes them, hot whipped and aching.'

Walter, who had left the room to visit the closet, came back in, his breeches already removed and shirt drawn up around his waist.

'I have to give it you,' he explained, replacing his maid in the tub, 'as all part of your preparation for what, I am certain, lies ahead.'

'Give it me, then,' Flora offered. 'As hard as I am likely to receive.'

Walter penetrated her with a single thrust and the shock whooshed from her mouth. Helena threw her arms around Flora's waist and held her still, but found the sight of her swaying breasts too much to resist. While Walter rode with long steady thrusts, the maid reached under Flora's arms and weighed the breasts in her palms.

'You could suck my nipples,' Flora suggested in a furtive whisper.

'Do as she requests,' Walter commanded, hearing her rasping plea.

Helena ducked beneath Flora and craned her neck upwards, closing her lips around the throbbing nipples and sucking them in. Walter began to ride harder, butting her tender, whipped bottom with his pelvis and groin. Flora's bent body rocked under the impact of smacking flesh on flesh, her fingers wormed around the taps. Then came a long and unexplained pause while he pulled out of her, splashed his hand beneath the water and was as quickly back in again. Now only one hand smoothed her flanks whereas previously there had been two. Helena continued with her playful dalliance, sucking and tonguing, licking and nibbling both breast and nipple.

Suddenly Flora gasped abruptly and hissed through her teeth at the burning pain going through her back. The organ inside her stopped its violent stabbing to allow the pain to sink in, and Flora to feel it more acutely. Then he dealt her another blow, plunging his organ back in immediately it was delivered. And so it went on, plunging and slashing, both organ and cane following each other, getting faster and faster. And all the while faithful Helena bit and ground her teeth over the throbbing nipples.

Flora was thrown into confusion, not knowing which either hurt or pleased her the most. Her back and flanks were on fire from the repeated blows, her nipples were sore and pained, but between her legs was all fire of a different kind. She knew that her orgasm was not long in coming.

'Oh, sir,' she panted, 'never have I had it like this!'

Crying and tear streaked, her face flushed, her breasts swollen and throbbing and her bottom in agony, she clung to the taps until her knuckles went white. The cane was trailing away as Walter rose towards his own fulfilment. Inside, Flora felt his shaft suddenly heat and swell; she was sure it had grown another inch.

With a grunt she braced herself and, legs and arms rigid, she felt him empty into her with a gush. Helena fell away and sank to her haunches, her lips sore from so much sucking. Her trembling fingers loosed the cords and Flora collapsed sideways into the tub

'You have done well,' Walter complimented. 'I am sure that you will be able to cope with anything that Effie throws at you. Now you may rest and Helena will administer to all your wants, whilst I retire to work out my plan.'

CHAPTER FIFTEEN

'How long do you intend to keep me chained like this?' Olivia asked Effie.

Effie gave her a look of contempt. 'Until you've learned your lesson. You were coming on nicely, proving to be a good actress, which is why I sent you to one of my best and most lucrative clients,' she paused and tested the chain running from the ring in Olivia's labia. 'Then you had to go and do a thing like that. I can't understand you at all.'

'I don't want to stay here any longer,' Olivia protested, trying to sit up.

The chain that had been fastened to the ring passed under her legs and was secured to a broad metal waistband that had been padlocked to the wall. Her hands were at her front, shackled to her waist. Charlotte had been given the task of feeding her gruel from a bowl, and as soon as she had recognised Olivia was determined to make her life an abject misery. She had it in her mind that Olivia had seduced Henry, and was taking her revenge. She stood behind Effie, porridge and spoon in hand.

'You'll stay here until I'm satisfied you can be trusted, which will be some considerable time. However, I can relieve your suffering for a short while. We have a new girl amongst us, about the same build and height as Sappho, ideally matched for this evening's entertainment, and you shall be the prize.'

She smiled at that and motioned Charlotte forward, then made her way back up the cellar steps.

'Serves you right,' Charlotte said, shoving a spoon of evil tasting stodge into Olivia's mouth. 'I knew you'd come to a bad end. Henry said it was written all over your face.'

'Bugger Henry,' Olivia replied, spitting the liquid over Charlotte's front.

Charlotte recoiled and hurled the bowl across the cellar. It bounced over the stone flags and landed upside down in a corner, and was immediately seized upon by a host of rats. Watching them, Olivia shivered and drew her knees tight to her chest.

'I'm going to whip you for that,' Charlotte promised. 'Mistress Effie said that I was to keep you under control, and that I shall rightly do. Put your knees down.'

Olivia, seething with rage, slowly lowered her knees, stretching her legs in front of her. Her back was against the wall and her hands clasped over her belly. Charlotte picked up a length of leather strap that had once been part of a harness and thrashed it into the floor. A cloud of dust rose, and through it Olivia saw the rats bolting for cover.

'Lift your hands up, wretch!' Charlotte commanded, imitating the forceful voice of Effie.

Olivia raised the shackles to her chest, exposing her thighs and belly. The strap lashed across her upper thighs and she screamed. Charlotte's eyes flashed like a lizard's eyeing its prey. Naked and defenceless, Olivia turned her head away from the eyes that she was sure betrayed insanity of some sort.

'You like this, don't you?' Charlotte questioned, as she hit her again. The strap made a hollow slapping sound as it lashed just under Olivia's navel.

'What's the matter with you?' she replied. 'Has Henry lost interest in you all of a sudden?'

'Bitch!' Charlotte screamed, and lashed her again across the belly, landing the strap across the top of her mound. She grinned like a maniac and delivered several blows in quick succession, leaving a pattern of thick, deep welts across the shaking belly.

Olivia squirmed from the force of the blows; each stripe seemed more vicious than the last, coming at full strength, landing only on her belly, one on top of the other. Olivia writhed and contorted, fighting desperately against the sickening chill inside her stomach. No matter how much she was beaten she would not give Charlotte the satisfaction that she sought.

She let her head roll against the wall, emitting a series of harsh groans. Her mind had emptied of any coherent thoughts, and was aware only of the whistling strap and the excruciating pain passing through her belly.

'You're holding back!' Charlotte hissed. She stopped to wipe the sweat from her brow and regarded the red welts striping Olivia's stomach.

To Olivia's great relief the strapping ceased, and when she opened her eyes she saw that Charlotte had left the cellar. The strap lay abandoned on the flags.

One by one the rats came slithering out of their holes and scurried towards the upturned porridge.

But hardly had they begun to lap up the gruel when Charlotte returned carrying a pint pot. She knelt beside Olivia and raised the rim to her lips.

'Drink,' she whispered, almost kindly. 'You must be thirsty after such a whipping.'

Olivia drank a little and took away her head, but Charlotte kept the pot close to her lips. 'All of it,' she said darkly. 'Drink every drop, or I'll whip you so hard you'll...'

She did not finish her sentence, but forced the entire contents of the pot down Olivia's throat. It was porter that she drank; thick strong porter that filled her stomach and made it swell and gurgle violently.

The strapping began again, but much worse than the last. The searing pain returned and Olivia begged for respite, but none came. Charlotte went on beating her and always on her belly. Lash after lash echoed around the cellar, and from each Olivia groaned with increasing agony.

'Please stop,' she wailed. 'I've had enough.'

Charlotte let the strap fall by her side. 'You can put an end to this yourself,' she smiled, flicking the end of the strap lightly into Olivia's navel.

'What do you want?' she asked, choking back a tear.

'I want to see you empty your guts.'

Olivia blushed red. 'Never!'

Charlotte was about to apply the strap again, but thought better of it and hurled it away into the shadows.

'How about me sitting on you,' she laughed, standing over Olivia and raising her skirts.

Olivia watched them lift until her bare thighs shone in the dim light. She went on lifting them until she bared her fork and bottom. Her hand went between her legs and rubbed her slit. Olivia saw a hot flush spread across her face.

'Put your tongue in my cunt and I'll let you go,' she said, now standing directly over Olivia.

'Is that a promise, or just another of your lies?'

Charlotte slapped her face. 'Up to you. Either you do as I want or I'll sit on your belly and ride you. See how you like that.'

'Doesn't Henry do it to you any more?' Olivia taunted, knowing that with so many other women freely available he probably didn't.

'None of your business!' Charlotte retorted, the excited flush turning to one of anger and frustration.

'I wouldn't be at all surprised if he's rogering Rita or Dora right this minute,' Olivia continued, forgetting that in her shackled position it was not a good idea. 'Or Sappho, for that matter. You couldn't match her if you tried.'

'Neither could you. I'll wager you're still a virgin.'

'That's why I'm ringed, so no one else can foul me.'

Charlotte cast her a sinister flash of her dark eyes as if she knew something that Olivia did not.

'So, you won't do as I ask,' she said thoughtfully.

'How do I know I can trust you?'

'You don't.'

'Then go to hell.'

The blow that Olivia thought would knock her senseless never came. Instead, Charlotte lowered herself to her knees, straddling Olivia's middle. Her bare bottom slowly descended and stopped just above the churning stomach. For a full minute she allowed her pert buttocks to hover, and by swinging her hips let the cheeks graze lightly over Olivia's belly. Her hands wandered over her breasts, pinching the nipples and fondling them. Olivia could not resist the flush of excitement that crept across her face.

'It's not me that will be in hell,' Charlotte observed, 'but you.'

With that she dropped like a stone, crashing the full weight of her body on to Olivia's stomach. A loud belch burst from Olivia's mouth and Charlotte bounced up and down, watching with great satisfaction the contorted grimace of agony as Olivia's bladder rapidly emptied.

'You've pissed yourself!' she laughed gleefully, rocking to and fro and slapping Olivia's face between whiles.

She would have stuffed her fingers into Olivia's mouth in the hope of making her vomit, but the dramatic entry of Effie cut that short.

'What on earth d'you think you're doing?!' she bellowed, aiming a kick at Charlotte's breast.

'She wouldn't eat her gruel,' Charlotte lied, without turning a hair.

'That does not give you leave to soil her. I want her fresh for the entertainment.' She looked at the lake of urine floating around Olivia's bottom and thighs and her nose emphatically wrinkled. 'Have her washed and brought upstairs directly, naked and chained if you please.'

She stomped back up the steps leaving Charlotte to carry out the humiliating business of having to wash Olivia, which she did by dragging her to a stone sink and forcing her to squat in it while she pumped the handle, muttering obscenities as she did so.

Olivia's stomach still ached as Charlotte took hold of the chain and led her upstairs to the theatre, where an assembly of gentleman were already seated. Olivia waited in the wings while Effie, dressed in a toga that left her breasts bare, announced to the audience that the play was about to begin. A gladiatorial contest it seemed, between Sappho and her opponent; a fight to the death with Olivia the willing slave as the spoils.

A further announcement told the audience that the victor would bugger and whip Olivia, after which she would be put up for auction. The men stirred in their seats while Olivia stood in a state of near shock.

'You are about to lose your virginity,' Charlotte informed her happily. 'I do hope the black girl wins.'

Olivia, waiting to be called on stage, edged nearer the curtain and watched as the contestants were readied for battle. Effie certainly did not lack imagination. Sappho was wearing a skirt that barely reached to mid-thigh. Through the thin cotton her magnificent flanks and buttocks flexed hard. The rest of her body, now gleaming with oil, was naked except for a broad brass waistband studied with jewels. In her right hand she carried a whip, knotted at intervals and divided into four thongs at the end.

Her opponent had her back to Olivia, and in her hand was a thick, heavy cane; one blow from that would be enough to leave a welt as deep as a finger. She was as tall as Sappho and just as strongly built and likewise skirted. Apart from that, she too was naked and her skin freshly oiled. The muscles in her powerful arms and back rippled as she stretched her arms outwards, displaying splendidly proportioned limbs.

'She'll bugger you as well as Sappho,' Charlotte said, on an afterthought.

But Olivia did not hear her, for now she was summoned on stage, her hands chained to her breasts, and between her legs the ring had been shown to its best advantage by having extra links added to it, and another length of chain that passed under her legs and was pulled tight between her bottom-cheeks.

Tall and slender and as slim as a young girl, she brought the audience to a hush. Four and twenty pairs of trousers bulged at the groin, longing to be the first to penetrate her. The ring would be ceremoniously removed prior to her deflowering, Effie informed the audience. Amid a deafening cheer, Olivia was pushed to the front of the stage and stood there for their inspection. She blushed and lowered her head, hiding her face in her hands while the eyes of the men devoured her. Effie left her alone, knowing full well that a bashful and frightened virgin was more desirable than any wayward whore. She let her stand there for a full ten minutes while the female gladiators put on helmets and took the painted shields that Rita passed through the curtains. The contest was going to be a savage one, with little if any quarter given.

Olivia was hustled to one side of the stage and made to sit on a stool, facing the audience with her legs spread wide open. Her hands were freed and put behind her head, thus lifting her breasts and thrusting forward her nipples. She could see many of the men licking their lips with anticipation.

'Let the contest commence!' Effie announced grandly, and she stepped aside.

Sappho was the first to strike, deftly sending her whip under the legs of her opponent, whose face Olivia had not yet seen. The woman gave vent to a loud shriek and hopped through the air. Her skirt was already ripped asunder and hung in shreds from the next lash which soon followed. But as Sappho delivered another, she caught hold of the whip and wrenched her forward, and in one swift movement tore away the cotton skirt. Sappho, completely naked, paused with surprise, and the heavy cane whistled into her backside.

A cheer went up as the sound of cane on bare flesh echoed to the back of the auditorium. Sappho rubbed the painful weal forming on her bottom and rushed forward, landing her whip with full strength on the other woman's back. And so they continued, lashing and caning each other, producing dozens of welts and stripes, tearing their flesh and uttering deep-throated cries of pain.

The weapons were soon abandoned as their tempers rose and they resorted to a wrestling match, each trying to humiliate the other. Sappho grabbed her opponent around the waist and hurled her to the ground, landing her on her back. With the speed of a panther she dropped to the floor and placed her heels on the woman's calves, forcing the legs open. A pelvic bone cricked and she screamed with pain. The men in the front row stared agog into the gaping sex of the spread legs. Then with a flash of her arm, Sappho fisted her in the groin.

The woman howled and doubled up, hands clutching her mound. When Sappho made to leap on her stomach she rolled out of the way and scrambled to her feet. One arm went around Sappho's neck and levered her backwards against the knee pressing in the small of her back. The sight of Sappho's magnificent body bent backwards was breathtaking. Her huge breasts thrust outwards and upwards. Her powerful thighs hardened like rock as she struggled to free herself. This she did with an elbow in the woman's ribs. The knee fell away and both women tumbled to the floor.

Olivia watched from under lowered brows as the woman gained the upper hand by getting on top of Sappho and pinning her arms behind her head. With her free hand she belaboured the sweating black breasts by punching and slapping them. Olivia was certain that under the rain of blows the mountains of wobbling flesh had swelled. The nipples certainly had, and the woman leaned forward and bit them between her grinding teeth.

Sappho, however, was not yet finished. She gathered her strength in her loins and bucked her bottom from the floor, sending the woman flying head over heels. Hot in pursuit she leapt on top of her, executed a spin in midair and landed with her bottom on the woman's face. Olivia heard a muffled grunt and lifting her head, saw the splendid buttocks of Sappho submerge her opponent deep into her cleft.

Glad of the rest, Sappho moved her hips slowly to and fro, visibly relaxing while the woman beneath her had little choice but to suck the parted slit.

Sappho took off her helmet and threw it into the audience, then wiped the sweat from her brow. She shot Olivia a knowing look and flashed her a wide smile, as if to say, 'soon you'll be doing this'.

Olivia looked at the floor, wondering if Sappho would use a phallus on her, or would she employ her fingers to split open her bottom. Her own fingers strayed to the ring in her labia and the links that hung there. Who, amongst the men in the audience, would be the first to deflower her, and would he really take her in public. If he did, Olivia's shame and degradation would be complete. From that moment on she would be public property, available to any who chose to take her for a price.

She swallowed a tear and forced herself to look at the contest that surely must be close to an end. Sappho it seemed, was lost in her mounting orgasm for her eyes had closed and her head was thrown back mouthing harsh groans and sighs. Olivia watched her teasing her own nipples, thumbing and rolling them, gasping for breath as she did so.

The legs of the woman beneath her were wide open and facing the audience. Already she was dribbling her juices from the pleasure of sucking the dark, sensuous slit of Sappho. The men stood up and stared in silence as the outer petals quivered between her fork. It was just possible to hear the sucking noises her slit made as she rose towards her orgasm.

But just as the audience, Olivia, Effie and all, thought the two women were sexually exhausted, the woman underneath gave a massive heave of her arse and tumbled Sappho to the floor. In a trice she snatched up the nearest weapon, the whip, and lashed it into Sappho's rump. The audience gasped in amazement at this sudden display of newfound strength, and went on gasping as the whip fell in rapid strokes, catching Sappho totally unawares, hitting her erect nipples and swollen breasts.

No matter which way Sappho twisted and turned the whip kept on lashing, particularly between her legs, cutting her aroused lips and clitoris, making her shriek with pain.

The woman had her back to Olivia and had lifted the visor of her helmet.

'Are you done?' Olivia heard her demand as the whip fell between Sappho's thighs.

'Take her!' Sappho moaned, a river of juice pouring from her slit.

Neither Olivia nor the men could believe that the whipped and exhausted Sappho could climax again. But climax she did, writhing over the floor in a sexual coma, while the victor strode towards Olivia and lifted her from the chair.

'Bugger her now!!' the audience cheered, knowing that as soon as the woman had taken her pleasure, the auction for Olivia's virginity would begin.

The woman turned Olivia's blushed face away from the audience and whispered an instruction in her ear. Olivia turned slowly back, then went limp. The shock had rendered her unconscious.

CHAPTER SIXTEEN

Olivia awoke to the familiar sounds of panting and gasping coming from the next room. She sat up and tried to recall the events of the previous night. She could remember that she had been punished by Charlotte, had wet herself, and then scrubbed under the pump before being taken to the theatre. There had been a sort of contest and the winner ought to have had her. There was also, she remembered, talk of an auction in which she would have been given to the highest bidder.

She reached between her legs; the ring was still in her labia and there were no signs of penetration having taken place. She was still intact. The noise coming through the flimsy partition grew louder and more energetic. Someone was being well rogered.

Olivia crept to the wall and peered through a hole in the plaster. Now she remembered. Flora had rescued her from the clutches of Sappho and losing her virginity to anyone willing to pay for it. She pressed her eye closer to the hole and saw a figure she knew well. Henry was having Flora from behind; Olivia could clearly see his shaft diving in and out of her slit. His hands were roving all over her bottom and reaching under her body for the enormous breasts that swayed pendulously to and fro.

Flora, red-faced and sweating, looked over her shoulder and asked very politely if Henry would like her on her back for a change, which seemed to indicate that he had been taking her bottom for some considerable time. He ceased his thrusting and drew out of her, allowing Flora to roll over, legs spread and toes pointing to the ceiling. He chuckled and threw himself between her legs. Flora grunted and raised her bottom from the mattress by using her powerful arms as levers.

There came another grunt, followed by a mighty shove of her hips, and Henry was engulfed to the hilt. Olivia, marvelling at the ease with which she swallowed him, watched to see what would happen next. It happened with terrifying speed; her long legs closed around his waist and locked over his back. Olivia could see the muscles of her thighs flex as her grip tightened, crushing the air from his lungs.

'Release me, you stupid bitch,' he grumbled.

Remembering how she had suffered at his hands, Olivia felt a cold chill pass through her stomach. Then she suddenly realised that the chains which had bound her hands and had gone under her legs were no longer in situ. She was free to move about as she pleased. Perhaps her time as a prisoner had been served, or was it merely that they had been taken away prior to being sold? But this was not the time to dwell on that, for Henry was riding Flora and exhausting himself in the process.

His toes were jammed into the bed-end and he was using all his strength to ride her. Between the mad pumping of his hips he paused to feast himself on her breasts, lowering his head and sucking her aroused nipples and squeezing the blazing flesh. That was one thing Olivia clearly remembered about Flora; in the height of passion her chest and breasts always turned scarlet, and her mouth was always fully open emitting stentorian grunts and groans.

'Oh my God,' she moaned. 'How you ride me. I can feel every inch of you. Oh my God, yes!'

Henry propped himself up on his elbows, his face dripping with sweat.

'I could roger you a lot more if you'd drop your legs,' he complained.

But Flora stayed where she was. 'Better this way,' she gasped. 'It makes me tighter inside.'

And she dug her heels deeper into his back and started drumming them, a sign for him to begin again.

'I should have had you chained,' he said, lowering his torso until his chest flattened her breasts. 'In fact, I think I will.' He started to call for Rita to help him chain Flora to the bed, but a powerful squeeze of her thighs stopped him in mid-sentence. His temper rising, he delivered a resounding slap across her face and another on the side of her head. Then he propped himself up again and commenced hitting her breasts. Henry hadn't changed, it seemed.

But Flora was not as meek and compliant as Olivia, or as docile as Charlotte. Her legs crushed hard into his ribs and Olivia watched spellbound as he fought desperately for air. Flora gave no quarter, but went on crushing him until his face turned purple, and with a muted gasp he fell over her, lifeless.

Olivia scrambled back into bed; Flora may have saved her virginity, but murdering one of the household into the bargain was taking matters too far.

She heard the heavy thud of Henry's body hit the floor, and in the next second Flora was in her room, her eyes wild with excitement.

'Get dressed,' she said, still breathless, and reaching for her own clothes.

'Flora, I don't understand,' Olivia cried. 'What are you doing here? And why have you killed Henry?'

'I haven't killed him,' she snorted, pulling up her drawers. 'And I'm here to save your hide, but there'll be little chance of that the way you dawdle about. Now for fuck's sake...' and she tossed Olivia a pair of drawers and a corset.

When Olivia had hurriedly dressed, Flora led her along the passage and down the stairs into the yard.

'Are we escaping?' Olivia asked, dazed and still not quite able to take all this in.

'D'you want to stay here?' Flora replied, exasperated at her naiveté. 'If Effie had her way you'd be fucked rotten and I'd have the skin off my arse. Now up you go.'

Olivia climbed onto Flora's back and heaved herself over the top of the yard wall and found herself, after a vigorous shove in her behind, lying on the pavement of the adjoining street. Flora landed beside her, swore an oath that would have made a navvy blush, and grabbed Olivia's hand.

When, after tearing through a maze of back alleys, they reached a busy thoroughfare, Flora slackened her pace.

'Your uncle sent me,' she informed Olivia. 'And what I haven't gone through, dear God, what with having to fight that Sylph... Syph...'

'Sappho,' Olivia corrected.

'Sappho. And having to sleep with any girl who took a fancy to me, not to mention flogged and whipped.'

'I thought you liked sleeping with women,' Olivia interrupted.

'So I do, but not when I'm chained up and unable to take my own pleasure.'

'Did Effie have you?'

Flora shot her a dry look. 'What d'you think?'

'And Charlotte?'

'Don't be stupid. Anyway, I had to lay her out before I could have her lover. I may have broken her jaw. Still, you can't have it all ways.'

'Why was it necessary to choke Henry?'

'Would you rather he fucked you?'

'I was supposed to be auctioned.'

'So you were, but a bargain was struck long before that. He was quite rich, it seemed.'

'But not now?'

Flora laughed to herself and hailed a passing cab. When they were safely heading along Oxford Street, Olivia asked Flora how she had found her way to London and into her uncle's house.

'I was streetwalking and saw you go by in a handsome carriage, and it didn't take long to find out where you were. I guessed you were in that line yourself'

'I'm not a prostitute,' Olivia interjected.

'As good as. Anyway, there I was starving and penniless and having walked all the way to London.'

'Should have caught the train,' Olivia grinned.

Flora ignored that and told her how she had finally knocked on Walter's door, and how he had taken her in and sent her to rescue his niece.

'I'm very grateful to you,' Olivia replied. 'And I shall see that you are suitably rewarded.'

Flora said nothing and gazed absently out of the window all the way to Berkeley Square. It was Walter who greeted them as the cab drew up.

'I'm home!' Olivia exclaimed excitedly.

'Yes, and after causing a great deal of trouble. Get upstairs to the parlour and take off those disgusting rags.'

Olivia, surprised at this unwarranted outburst, went upstairs and took off her dress.

'All of it,' her uncle said, coming into the room.

Olivia took off her drawers and corset and stood naked before him. Walter seated himself in his favourite chair, and for a while contented himself with running his eyes over her fine body. She ignored the erection that rose in his trousers.

'Over my knee, Olivia,' he said suddenly.

'What?'

'You seem to think that being sent on an errand gives you licence to go roaming all over London and lapsing back into your old ways. Well, we'll see about that.'

'I didn't go roaming, I was abducted.'

'Are you questioning me?'

'I was just explaining that I...' Her voice trailed away under his penetrating eyes. 'No,' she said sullenly, and made her way reluctantly across the carpet.

'Over my knee!' he shouted, seeing her hesitate.

'Are you going to spank me very hard?' she asked timidly.

'Very hard,' he assured her.

Her head lowered in submission as she stepped forward and placed herself over his knees, bottom up, bare and vulnerable. As she did so, Flora and Helena came into the parlour, showing no surprise at Olivia's embarrassing predicament. Judging from the way they stripped off their clothes one might have thought that their presence was expected.

'Flora, be so good as to hold the head of my wayward niece,' Walter said, and then turned to his maid and instructed her to grip Olivia's ankles.

When the two women had obeyed his instructions, he placed his hand on Olivia's bottom and gently patted the cheeks. The other hand rested between her shoulder blades, then without any warning the hand that had been patting her lifted and fell with extraordinary force. Olivia shrieked, her face contorted with pain, and her body jerked forward, pushing her face directly into Flora's breasts.

Walter waited for the pain to subside before hitting her again, another resounding slap, which this time made her legs jolt, but the maid held her ankles firmly together. A slap from Uncle Walter was no light thing, and both women watched with undisguised delight as Olivia's bottom began to redden. The third slap was delivered with a full and wide swing of his arm at which even Flora winced. She watched as the imprint of Walter's hand slowly manifested itself across the left buttock.

'Hold her still!' Walter commanded, and raised his hand for the next blow.

'Let me put her head between my tits,' suggested Flora.

'Better if she sucked your teats,' added Helena, slyly pushing apart Olivia's ankles.

Walter shrugged. He had not intended that his assistants should also enjoy themselves, but if that was their want, he would not argue. He nodded to Flora who raised Olivia's head, and then to everyone's surprise, kissed her full on the lips.

'I'm sorry,' she apologised, after keeping them waiting. 'It's been a long time since Olivia and me have done that. Isn't that so, Livy?'

Olivia murmured her agreement and looked pleading at Flora, her saviour. All her sufferings in the House of Correction were behind her now. She had forgiven the cruel treatment Flora had dealt her.

'It has been a long time,' she repeated, in a low, husky whisper.

'You may do with my niece as you wish,' Walter said knowingly, 'but between her legs is strictly out of bounds.'

Helena looked crestfallen. 'I know that she is being kept for her lover, but surely a tonguing would do her no harm.'

Walter considered that and nodded. 'No fingers, just your tongue.'

Then he sent the flat of his hand slapping into Olivia's right buttock. A harsh grunt escaped her lips as Flora lifted her breast and forced the nipple into the open mouth. Olivia sucked greedily on the teat, drawing it right in and as much of the breast as she could.

While she went on sucking, Walter went on slapping her harder and harder, turning the cheeks a blazing red. At the tenth slap tears were running from her eyes and wetting Flora's breasts.

'I think she needs a little air, sir,' Flora spoke softly, and lifted Olivia's head away from her swollen teat.

Her face was red and filled with desire. How so different from their first meeting in the courtyard and her reluctant coupling in the dormitory. Now she could suck away for as long as Flora desired it. Her head was eased back into position and she attacked the other nipple, eagerly rolling her teeth over the teat and flicking her tongue around the pimpled disc.

Hers was not the only tongue eagerly pursuing its devotions. Helena had slid Olivia's ankles wide and had angled her head into the open fork. The metal ring did not prevent her from finding Olivia's clitoris and teasing it to distraction.

Walter would have gone on slapping Olivia, indeed he could have punished that pert bottom until he was exhausted, but now his hand rested lazily on her back as he listened to the sound of mounting orgasms.

Always a keen observer of young women in the throes of passion, he looked and listened with intense fascination as each of the women became more intent on satisfying themselves. The sounds coming from Olivia's throat were no longer those of agony, but of undisguised pleasure. The harsh grunts were soft purrs, the misty look in her eyes not of anguish but of lustful longing. The effect on Flora was equally plain.

'My love, my love,' she moaned, from trembling lips. 'If only you were between my thighs...'

Waiter felt his own erection prodding into Olivia's stomach, and one glance at Flora's face told him where it ought to be. But how to get out from under Olivia without breaking the spell? It didn't help his state of mind when he saw Flora put her hand between her legs and begin to rub to and fro. In those circumstances, time was not on his side. If Flora came before he could enter her, or worse, he shot his own bolt, he would lose all credibility.

With consummate skill and long practice with Helena, he lifted Olivia's bottom from his thighs and slid sideways across the chair, and at the same time lowered her back again.

'What's going on?' Flora breathed.

It was Helena who answered her question. 'Master's going to have you,' she said, planting a kiss on Olivia's burning bottom.

Before Flora could take that in he was behind her, aiming his cock into her soaking silt.

'You're going to fuck me?' she asked, wide-eyed.

Then her hips jolted as Walter plunged savagely into her. It took only one thrust to fill her; she was so wet and hot. Helena watched with mixed feelings of jealously and want as Flora gasped and panted in time with Walter's thrusting. Flora's hips moved in accordance with each powerful jerk of his pelvis as he rode into her with long, slow strokes.

Helena was quickly back between Olivia's legs, burying her face in the deep, dark slit, feeling the heat of her cheeks against her face. Olivia was like a furnace inside, and when Helena found again her swollen clitoris she let out a loud howl and sucked all the more harder on Flora's teat.

Suddenly, she drew back and looked up pleadingly into Flora's flushed face. 'Hit me,' she whispered.

Flora did not at once hear her, for now Waiter was taking her with longer and faster strokes. He had lifted himself up to make his shaft glide against her clitoris, and the feeling of that was unbearable. All she could do in reply was clutch and tear at Olivia's hair.

'Beat me!' Olivia shrieked. 'Beat me as hard as you like, but just beat me!'

'Do as she says,' Walter instructed. 'Beat her hard, if that is what she wants,' and he slipped his belt from the loops and passed it over Flora's shoulder.

She took it and without interruption landed it on Olivia's back. The belt struck just as Helena's tongue touched her excited bud. A shiver shook the whole length of her body and the belt whistled into the small of her back. Fortunately, Helena's head was well under Olivia's legs and in the safety of her fork when the belt struck again. The end of it lashed around hips and buttocks with such force that Helena felt its reverberations go through her own shoulders.

Flora felt the same go through her breasts, for Olivia had planted her mouth firmly on both nipples and was sucking as if her life depended on it. She had placed her hands on the sides of Flora's orbs and crushed them together, the nipples had touched and Olivia had taken them both.

Flora was suffering more than anyone else in this sudden and unexpected orgy. She made tremendous efforts to whip Olivia, and indeed had done herself great credit in the way she striped her back and buttocks. But her strength was failing. It would not be long before both she and Walter climaxed. Inside she could feel his organ suddenly heat and go rigid. It rubbed hard against her clitoris and then, with a wild shriek, she flooded her juice from her slit. Walter emptied into her a second later, and was no less forthcoming in his own emissions. A barrage of darting spurts filled Flora's hot, dripping tunnel, and with a groan she let the belt fall haphazardly over Olivia's back.

It lay there like a dead serpent; the end trailing between Olivia's bottom-cleft, the buckle resting between her shoulder blades. She also was fast approaching orgasm. Helena was almost demented in the way she flicked her tongue into Olivia's slit. There seemed to be no pattern or control. She let her tongue go where it would, and to Olivia it was as if a thousand tongues were torturing her, so fast did Helena move.

When Olivia came it was with muted sobs and moans, a quaking of her body and trembling lips.

'Dear God,' she whimpered. 'Help me. Flora, help me.'

Flora was quickly down on her, kissing her full on the lips, pushing her tongue to the back of Olivia's throat, pressing their heads so hard their jaws ached. She went on tonguing and kissing until Olivia was spent. Only Helena had not come, and she drew back from Olivia's drenched fork and wiped her lips with the back of her hand.

'This isn't fair,' she complained.

And neither was it. Olivia and Flora, still flushed in the afterglow of orgasm, lay panting on the carpet. Walter had seated himself back in his chair and was gazing proudly at his organ; it was still erect.

'Sit on me,' he commanded of Helena. 'If you would be put out of your misery.'

The maid clambered up onto the arms of the chair, which in its design could have been made for the purpose to which it was now being put. Her knees rested on the fabric, thighs well spread, and between her legs the slit was open and wet. With as much skill as her master, Helena lowered herself, spreading her bottom until Olivia, now watching in amazement, thought it would split. Then, with Walter's plum just inside her, she jerked her knees from the arms and took him in a single drop of her hips.

Flora, who had recovered somewhat, reached for the belt and stole up behind Helena. She lashed without respite, covering the maid's back with a dozen welts in less time than it would take to even think about it.

'Lay them on hard!' Walter exclaimed, breathless at this sudden and unexpected bonus.

Helena wriggled under the force of the blows, twisting her hips and bottom as each lash cracked against her skin. She came much sooner than she would have liked for Walter, thrilled at the sight of her grimacing face and the cries of anguish that filled the room, was as hard as a rock.

But if she thought her torments were over after she had climaxed, she was profoundly mistaken. Flora handed the belt to Olivia and stood back, arms folded across her chest, legs together as if she were back in the House of Correction ordering a punishment. She could not forget with what authority she had beaten, and had commanded others to beat her charges.

'Complete the punishment,' she said to Olivia, in her old familiar gravelly voice.

Walter looked over Helena's shoulder. The sight of his niece, naked and holding the belt, was too much. 'Do as Flora commands,' he said. 'Give Helena a good beating.'

He took Helena under the arms and lifted her clear of his organ, and threw her over the back of the chair. Her bottom rested on the uppermost rung, her legs spread over the arms.

'You can't miss from here,' Flora observed, staring into the maid's open fork.

'You want me to beat her there?' Olivia asked, following her intent gaze.

'Of course. Or have you forgotten how you were whipped and the effect it had on you?'

Olivia blushed. She had not forgotten.

The belt sang into Helena's fork, catching her in the open slit. Another four strokes struck her swollen pudenda with unerring accuracy.

'I can see that your spell in prison was not entirely wasted,' Walter reflected.

Olivia, surprised at the pleasure there was to be found in beating the maid, continued with her strokes. Up and down her back she went, forming a perfect ladder of welts, each one directly below the other until she reached the out

147

swell of Helena's hips. She stopped for breath and looked at Flora and Walter in turn, wondering if she had delivered enough.

'And her bottom,' they said, almost in unison.

Olivia lashed the raised buttocks until she had no strength left and Helena hung lifeless over the chair.

'I've killed her!' she exclaimed, rushing round to where the maid's head hung between her trailing arms.

'I doubt that,' Walter replied dryly. 'It would take a great many more stripes to finish off Helena.'

'You mean, that you beat her like this all the time?'

'Only when she has been disobedient or rude to my guests, which I am sorry to say does seem to happen with alarming frequency. That is why she is beaten regularly.'

'As were you,' Flora reminded her. 'You were one of the worst of my charges.'

'Was she as disobedient as you claim?' Walter asked, intrigued.

'Not so much as disobedient, more unwilling, I should say.'

Walter looked at the ring in Olivia's labia. 'Did you promise to obey the man who put that ring in you?' he asked.

'I did, but in truth, I never saw his face. All I know is that he promised to marry me when the time came, and the ring was to keep me pure.'

'But you did let men whip and feel you there, before and after the ring was put on you.'

'That was only because I had too. It was my job, but if I'd known I would never have complied.'

'I don't believe that,' Walter said thoughtfully, and casting an eye at Helena's punished flesh. 'You were ready enough to suck Flora's tits, and asked to be beaten into the bargain.'

'I can't help the way I feel sometimes. I wasn't always like this, not before I went into that dreadful prison and was subjected to all sorts of terrible things.'

'But you did participate. Flora has told me all about you. I know everything.'

'I think she's learned a lot more since then,' Flora added, rather maliciously.

'I did suck men,' Olivia confessed.

'And you enjoyed it,' Walter said, mockingly.

'I might have, if I had loved the man in question.'

'If that be the case, you would also enjoy having it up your bottom, would you not?'

'I suppose so,' Olivia agreed.

'And in your other hole also.'

'It is more natural to have it there.' She paused and watched the maid heave herself off the chair.

She did not seem unduly damaged from the whipping, and when her feet were planted firmly on the floor she rubbed her bottom, smiling lasciviously in the process.

'You didn't do too badly,' she said, addressing Olivia. 'You made me feel quite excited.'

'Are you ready for more?' Walter asked. 'My niece seems insatiable.'

'I am not insatiable,' Olivia snapped. 'You make me sound as if I can't pass a day without wanting a man's thing up my bottom, or in my mouth, or... or anywhere else.'

'Calm yourself, Olivia. I was merely testing you. For soon you shall meet the man who ringed you, and I have no doubt that he will be glad to hear of your fidelity under such difficult circumstances.'

'Who is this man?' Olivia wanted to know.

'His identity he wishes to keep a secret. And for a while you must be content with that. I have appointed Flora as your maid in waiting.' He smiled at Flora, a broad appreciative smile that suggested she was much more than just a maid in the household. 'And I have no doubt that she will keep you safe, and until you do meet your future husband I have allowed Flora to share your bed, unless of course, you have any objections.'

'None at all,' Olivia replied, too startled to offer an objection.

'I have instructed Flora that she is never to leave your side, and as a reward for her loyalty both to you and me I have permitted her licence to take you whenever she pleases. Up your bottom, of course.'

'She did rescue me,' Olivia agreed. 'And for that I shall always be grateful. But does my gratitude have to extend that far?'

'How else could you repay her?' Walter asked. 'You have no money of your own, or property. I should think that Flora's request was quite a modest one, considering the immense danger she faced in bringing you here.'

'Why didn't you summon the police?'

Walter shifted uneasily. 'That was not possible under the circumstances. I doubt if they would have been able to rescue you, and besides, I have no desire to do Effie any real harm.'

'Real harm?!' Olivia exploded. 'You should have seen the things she made me do. She deserves to hang!'

'Hush, girl. I will hear no more of your hysterical outbursts. What has been done cannot be undone. There is no need to pursue the matter. You are now under Flora's care, see that you are well behaved, and obedient.'

Olivia, excited at the prospect of meeting her mysterious lover, obeyed her uncle's wishes to the letter. Every night she bared her bottom to Flora, who took her repeatedly with a huge phallus strapped to her waist. To open Olivia wider, she requested that she keep the phallus inside her for a while, and when her anus had sufficiently opened, she produced another, bigger than the last, and every day or two the size was increased until her bottom would stretch no more.

'Are you pleased with me?' Olivia always asked, after Flora had buggered her.

And always the answer was the same. 'Very, but next time hold back your climax just a little bit longer.'

Flora often tied Olivia to the bed frame and whipped her bare bottom; sometimes she spanked and caned her, and more often than not expected her to suck the phallus that had been fresh in her bottom. Olivia was totally unaware that all this was on her uncle's instruction. She was being prepared for her lover.

Chapter Seventeen

One morning soon after Helena escorted Olivia to her uncle's parlour. She was naked, a situation she was coming to accept as nothing out of the ordinary. The maid was dressed only in her drawers, and led her mistress into the centre of the room. The furniture had been previously cleared to create a space before a blazing fire.

'Please kneel, miss,' Helena said kindly, indicating the hearthrug.

'Now what's happening?' Olivia asked.

Helena removed her drawers with a dexterous sweep of her hand. 'I'm only obeying my instructions, miss,' she replied, tossing her drawers over the end of the sofa.

Olivia watched her go to a cabinet where Walter kept his private papers, and return with a large Oriental jar. When she took off the lid, a sweet, aromatic perfume drifted into Olivia's nostrils. She scooped out a thick syrupy grease and inhaled its vapour.

'I have to cover you with this,' Helena informed Olivia. 'Will you now please kneel?'

Olivia stepped backwards closer to the fire, savouring its warmth on her bottom. On the mantelpiece stood a decanter and glass that Olivia insolently filled. She was unused to her uncle's brandy, but nevertheless swallowed it in a single gulp. Then she poured another.

'Will you please hurry, miss,' said Helena, looking decidedly worried.

Olivia lifted the glass to her lips and sipped with deliberate slowness. 'Not until you've told me what all this is about.'

'All I know is that I have to grease you in preparation for your...'

'My what?' Olivia snapped, draining the glass.

'Please, miss, I can't say.'

'Then I shan't do as you wish.' And she lifted the decanter, and looking over the rim took a bold draught.

'But the master said that—'

'I know what your master said. But what he wants and what he gets are two different things,' and she belched loudly.

Helena was about to utter another fearful protestation when Walter came into the parlour. The sight of Olivia leaning on the mantelpiece, decanter in one hand and his favourite brandy half gone was too much.

'I thought I ordered you to prepare my niece,' he said, turning on Helena, who visibly trembled.

'I asked her to kneel down, but she wouldn't, sir. She just helped herself to the brandy.'

'And you just stood there and let her do it in flagrant defiance of my instructions.'

'But there was nothing I—'

'Did you try to prevent her?'

'No, sir.'

Walter regarded his maid with utter contempt. 'Then put yourself over the back of that chair.'

With lowered eyes, Helena walked to the nearest chair and leaned over its back. She straightened her arms and planted her hands firmly on the seat. Her legs were still together, as straight as ramrods, but trembling at the thighs and knees. Even from where Olivia was standing she could see the flesh of the maid's buttocks quivering with terror.

'It was all my doing, uncle,' Olivia interjected, replacing the decanter on the mantelshelf.

'Rubbish! She had her orders and disobeyed them. Now she shall be justly punished. Fetch me that cane.'

Olivia followed his gaze to the cabinet where a cane hung from a hook at its side.

Olivia fetched it, but instead of handing it to him she pleaded again on the maid's behalf. But her uncle would have none of it and snatched the cane from her hand.

'Kneel on the rug as you were supposed to do in the first place,' he commanded. He flexed the cane in his hands, letting one end go so that it whistled ominously through the air. Helena winced at the sound. 'When I have finished with this wretch she will oil you,' he told Olivia. 'And you will do as you are told. Understood?'

Olivia nodded dumbly and dropped silently to her knees. She watched, overcome with guilt as the cane slashed into Helena's backside. He delivered half a dozen more in rapid succession, slicing into her buttocks and tops of her thighs. Poor Helena yelped and sobbed, tossing her head with pain and digging her fingernails hard into the seat.

'Keep your legs together,' Walter growled, when her feet shuffled slightly apart.

He went on beating her, beginning on the sides of her thighs and knees and then progressing downwards to her calves, halting only when he reached her ankles. The cane would have ascended again to her buttocks but he thought for a moment and said softly, 'Lift your left foot.'

'No!' Olivia shrieked. 'Not there. For pity's sake, uncle. Not her feet!'

Walter turned to face his niece. 'If you had not been so disobedient this would never have happened. And since you are now so concerned, you shall assist me. Take her off that chair!'

Olivia knew not to disobey any further, and went sadly to the maid. She put her arms under Helena's shoulders and lifted her from the chair back.

'I'm sorry,' she whispered, raising the whipped body upright.

Helena made no reply but hobbled to the centre of the carpet. Her bottom and backs of her legs were a blazing scarlet.

'Lie her on her back,' Walter said.

Olivia lowered the sobbing girl to the floor and looked up at her uncle, her eyes wide and pleading. But the effect was lost. Obeying his instructions, Olivia slid her arm under the maid's knees and raised them to her chest. Then she fetched a length of curtain cord and tied it around the lifted ankles. When that was done she used her bare hands to hold them in place. The maid's feet were close together, soles facing upwards, toes flexing in fear.

'A little trick I learned in Constantinople,' Walter informed them both. 'Usually, the slave would have her feet secured in a pair of stocks, but on this occasion we shall have to improvise. Won't we?'

'There must be some other way she could take her punishment,' Olivia suggested.

The cane fell with a mighty swing, but landed not where Olivia thought it would, but hard on her own bare back. She shrieked and jolted forward, letting go of the maid's ankles.

'That was for daring to be so presumptuous,' Walter said. He gave his niece another square across the shoulder blades, but much harder than the last. 'And that was just for the pleasure of thrashing you. Now take hold of her ankles and lift her feet high enough so she can receive the full strength of my arm.'

Olivia closed her eyes as the cane whistled onto the soles of Helena's bare feet. The shock was so great that her whole body juddered across the carpet. The scream that escaped her lips was deafening.

'This is evil!' Olivia said emphatically, watching a livid stripe spread across Helena's soles. Her toes were flexing back and forth, opening wide and then closing tight.

'The English have much to learn from their Turkish counterparts,' Walter observed. 'I saw a slave girl, about your age as it happened, strung up by the ankles and whipped senseless. It was quite a revelation, the way her body twisted and turned. Forty strokes I think she had.'

'What on earth for?' Olivia uttered.

Walter shrugged. 'The coffee she brought her master was cold, I believe.'

'Hung upside down by her ankles, and feet whipped just for that?' Olivia gasped.

Her incredulous reply was drowned by another blood-curdling shriek from Helena as the cane whipped into her heels, and fell again just as rapidly onto the balls of her feet, just beneath her toes. Helena writhed in agony, throwing out her arms and rolling her head from side to side. Walter gave her a dozen more on the instep where the flesh was at its most tender and its most sensitive. Helena had ceased to scream and now lay inert, groaning and dribbling.

'One more on her toes and she can get up,' Walter said, touching his maid's toes with the tip of the cane.

Olivia turned her head away as the cane fell with incredible precision, right on the underneath of all five toes on the left foot. Then he struck the right, and idly lashed across Olivia's bottom.

'They say that when a woman has been soundly thrashed she is all the more better in bed,' Walter observed. 'Remind me later to give Flora a thorough good beating,' and he placed the cane carefully on the table.

Olivia, wiping away her own tears, untied the cord from Helena's ankles and let the bruised feet fall to the floor.

'Now be about your duties,' Walter said to the maid, who heaved herself painfully from the carpet.

'Would you mind telling me why I am to be greased with that, whatever it is?' Olivia asked.

Walter glanced over his shoulder as he made for the door. 'You will shortly have a visitor, and the oil will assist his intentions. That is all you need to know.'

Helena, who had no desire to be whipped again in such a fearful manner, took up the jar and scooped out a fresh dollop. Olivia offered no resistance when she began smearing it over her breasts. Her touch was light and gentle, the oil cool and soothing as Helena began circling her fingertips over the mounds, moving closer towards the nipples which by now had risen erect.

'Your visitor will love these,' Helena sniffled, giving the buds a tender squeeze.

'Who is my visitor?'

'Don't know, miss,' she replied truthfully, and went on plying the oil.

Olivia gasped as it started to sting her nipples. Indeed, it seemed as though her whole breasts were tingling. Her head went back, and open-mouthed she gasped for air. Helena temporarily put aside the jar and placed her own hot mouth on Olivia's panting lips. It was as if her searching tongue would never kiss Olivia that way ever again, and Olivia sensing this opened her mouth wider.

'I think I owe you this,' Olivia muttered when they broke for air.

'No need to mention it,' Helena replied. 'It is my place to be whipped when my master feels it right and proper to do so.'

She replenished her fingers and rubbed the oil between Olivia's breasts and over the mound of her stomach. In particular she coated the naval, filling it with a generous dose, and then continued to smear it all around her belly. Inside, Olivia was quivering. Her love tunnel seemed on fire, and yet there was a peculiar chill about it, and she shivered.

'What is this ointment?' she asked, looking down at her trembling nipples.

'I think it's something the master brought back from his travels in the East, miss,' Helena replied, tipping the jar into her palm.

'From Constantinople?'

'I think so.'

'Where he saw the slave girl hung up and whipped on her feet.'

153

'That and other things, miss.'

Olivia was about to ask what things when a sudden thrust of Helena's fingers made her catch her breath.

'Oh God. You put it there,' she gasped, clenching her fists.

'Only doing what the master says, miss.'

Olivia's mouth opened, but this time Helena did not kiss her but went on dutifully inserting her fingers into Olivia's vagina. She reached deep inside, coating the walls with the oil and then taking them out again for a fresh dipping into the jar.

'Please stop,' Olivia sucked her breath with a hiss.

'Not until you're full, miss,' and the slim fingers were back inside, wiggling all the way up to the womb.

Helena obeyed her instructions to the word and kept on inserting her fingers full of oil until Olivia's tunnel was filled.

'Have you finished?' Olivia said tearfully, for inside her flesh was experiencing that curious hot and cold sensation that had hitherto plagued her breasts.

'Only just begun, miss. I have to cover all of you. Will you please open your legs a little wider?'

Olivia shuffled her knees across the rug and felt the maid's hand go under her legs and rub slowly to and fro. Her palm had been covered with the oil which she now ground into Olivia's labia and pubic mound. Olivia cried out when the maid pinched her clitoris between forefinger and thumb. Her other hand had taken a fresh palm of oil and was rubbing it again over the aroused breasts and nipples.

'Now your bottom, miss,' Helena said, taking her hand away from Olivia's sex.

'Thank God you've finished there,' she replied, falling forward onto her hands.

The maid said nothing, but twisted her lips into a knowing smile and upturned the jar over the base of Olivia's spine. The oil ran like lava between the buttocks, slowly burning its way through the deep cleft and halting where it met a tuft of thick, tangled pubic hair. Helena put her hand on Olivia's bottom and began moving it round and round over the cheeks, leaving not an inch of skin untouched.

'May I be permitted a liberty, miss?' she asked. Olivia murmured her consent. 'You have such a beautiful bottom, I'm not at all surprised that so many men want to take advantage of it.'

Olivia blushed with pride at this unexpected compliment, and then suddenly grunted. The maid had thrust her oiled fingers deep into her anus, and was wiggling them inside her as she had done with her vagina.

'Do you have to fill me there as well?'

'Everywhere, miss,' the maid laughed, and gathered her fingers for more oil. 'Will you please relax a little?' she asked, as her fingers went in again to the knuckle.

154

Olivia could not reply. Her tongue hung out of her mouth, and she made a warbling sound from her throat, for now Helena was using her free hand to slop a generous amount all around her labia and clitoris. Ignoring the groans and grunts, she ran her greased palms up and down the insides of Olivia's thighs, making sure the long length of flesh was well covered.

'If you keep doing that I shall release my own juice,' Olivia stuttered.

'Oh, you mustn't do that, miss. The oil is only to prepare you for what is to come.'

'I... I think I'm coming.'

Helena took away her hand, and for no particular reason gave Olivia's left breast a hard slap. The frantic panting of Olivia suddenly stopped.

'Why did you do that?' she gasped.

'To distract you, miss.'

'Do it again,' Olivia groaned. 'I'm nearly there.'

Helena slapped her breasts with as much strength as she could muster. Beneath Olivia's body they swung to and fro like a pair of bells.

'Shall I smack your bottom, miss?' the maid asked, lifting her hand high in the air.

'You will do no such thing!'

The male voice behind made Helena freeze. Olivia remained on all fours, her breasts slowly settling back into place.

'Get out!' the voice ordered Helena. 'Your master awaits you in his room together with Flora, whom you are required to thrash and oil!'

Helena stood up and reached for her drawers.

'Leave those and get out!' the man barked.

Helena fled naked from the parlour, clutching the oil jar. The man waited until her footsteps had died away on the staircase, and then came closer to Olivia.

'Remain where you are,' he said, his voice softening.

Olivia obeyed, her whole body still tingling from the oil. Under her legs a small pool was gathering where the oil had mingled with her own juice and was dripping from her vagina.

'The maid has served you well,' he remarked, regarding the pool.

Olivia said nothing, but listened to the sound of clothes coming off and a movement close behind her.

'Who put this ring on you?' he asked.

Olivia felt the touch of his thighs against the backs of her own, and she shivered.

'A man who has proclaimed me for his wife,' she replied.

'And its purpose?'

'To keep me pure, sir.'

'And are you pure?'

'Indeed I am, sir. For no man has ever penetrated me there. Nor will he for as long as I am ringed.'

His thighs pressed closer and harder against her. She was sure she felt his hardened organ between her buttocks. It began to slid up and down in the cleft, a task made easier by the liberal amount of oil that Helena had put there. The effect of the oil could be plainly felt on the man, for his organ had stiffened and was larger than any Olivia had ever touched or sucked.

'Given the opportunity, would you have this?' he asked.

'Indeed, a short while ago I would have begged for it,' Olivia replied.

'But the ring would have prevented that.'

He reached under her and fondled her breasts, making them slip and slide from his grasp. He paid particular attention to her nipples, pinching and squeezing them, feeling the buds swell in his fingers.

'Why are you teasing me?' she gasped.

He made no reply, but took his hands away and slipped one of them between her legs and, with studied motion, began sliding it over and around her slit. Olivia choked back a tear and involuntarily squeezed her bottom-cheeks together.

'How do you feel now?' he asked, slipping a finger inside her.

'I am in hell,' she muttered.

'I can relieve you from your suffering, if you will agree to do as I command.'

'What is it?' she sobbed.

'First I will blindfold you, and then put you on your back. Then the ring shall be removed and your dearest wish granted.'

'You want to take me?'

'That is what you want, is it not?'

'Only from my intended.'

'Would you resist if I were not that man?'

Olivia hesitated. 'If you are not he, then I should be pleased to take you in my mouth or up my bottom, but I could not permit you any other place.'

He gave her bottom an affectionate slap. 'Your loyalty is more than I ever dreamed, Olivia.' And so saying he seized her hips and span her over.

'You?' she gasped.

When after what seemed an eternity she came out of her swoon, it was to find that she was lying with her legs spread and the ring already removed. A cushion had been thoughtfully placed under her bottom.

'Would you care for a brandy?' he asked, kneeling beside her. 'Your uncle tells me that you are quite partial to it.'

Olivia shook her head. The effect of the oil had not worn off, and inside she still tingled.

'It was you who helped me escape from the Reynolds,' she uttered, blinking in disbelief.

'And it was I who ringed you.'

Olivia thought she would pass out with shock. 'I don't understand. Why did you not keep me with you instead of letting me escape and be taken by that horrible man on the train, and then...?'

He closed his hand over her mouth. 'It was not possible. I was then married to another, and was on my way to London. I only found you by chance, and helping you escape was all I could do at that moment.'

Olivia let him put his hand between her legs and rub it gently over her labia. Already she was wet with longing.

'Who are you?' she asked, reaching down and pressing his hand harder.

'Your cousin, Rupert,' he replied, taking her hand and closing it around his organ. 'I have known about you for years, and longed to meet and marry you. When your uncle told me that you had come by accident into his house I was determined to make you mine. While I was ridding myself of my wife I little thought that you would be abducted.'

'It was as well you ringed me, or I would have been deflowered many times over.'

'You can thank Flora for helping me,' he said.

'Where is she now? I must show her my appreciation.'

'At this moment she is being whipped and ridden by your uncle, and no doubt will be for many years to come. You will have time enough to thank her. But for the present...'

He leaned over her and started sucking her nipples. Olivia reached clumsily under her bottom and guided his organ between her legs.

'Why was it so necessary to cover me in all that oil?' she asked, nudging the head of his organ into her slit.

He laughed to himself. 'I had no idea that you would go into a swoon. I thought you would be so worked up with the oil and seeing me that you would be like a bitch in heat, instead you laid like a corpse.'

'Sorry,' she blushed.

'I shall have to punish you for that.'

'Before or after you have taken me?'

Without waiting for an answer, she lifted her knees and threw her legs over his back. If she was surprised at how easily he penetrated her it did not show on her face. The oil was still lingering in her vagina, and what with her own juice flowing like a torrent, he took her as naturally as if she had taken a thousand. He rode her until sheer exhaustion brought them both to the brink of collapse.

'Shall I be your lawful wedded wife?' she asked, after he lad dismounted.

'The documents are already drawn up,' he said, licking the sweat from her breasts.

'And you expect me to honour and obey?'

'Of course.'

'And in return you will keep me in the manner to which I lave become accustomed?'

'Naturally.'

Olivia wriggled free from his grasp and left the room. She returned wielding her uncle's cane, which she placed neatly in its hand. Then she prostrated herself over the back of the chair, bottom up and legs wide apart.

'You may begin now,' she said softly. 'In the manner to which I have become accustomed. And afterwards I shall fetch the oil, providing that I have been suitably treated.'

Rupert raised the cane high above his head and sent it whistling into her bottom.

Olivia looked over her shoulder, and said with a devastating smile, 'Harder... much harder!'

The Adventure Continues...

Also available to order as a paperback on **AMAZON**

There was a pause while he patted her bottom with great appreciation. Then without warning he smacked her with the full strength of his arm. The shock of the blow almost sent the wad flying from her mouth, but he had stuffed it in too well for that to happen. He struck again with even greater force, and he went on spanking all over her bottom, until it blazed a magnificent hue of bright scarlet. Olivia could feel his thin penis rising against her tummy.

Abandoning her philandering husband, Olivia enters a world rife with superstition and depravity: the convent of Saint Dulcinea, behind the walls of which persist strange and perverted rituals reminiscent of the Middle Ages, when harsh discipline and torture ensured absolute obedience.

Under the constant supervision of the nuns she is subjected to continual punishment and humiliation. Gradually she learns the true and terrible purpose of their intentions, which are not for her benefit, but to ensure the survival of the convent.

Olivia is driven to desperate measures, but the nuns are always one step ahead. Perhaps there is no escape from the dark terrors of the Dulcinites...

www.ingramcontent.com/pod-product-compliance
Lightning Source LLC
Chambersburg PA
CBHW020354130626
46549CB00006B/2290